NORTH OF ELYSIUM

I0539281

PUBLISHED BY
JERRY J. K. ROGERS

E-book ISBN: 978-0-9905826-3-2

Pring ISBN: 978-0-9905826-0-1

DEDICATION

It is with fond remembrance that I dedicate this book to
Lenny and Linda Estrada.
Their bright and sunny dispositions always imbue
a wonderful fragrance of memories.
Their encouragement made it seem as if anything
was possible; their joyful personalities and wonderful smiles
were a true blessing for a somber world.
Lenny and Linda, you both will be missed.

CONTENTS

RISE OF THE SPIRIT TRACKER

O n a solitary pier of a small coastal town in western Africa, Villagers who were fishing, taking a stroll, or watching the murky waters roll onto the rocky shore from the mild breeze, noticed a menacing backlit, sun-infused, orange, and gray cloud form off in the distant sky. The disturbance first appeared as a simple billowy puffball. Within minutes, it grew into a bulbous thunderhead, covering most of the horizon. In the center, where the gray was darkest, a jagged tear formed in the sky, an eerie rip suspended over the ocean. An opaque and misty orb, followed by a long smoky contrail, spat out of the breach, and streaked through the air towards the pier.

Onlookers froze in fear and awe, observing the mysterious phenomenon, except for one man. He ran to his cart sitting at the end of the pier and extracted a bow and arrow. The murky beach ball-sized orb, bouncing down the pier's aged wood planks, transfigured into the semblance of a snake, craning its head as if searching for prey. It spotted a German Shepherd puppy whimpering and backing away, prostrate on all fours. The vaporous creature moved with lightning speed and entered through the canine's nose. The dog's blue eyes turned yellow; it stood erect on all fours, surveying the scene while releasing a guttural growl.

"Move away from that dog," the man shouted.

The puppy snarled, sounding throaty and guttural, as if it should come from a larger beast.

The villagers scattered.

Arming his bow, the African drew back on the string, leveled, and targeted the canine. The puppy again snarled and then turned from the crowd, running down the unpaved street with unnatural speed.

The African knew he had only one shot. Leading his target, he released his fingers, freeing the arrow. The barbed projectile found its mark. The spirit-infused creature rolled onto the dusty road. The tall, thin, pitch-skinned African rushed over to his wounded prey and dropped his bow. He picked up the animal by the scruff, making sure he was now face to face with the creature. The canine's life ebbed to nonexistence. The African picked up his bow and strolled towards his cart near the pier.

"Why risk coming into this world this way?" The African asked, knowing he wouldn't receive an answer.

A growl rumbled in the dead beast's throat.

Impossible, the African thought; *the evil spirit should have departed.* He killed the beast, believing he had forced the malevolent personality occupying the canine to commute to the next plane. This occurred in the past, three, seven and ten years prior, each time one tried to enter this world through similar means.

The African recognized this wasn't the usual malevolent supernatural essence attempting to manifest itself within a creature in the world. Nor did it pass through in the same way as previous entities. Could this be the manifestation of a major daemon, even that of a destroyer?

The spectators second-guessed that they had envisioned a semblance of a snakelike, jade-colored vapor extrude from the dead puppy's mouth. The ethereal substance then billowed into the form of an enormous serpent and disappeared from their sight. In the eyes of the African, the creature, still visible and terrifying, wrapped itself around him with whirlwind agility. It squeezed as if it were a supernatural anaconda. The spectators observed the African standing rigid; his breathing became labored. The one man brave enough to walk up to the statue-erect African was a swarthy, crackled-skin, elderly fisherman named Sogundu. He attempted to poke the younger African, but fear and dread flooded his soul.

He backed away.

In the fading light through the sparkle of his life, the African viewed the serpent's face on the end of its misty body as it moved in front of his face; the ethereal creature smiled; it twisted tighter.

"You have not seen the last of me," the African said. He exhaled his final breath and fell to where the pier married the shore.

The onlookers heard the clap of thunder rumbling through the gray clouds. Another rift formed in the sky, outlined in murky turquoise along its boundary. The fissure then sealed itself. The ominous clouds dissipated, and the aquamarine sky returned.

The African lay lifeless. The old man, Sogundu, and another villager attempted to provide first aid.

Men who respected the fallen villager carried his body to a large two-room mud-made abode. The wife, the tallest woman in the village, sat in the doorway milling corn; she witnessed prominent villagers carry her husband's rigid body above their heads. Nila, her sixteen-year-old son sitting next to her, froze in shock, his dark face and brown eyes staring at his father's lifeless form.

Supporting the head was the chief of the small community. He considered it an honor to take part in the procession. "We're sorry, but your husband."

"I can see what happened to my husband. He died doing what he was destined to do," the wife interrupted, suppressing the urge to scream and cry out, wanting to maintain her composure by presenting a strong countenance. "I saw the clouds and was worried about what they showed."

The wife turned to her son, still paralyzed, unable to comprehend what he was witnessing. Her dark brown eyes stared into Nila's. The thought of "this isn't happening" repeated over and over in her mind.

"There are days when evil journeys in and out of our world," she said. "It feels empowered to move between planes. Your father's fate was to contain the forces that had caused evil influences upon men."

"I don't understand," the sixteen-year-old responded. "My father is dead." His emotions now radiated pain as if festered with sores.

Nila's mother ignored her son and turned to the chief. "Did my husband fight well?"

"He did," the village chief acknowledged.

"Yet my son's training is not complete." *Would my son be called upon to complete what his father couldn't?*

Before the daylight withdrew, nightfall crested along the horizon. Eight pallbearers laid the African to rest in a freshly dug grave. After shoveling hardened dirt, rocks, and stones over the shrouded body wrapped in a canvas swaddling cloth, the chief placed a simple cross at the west end of the grave mound.

Nila's sight blurred from the sheets of tears covering his eyes. He gazed upon the emotionless stone face of his mother. "Mother, why don't you cry?"

Nila's mother returned a tender smile. "It seems you're doing enough crying for both of us. Besides, it's hard to cry when I know I'll see him again in the next life. Your father may be absent from this body, but he is to be face to face with the Great Creator. One day, I will join him, you will join him, as death comes upon us all."

Her heart swelled with loss, as if her emotions fell into a bottomless pit; her eyes were now overcome with an onslaught of tears. Soon, they became two desert orbs unable to cry anymore.

Minutes later, she and Nila wandered back to their dwelling. The village chief stood waiting by the abode's front entrance. He approached Nila, placing his hands on the teen's shoulders. "Your father died too soon, but you must continue what your father had started."

The chief stepped back; his piercing stare focused on Nila's mother. "There is one who will finish teaching him."

"You can't send him...the son if he is too young is never called to finish what is to be done. It's passed on to another..."

"Hush." The chief interrupted, which shocked Nila. He'd never heard the village leader being disrespectful and breaking into someone's conversation. "I know what is to happen in a situation like this, but these are days where men are consumed by material distractions, and influenced more by the evil than the grace of the one on high. Many questioned whether it was wise for you and your husband to allow your son to sneak out on those nights."

"We did it so that he wouldn't be naïve to the detractors that exist. He always returned and stayed true to what his father taught him," Nila's mother said.

Nila wondered how his parents, although well versed in the modern ways of life and technology, rejected it. This also seemed true of the small fishing town that appeared overlooked by the progress of the world. Sometimes the surrounding towns and villages called his town "That-Place-That-Doesn't-Exist." The population being so introverted, Nila assumed they didn't accept the reality of technological progress. He snuck away from time to time, going to nearby villages or towns, making new friends and experiencing gadgets his village detested. Nila didn't know that his parents were aware he would do this.

"For that, we are thankful. But now another in the bloodline must continue what your husband has started."

"To take on daemons. He is not ready."

The chief's demoralized eyes and defeated expression descended, displaying a deeper level of distraught. "It is not a mere daemon that has killed your husband. According to the old man Sogundu, for an instant, he witnessed a Destroyer daemon itself."

"Impossible. My husband would've known what to do."

"Sogundu should know. It's believed to have entered our realm under the brazen pretense of a shameless and reckless minor daemon."

"And you want my son to take on the fight?" Nila's mother asked, unable to hold back from crying.

"He is of the bloodline; when a destroyer enters the world," the chief had started before Nila's mother interrupted him.

"I know what it means. I'm aware of the history," she said. As much as she wanted to resist, there was no option but to concede to the chief's insistence. It was her son's destiny to follow in the path of his father, just as his father had before him. Such was the path of their ancestors; such was the path for her son.

"Why do you cry now, mother?" Nila asked. Still experiencing the trauma of losing his father, he was oblivious to the entire earlier conversation.

Nila's mother sniffled and attempted to wipe the tears from her eyes. "You're having to do so much before you have a chance to grow up, meet a young girl, get married, and experience the pain and joy of raising children." She didn't mention the reason for her crying was that he would head out and may not see him again until that blessed day. Nila's mother would lose two whom she loved.

"I'll get married; I'll have children, won't I?" Nila asked.

Nila's mother stared into his bright brown eyes. "I see so much of your father in your face, blessing of my barren womb." *Is this how Hannah of the scriptures felt?*

Nila's parents considered themselves fortunate to have been able to conceive him before they were to enter the sunset of their lives. They were in their late-forties when Nila was born, both thinking maybe a child wasn't in the Great Creator's plan for their lives. They both presumed there could be a special purpose for him.

The village chief dispatched the old man, Sogundu, to spend time with Nila. When the time came, Sogundu first explained to him how his father had died. Then he described the "special hunts" accomplished by his father, not for meat, but for daemon-possessed creatures attempting to enter this world and cause havoc upon men.

After a few days, Sogundu came up to Nila as he tended the family's garden. He instructed Nila to pack a small suitcase.

"My mother needs me. Why do I have to leave now?" Nila asked as Sogundu stood next to him near three short rows of corn.

"Because you need to worry about more important things in this world."

Nila's eyes enlarged with ire. "My mother is important." He dropped his gardening tools and rushed inside the small abode up to his mother, who sat at the small dining table mending a shirt.

"Mother, Sogundu wants me to leave here."

Nila's mother stuck herself with the sewing needle, distracted. She glanced up at her son. "I know. He informed me of this a couple of days ago when I went to the market."

Sensing minute pain, a small spot of blood formed on the tip of her finger. She licked it off. "Now don't argue. You must do as Sogundu says." The sheen in her eyes reflected her attempt to suppress tears.

Nila didn't know how to respond. After getting over the shock, he replied, "I'm not leaving. You need me, especially since you've been feeling sick each morning since father died."

"That is none of your concern, and if you want to honor me and your father, you will do what Sogundu says, and mind those who are your elders. I'm trusting they will help you through this."

Nila's mother placed the shirt, needle, and thread on the table next to her, stood and went over, giving Nila a hug. "Honor us; that is the greatest love you could show your father and I."

Calm embraced Nila. His mother's words, spoken with a gentle tone, washed away the tense irritation that had welled within him.

Sogundu told him he needed to journey from the land he grew up knowing so well to other regions on the continent. In time, there was a possibility of traveling across the sea. Sogundu informed him that before his birth, his father had once journeyed to a distinct town in Spain. Providence would reveal his future path.

The next morning, Nila filled a worn suitcase gifted by Sogundu with a few outer garments, undergarments, socks, and a single beige sweater, the only clothes he owned, and a copy of the Great Creator's holy writings. Sogundu directed him to leave nothing behind; he was to focus on the future that was before him.

"How am I to pay for my travels?" Nila asked of Sogundu. He shoved three pairs of faded pants and three shirts into the suitcase. "You know we have no money."

"There's a missionary from a religious order willing to help in case this day was to come. They will pay for your trip up to your destination, plus some additional living expenses."

"And where am I to travel?"

"The outer border to the way of life hereafter."

"Am I to die?" Nila questioned, raising his voice filled with apprehension.

"No, not until the appointed time by the Great Creator. You will head to the boundary where the hearts of men lead. For some, the way is blissful and beautiful. For others, the land is barren and unforgiving. What you face is stronger than you can ever imagine," Sogundu explained.

Why didn't Sogundu just say that? Nila wondered. "Then how can I succeed?" He asked.

"Be yourself, but enough of this. It's time for you to go."

Be myself. How is that going to *help me?* Nila thought as he double-checked his suitcase. "None of this is making any sense."

Sogundu placed his hand on Nila's shoulder. "I know this is difficult for you, but there are days in our lives when the weight of uncertainty is replaced with the heaviness of unrest."

Nila's forehead crinkled, his lips furrowed. "What does that mean?"

"Say goodbye to your mother. You must leave."

Nila hugged his mother, not wanting to let go. She found it hard to let go herself, but with a gentle nudge, ended their embrace. He suppressed the urge to cry, and departed the house to begin his trek, following the directions given by Sogundu. Nila's mother watched as he walked out of town, joyful at his strength not to look back.

Somber with the loss of her husband and exodus of her son, her eyes were two desert-like orbs, unable to bear more tears.

"I wish we hadn't allowed him to visit the other towns; we had so much more to teach him," conceded to Sogundu.

"No, what you and your husband did helped. You both have done well," Sogundu responded with pride. "He will be better prepared than those before him. Yes, you have done well, and Nila, he will do well."

"I wish his father had more time to teach him what he needed to know."

"Sometimes the best lesson to offer is experience."

"I thought you said there was going to be someone else to help him."

"There will be. I'll head over to the next town and send a message to let him know of Nila's arrival."

Nila journeyed for two days, walking down a less traveled dusty, parched, compacted gravel and dirt road. Sometimes the road passed through a patchwork landscape of forest or heavy brush; other times, savanna grassland. Every so often, an old truck aged with rust, or a small car belching blue-tinged exhaust, stopped to offer Nila a ride. Sogundu told him not to accept a ride from any passersby. He emphasized, let passersby be passersby. Each one is to complete their own journey.

Arriving in the city, Nila followed the instructions verbatim given to him on how to find the missionary. He found the small church, but the staff informed him that the missionary had retired; he was living with his wife several streets over in a temporary residence. Nila continued on to the missionary's home. He walked up to a large cottage made from irregularly sized planks of lumber and corrugated metal sheets. A small fenced, mud-strewn lawn with patches of trampled grass surrounded the house. A rooster, chickens, and a goat wandered about unconstrained behind the three-foot high enclosure. A slender white male in his early fifties, with an uncombed beard streaked with gray, stood erect in the doorway, smiling. The closer Nila approached, the larger the missionary's smile grew.

"Nila?" the missionary asked when Nila approached the fence entrance at the front of the house.

"Yes."

The missionary's grin exploded into a capacious smile, exposing white teeth with a tinge of yellow. They were as close to whiteness as Nila knew that could exist for teeth. "I've been waiting for you. My name is Parsons. Please come in."

Nila entered the home, amazed that it was larger on the inside than what the outside suggested. The house contained a limited interior size, having a constricted living room, a small dining room and kitchenette area, and the trifling semblance of a bathroom. Another door at the rear led to a nearby outhouse. The main bedroom seemed substantial; the guest room where Nila placed his suitcase was half as spacious. The furnishings throughout the house were simple pieces of handmade furniture.

Parsons' wife offered Nila a small meal that he accepted with delight at being hungry from his long walk. He had exhausted his limited rations hours earlier. After he finished his meal, Parsons started a conversation. "I'm sorry about your father. Sogundu passed on to me what had happened."

"Yes, my father told me about daemons, but he never explained Destroyers."

"It was your father we believed who would make this journey. It shows that the old man, Sogundu, and myself were preparing for the return of the wrong Destroyer."

"Who or what is this Destroyer?" Nila asked.

"It's hard to explain. Only the Great Creator understands its dominion and workings. We know how to stop them, if possible."

Another question came to Nila. "Are you the one Sogundu says he saved?"

Parsons chuckled. "The old man says he saved me, huh?"

"Yes," Nila answered.

"Funny, I remember it differently. It was I who saved him."

"He says he saved you from a band of local thugs under a ruthless warlord."

"Yes, he's correct. He delayed what was not my time. Sogundu kept me from being killed, and my meeting with our Redeemer and Great Creator, but save me, he did not. I don't consider the mortality of this physical life to be important. Nila, my soul is prepared, and if to die during my missionary work, so be it. But it was I used by the Great Creator who saved him."

"I don't understand. What happened?"

"I saved Sogundu from the influence of a Destroyer daemon when one breached into our plane."

Nila's expression of confusion told Parsons a question was forthcoming.

"Influence of a Destroyer from the breach?" Nila asked.

"Ah, you may be more enlightened than most sixteen-year-olds, but remember, my background differs from yours. The Destroyer entered this world and possessed the old man, Sogundu. He was the ruthless warlord he mentioned, only much younger. He is now considered a new spiritual creation."

Nila's narrow eyes popped wide open.

"Only he and I know the true fullness of his past these days," Parsons continued. "Upon our first meeting, he would've killed me, but I knew he was not himself. The daemon that possessed him, I discerned, was one of great magnitude."

"How did you defeat the Destroyer?"

"You'll learn that you cannot defeat the Destroyer, merely prevent it from causing further damage. Your faith is your greatest ally. But enough of that; you must be tired. Tomorrow, I'll teach you what you need to know to survive in the world. And over time, we'll learn where it is you are to travel."

"I'm not going to leave right away?"

"No, we must teach you what your father couldn't."

A new spirit tracker would arise.

PREPARATION

M onths passed; a year and a half, to be exact. Nila became accustomed to his new daily routine. Waking up an average of an hour before dawn, he fed the chickens, milked the goat, or took care of the chores Parsons had assigned the night prior. Today, it would be to fix the fence at the rear of the property. Afterwards, he ate a breakfast of corn gruel accompanying a small portion of fruit, and a small egg omelet filled with sardines. Nila next undertook a light body wash to clean off the sweat and remove the flourishing body odor instigated by his morning chores.

Nila then attended the missionary school. The days of teasing by the younger students in class for being the tallest weed in the blades of grass were behind him. It hadn't disturbed Nila; he had learned humility to know he would soon prepare how to contend with a daemon, and not to worry about the taunting he received from his classmates. Yet, when they realized he comprehended the lessons with ease, the students, even his harassers, sought him for tutoring. Nila was patient and considerate of his classmates. They soon nicknamed him "ach-gadolu," big brother.

Nila's teachers had underestimated his literacy, assuming he hadn't grown up with any education, believing him nothing more than a farm boy from a small remote town. After seven months, impressed by his knowledge, they moved him to the high school level class. Nila's mother had homeschooled him apart from the days his father took him on a hunt, at least the hunts his father allowed for him to accompany.

There were several hunts where his father would be gone for two to three weeks. This occurred after strange weather phenomena, followed by a visit from Sogundu. The two men then dismissed Nila from their discussion. When he asked why, they'd tell him children weren't meant to know such things. Nila considered it odd that after some of his father's mysterious hunts following Sogundu's visit, he wouldn't bring any game meat back. His mother didn't care; she'd tell her husband, "You did well for the greater good in service of the Great Creator."

Nila thought back to one hunt with his father when he was thirteen.

"You must remember, as a hunter, the prey you seek may not be the prey you hunt," his father would tell him. "Sometimes you may have to track the life within a life, a spirit possessing flesh."

"I don't understand, father."

"One day you shall. It will be a day when you learn of your true strength."

"Strong like you are, father?" Nila asked. Nila admired his father. And his father knew Nila had tried extra hard to impress him, but told him, "Blessed are your mother and I. To be my son, I couldn't be any prouder."

"You shall be strong in your own right, not like me. Focus on the gifts that are unique to yourself. Do you remember the one day back over the passing of twelve full moons ago? A visitor had come upon our town; you knew there was something unique about him, just as myself and Sogundu recognized there was something more?"

"I remember the visitor, because you and Sogundu said I had been gifted the same as you had, father," Nila said, feeling proud. He wanted to find ways to further garner his father's approval.

"It was then we realized there would be a day I would need to teach you what my father taught me, and his father taught him," his father had said. "For now, you are too young for me to tell you everything."

Nila remembered the visitor. The mysterious man had departed with him on a supposed hunt. They were gone for weeks. His mother made a comment regarding Spain. When his father returned, he mourned the loss of a newfound friend, but his hunt was successful.

Nila wished his father had taught him more.

Each week after church service, Parsons handed Nila a letter from his mother. Each week, the letter comprised the same message; she found it hard not having his father around. The village helped with the chores; they couldn't help her missing him. She also wrote about how she missed Nila, but understood his purpose was much greater than the wishes of an old, aging woman. She called herself old. Nila considered her young, even though she was fifty-seven. Nila sensed sadness in each letter. He pleaded to go visit her, but Parsons refused. He and Sogundu agreed it was best to continue his training.

When not in school, learning how to survive in the world, or doing his daily farm and household tasks, Sogundu had dispatched a Huntsman to help teach Nila the art of hunting, archery, and knife usage. When Nila first met him, he considered him imposing—tall, muscular, and unblemished mahogany toned skin. His broad face framed large light brown eyes that glistened as if golden beryl gemstones. The strands of his coal black hair remained in place regardless of the wind or activity. He carried himself with an air of confidence that fell shy of arrogance.

The lessons were far stricter and regimented than going out hunting with his father. At the beginning of his training, the Huntsman had him do running sprints, jump squats, push-ups and other aerobic exercises. They then spent time on the basics of nocking the arrow on the bowstring, and then pulling back, but never releasing. When the Huntsman sensed he was ready, Nila then learned how to aim, focusing on a target and release. Nila also learned the proper methods of transporting his gear while walking, running, or pursuing his prey.

During the next phase of his training, the Huntsman changed Nila's physical fitness workout routine. He performed his exercises while wearing his gear and until he was close to exhaustion. Then he was to fire off rapid volleys, not able to finish for the day until he hit his designated target three times in a row. Nila thought he was successful, hitting near the center every other arrow.

"You are nowhere near as good as others I have trained," the Huntsman said.

Nila thought otherwise but remained quiet, taught not to talk back to his elders.

As the training progressed, Nila struck the target's center eight out of ten times. "I'm getting pretty good at this."

"Just because you think you're ready doesn't mean you are," the Huntsman rebuked. "You hit the target, but you must hit it with accuracy each time. And you must still learn to hit a running creature, sometimes moving so fast that if you don't lead it properly you will miss, no matter your skills. To fail doesn't mean there's no meat on the table—it means someone's life, or their soul, is in jeopardy because of the daemon."

Nila remained quiet.

"Do you understand what I'm telling you?"

"Yes."

"Good. We'll call it a day."

Nila returned to the house. Parsons sat at the table reading a book.

"How'd your training go?"

"I thought I did pretty good using a bow and arrow, but the Huntsman didn't think so."

"What you learn from him is the best training any man could receive," Parsons said.

"Then how come he doesn't go after the daemon?" Nila asked.

Parsons' milky skin flushed, and nostrils flared. This was one of the rare times Nila had observed him angry.

"Forgive me, Parsons," Nila said. "I didn't mean that."

"Yes, you did." Parsons took a couple of deep breaths. "Otherwise, you wouldn't have said it. That's why it's just as important for you to focus on what you say, what you hear, and what you do. You may be frustrated, but you cannot afford to act rashly. Do you understand?"

Nila's head dropped.

"Nila, look at me," Parsons said, his tone now softer.

Nila looked up and stared at Parsons with doleful, downcast eyes.

"Do you understand?" Parsons asked again.

"Yes," Nila replied, above a whisper.

"Good, now go say your evening prayers and call it a night."

Over the next week, Nila became comfortable maintaining his breath control whenever he aimed at a target following a rigorous workout, confident he could strike a fly at twenty-five yards.

A question came to mind. "How can a simple arrow kill the daemon?"

"The arrow doesn't kill the daemon. It dispatches the vessel."

After more training, the Huntsman considered Nila skillful with basic archery tasks; the lessons turned in a different direction. He took Nila out on quick jaunts to get him accustomed to foraging and tracking through the woodlands and outback. During one excursion, the Huntsman instructed Nila to leave his gear behind. The two journeyed into the wilderness, past their normal training fields and into deeper bush where elephant palms exploded in size, and trees extending towards the sky resembled emerald skyscrapers with buttressed roots two stories tall.

The Huntsman taught Nila the importance of improvising and fashioning a weapon from whatever articles that may be available. Whether finding the proper stick or branch, and then using it as a club, or fabricating a crude spear, this would be a skill he may soon need.

One day after returning from school, mentally preparing for another day of intense training, Nila returned to Parsons' residence to find the Huntsman sitting with Parsons at the lacquered-finished dining room table flaking with age and heavily scratched with use. Both men's faces were stoic and emotionless.

"Sit down, Nila," Parsons directed, gesturing with his hand to an open seat at the table between the two men.

Nila sat. His heart pounded. His mind raced with worrisome thoughts. Did something happen to his mother? Did he do something wrong? He couldn't think of anything.

Parsons asked, "Nila, have you heard of the Valley of Hinnom?"

"No, I haven't. Where is it?"

"It's a way from your town, beyond the mangrove swamps and beaches of the coast, past the tropical forests, beyond the plateau, and amongst the hills bordering the highlands and mountains, many call it The Lost Land," the Huntsman said.

Nila's forehead scrunched. "Why is it called The Lost Land?"

"You'll soon learn why. Few from our land can visit and return. There is an extensive valley between this land and there. In the middle of the valley flows a river, a river called Purgo," Parsons answered.

"How come I haven't heard of this land or river before?" Nila asked. He was proud of having a firm knowledge of his local geography.

"What is the nickname of the town you come from?" Parsons asked.

"The Invisible Town, or the Town-That-Doesn't-Exist," Nila responded.

"The same holds true of this valley. It's not the only one. There are many like this one across our world," the Huntsman said.

"These lands are where your father would go from time to time on his hunts," Parsons added.

Nila's thoughts swirled in his head, trying to make sense of Parson's comment. "Why there?"

"It's there where two realms overlap, and it's there where daemons sometimes try to breach into ours by possessing animals. It was there your father searched for these polluted animals on some of his hunts," the Huntsman said.

"According to Sogundu, that is not how my father died. It was through different means that the daemon arrived."

"There are many ways a daemon, more so a Destroyer, may enter our realm, and when they do, they can be dangerous."

"How am I to know if a Destroyer enters?"

"One already has—the one that killed your father," Parsons interjected. "That's the one you must seek."

"But it's been so many months. How am I to find it?"

"Know this, daemons live outside our existence. What seems like weeks, months, or years to us could be seconds, minutes, hours, or days when you live in the eternal. Yet their presence is in the here and now. They may focus on one person at a time, as with your father. They may work with other daemons. They are dangerous, and you must be careful."

Nila fidgeted. "Am I the one to do this?" he said, with a shaky voice.

The Huntsman gave him a piercing stare, one Nila had never experienced before, even during the intense advanced sessions when he made basic and simple mistakes. "Hunter, you are the one. Of this, we are certain. But do not make the same mistake your father made."

"What mistake was that?" Nervousness still laced Nila's voice.

"When you slay a daemon-possessed beast within this realm, ensure the daemon is expelled. It's possible it may interact differently and act differently with each person it encounters."

"How will I know how to do this?"

"That's the one thing I cannot teach you," the Huntsman replied.

"Then how am I supposed to know what to do?"

"Know that the Destroyer, or any daemon, although bound by law, may not abide by the rules," the Huntsman said. "That's why one role of the Guardians is to help maintain the limits daemons have over this world. Daemons do not have free rein over natural law; but also know that the guardians of light are themselves limited in their abilities as well."

"How do the Guardians help?"

"In ways you may not realize. They inspire, teach, maintain order, or provide an opportunity not otherwise available; their ways are many. Sometimes it may be as simple as to serve and protect."

"And who are these guardians of light?"

Parsons jumped in on the conversation. "Some men call them ang..."

The Huntsman interrupted. "There's no need to tell him any more than I already have."

Nila considered this was the most information anyone communicated to him concerning daemons, guardians, or even providing a peek into the history of his father. It filled him with mild anxiety, not sure why this was important to know.

"But I have so many more questions," Nila said.

"Go get some rest," Parsons noted. "You have a busy day ahead of you tomorrow. Don't focus on questions you may have, only on what you've learned up to this point."

THE VALLEY

I t was four o'clock in the morning when Parsons woke Nila. Parsons' wife had made a small breakfast of two boiled eggs, grilled flatbread, and seasoned boiled potatoes, waiting for him on the breakfast table. As soon as Nila finished, the Huntsman knocked on the door. Nila wanted to brush his teeth, but the Huntsman showed there was no time to do unnecessary tasks when on such undertakings. While grabbing his gear, the Huntsman told Nila to leave it, except for food and water.

They walked for two hours. Nila believed they were traveling back to his village until they arrived at a simple bus station. They boarded a packed carriage destined for an outlying district. Exiting at a stop in a plateau town near the mountain region, they traversed through the edge of the savannah into a bush area thick with tall field grass. The Huntsman then led him down a small path leading from the main road, inconspicuous if one weren't watching for it or knew where it was located. Walking at a quick pace through the tall grass, up through palm fronds, elephant ear plants, black ironwood trees, and other thick foliage, Nila sensed a gradual incline. Cresting the peak of a small mount, a breathtaking view into an emerald valley of vegetation and a winding river flowing along the floor emerged. Before now, Nila had never known nor contemplated the beauty of his country. As he surveyed the opposite side of the valley, which appeared barren and rocky, a parched sensation momentarily battered his mouth and throat.

Apart from the sparse areas of growth beyond the mangrove swamps of the coast, Nila supposed the country's landscape would be barren. He'd heard stories of deforestation because of tree harvesting for timber or land clearing for grazing animals.

"Nila, that's the river Purgo. When you go down, no matter what happens, do not cross it. Do you understand?" the Huntsman pleaded.

"I do, but why?" Nila asked, wondering why there was apprehension in the Huntsman's voice.

"Just remember everything that Parsons and I told you yesterday. Even though things may appear normal, they are not. Then again, things are as they appear. The same goes for those whom you meet."

"Then how am I to tell the difference?"

"I'm glad you're full of questions, but now is not the time for them."

The Huntsman scouted along the crest for a few minutes, finding a cleared path down the side of the mountain. Though it seemed like they had scaled a large hill, Nila looked down into the valley and suspected the lush vegetation concealed the mount's actual height. The Huntsman stated the peak where they stood was the top of a small mountain. Nila had never climbed this high before.

The Huntsman stopped. "Follow the path down until you come across a road."

Nila, fatigued after walking for as long as they did, was astonished that the Huntsman didn't seem winded.

"Can we wait a few minutes?" Nila asked, catching his breath.

"No, the enemy will not wait for you; follow the path down."

Nila started navigating the path's steep descent, ensuring his footing was secure with each step so that he wouldn't slip and fall.

"What am I supposed to do when I get there?" Nila asked after taking several steps.

"Just follow it down. If you come up to a bridge that crosses the river, no matter what, DO NOT CROSS. You may drink from the waters, but DO NOT CROSS."

Not until the Huntsman made the comment about taking a drink. Nila didn't think about his encroaching thirst. His mouth became parched as he continued his descent down. Several flat rocks imbedded in the black fertile dirt proved hard to gather a sure footing. Nila made sure he cleared the slippery obstacles before asking his next question. "And then what?" he inquired, yelling out, keeping his eyes forward to make sure not to stumble.

The Huntsman chuckled. "You're like your father and grandfather when I trained them."

Nila froze in his tracks. *Father and grandfather. The Huntsman didn't appear any older than his mid-twenties. How could he have trained them both?*

Turning around, no one stood on the top of the mountain. Nila debated between going back up or continuing down. Continuing down won. Every several feet, he grabbed onto tree branches or the large leaves of short palms to help regain his balance. The steep decline eased at a couple of switchback locations where the trail hugged the side of the small mountain. Gauging the waning sun, Nila estimated he'd been traveling for over an hour before coming to an impacted dirt and clay road. He followed the winding pathway with his eyes until he came upon a narrow wood-planked bridge crossing the river. The downward slope from this point was going to be easier.

Nila arrived at the bridge. The setting sun, now low on the horizon, shone off in the distance. Its reflection shimmered above the river flowing on the valley floor between the shadowed mountainsides. The waters, the cleanest and pristine rivers he'd ever come across, were clear and appeared refreshing, almost too perfect. Nila was accustomed to waters muddied from migrating animals or the day-to-day activity from towns or villages not having adequate plumbing infrastructure. Local well waters were half as clean. Nila went to the bank, scooped his cupped hands into the river, and drank. His fatigue waned. He didn't know how to explain it, but his muscles rejuvenated, every sound was acute.

Perusing along the river, across the bridge, up and down the mountainsides, he was unaware of what to expect. Eyeing the wide path extending from the bridge, it trailed up the side of the mountain opposite the river. The terrain remained fertile only a few yards past the river. The further the trail went up, the landside evolved, becoming dusty, rocky, barren, and desolate.

The sun sank behind Nila; darkness settled over the valley. He glanced back up the road he had traveled, squinting through the waning evening sun. A figure approached. He soon made out a short, attractive female with a petite face, pale complexion, and straight brunette hair. Her hazel tinted eyes conveyed a dazed expression.

"Excuse me, am I supposed to meet you?" Nila asked.

The woman stopped and glared at Nila; her glazed over eyes scarcely blinked. "Where am I?"

"You don't know where you're at? You're at." Nila didn't know either. He'd concentrated on the landscape and environment, not actively listening.

"I'm supposed to walk toward the bridge and cross over."

"I don't know exactly where we are," Nila said. "We're next to the river..." The strange surroundings scattering his senses, he'd forgotten its name, though remembering the command from the Huntsman not to cross. "Where'd you come from?"

"I was in northern California...a small town a short way from Redding. I was sitting in a rental car...I took some...now I'm here...I don't understand."

The woman gazed at Nila; her eyes filled with sadness. She continued walking. When she came upon the bridge, the sparkling, clear flowing waters caught her attention. A burning, parched sensation had infused her mouth after she entered the valley. She stepped over to the riverbank, stooped down, and reached in to scoop up some of the pristine water. No matter where she dipped her hands, the water flowed around her hands, remaining dry, regardless of the number of times she tried.

The woman remained squatting motionless, longing for the flowing waters; her thirst became unbearable. She turned and stared at Nila. "I realize now that it's too late. The waters that give and sustain life once offered, I had refused to drink. Now I'm unable."

She proceeded to the bridge to cross the river.

"What's your name? Who are you?" Nila asked.

After a couple of steps onto the bridge, the woman stopped and turned around to gaze at Nila with her dulled eyes unable to produce tears. "Lost," she replied with dry, shriveled, and cracked lips that trembled. She continued across.

Nila fought the urge to follow her, again remembering the Huntsman's stern warning not to cross over the river, no matter the circumstances. The woman reached the end of the bridge and continued up the trail on the barren side of the valley. Nila turned from watching her to debate what to do next. A thought–the Huntsman said nothing about not being able to backtrack on the wide dirt and clay road to see where it led. With a full moon rising, the sun almost set, there'd be enough light to travel safely. Nila didn't want to risk camping out in an unknown land, unarmed and unfamiliar with the landscape.

There was no rustling of vegetation by small or large creatures. The sound of insects - muted. No wind or breeze flowed across the land. The only noise was that of his footsteps upon the earth below him. The quiet was unnerving. Moaning and wailing from a woman's voice echoing in the valley fractured the silence. It was a voice that sounded familiar, similar to the woman whom he had met. Looking back over his shoulder, no one was there.

Nila continued his trek. He reached the point where he entered onto the road from the path through the foliage. The moon's radiance illuminated his original path, but he felt more comfortable taking the main road. Approaching where the wide path peaked over the crest, and still a bit disoriented, Nila was unfamiliar with the changing landscape.

The road forked. To the right, the distant terrain in the moonlight appeared unfamiliar. Outlined in the dark were conifer and other forest trees he had never seen before, not knowing they were ponderosa pines, oaks, and elms. A mistrust of the landscape faded, where to the left and down towards the foothills of the mountain, by the side of the road, was a small campfire in a clearing of familiar savanna grass, elephant ear plants, short palms, and other foliage. Nila proceeded in that direction. He wasn't sure who he would meet, but risked going down. Approaching the dancing lights of the flames with flittering embers floating upward, a broad-shouldered, solitary figure sat by the fire. It was the Huntsman. Nila expelled a breath of relief.

The Huntsman noticed Nila's dusty and sweaty sable-toned skin. "How many travelers did you meet on the road?" he asked.

"Wouldn't you have seen them sitting here by the road?" Nila asked.

"Like you, they enter from different paths. How many did you meet on the other side?"

Nila assumed the Huntsman meant the other side of the small mountain. "One."

The Huntsman's facial response showed that wasn't the expected answer.

"One?" the Huntsman asked with apprehension. "Are you sure?"

"Yes, I'm positive."

"What about encounters with any beasts?"

"No beasts of any sort."

"Nothing at all? No snakes, no wolves, no bears, nothing?" The Huntsman asked with emphasis.

"No."

"Then the Destroyer is already being disruptive. So, what happened to this person?"

"Nothing, I was told she was in the north of California outside of Redding, and then ended up on the road. Then she crossed over the bridge."

"I see; I know that town."

"What does all of this mean?"

"It means that when we get back, we may need to have Parsons arrange for you to continue your journey. It seems where her path originated when she crossed may be important."

"What do you mean to continue my journey? Don't you mean to start my journey?"

The Huntsman reached over, placing his hand on Nila's shoulder. "My friend, you've been on this journey since the day your father died. Now rest. We have to wake before dawn and hurry back."

Parsons rushed to embrace both the Huntsman and Nila with a warm and firm hug upon seeing their arriving down the road.

"How'd it go?" he asked. "You've been gone for a little over two weeks. I was getting worried."

Nila stepped back and shook his head. "No, that's not possible. Two weeks? How? We've been gone for a little over four days?" They were to have been back sooner, but the bus on the return had broken down.

"Nila has to leave right away. The Destroyer is at work," the Huntsman said, not giving Nila a chance to wrap his head around the time inconsistency.

"Is Nila ready?" Parsons asked.

"That doesn't make a difference now," the Huntsman responded. "We can't wait. From what Nila explained with what happened, I think I may know where the Destroyer is operating. Once they start their mischief, they're territorial. Nila needs to travel abroad." He explained everything that occurred to Nila in the Valley of Himmon.

Nila, himself attempted to grasp everything that had happened hearing it again.

Uneasiness painted Parsons' face. "Must he go? His father gained more experience tracking closer in nearby countries and was older than Nila is now before he went abroad."

"Understand, Parsons, the boundary regions in the valley were empty. We have to act right away; otherwise, the long-term consequences are frightful."

"I understand what you're saying, my friend. I'm worried for Nila, that's all. Must he go so far, so quickly?"

"Can you make the arrangements?" the Huntsman asked.

Parsons hesitated before answering. "I'll schedule a church van to take him to the capital. They'll buy him some new clothes, luggage, and purchase his ticket when he gets to the airport. Where's he going?"

"It appears Northern California, to Elysium."

"California, all by himself. That's so far away," Parsons said with apprehension.

"I realize that he'll need help. I also need you to arrange for someone who had the same abilities as the one who helped Nila's father during his Spain trip."

"I have a friend of mine who's a monk at the same monastery of my Order down in Mexico. He should be able to find somebody to assist and escort Nila," Parsons said.

"Good, but tell him only what he needs to know. Somewhere along the way, he'll need to meet up with Nila before they arrive at their destination," the Huntsman said.

Parsons focused his attention on Nila. "Nila, I'm so sorry we have to send you out so unprepared like this. The Order will set up a prepaid credit card for expenses and anything else you may need once you get to your destination."

Nila's thoughts became unfocused as he tried to comprehend the conversation between the two men and determine what specific items Parsons had referenced. "Like what?"

"We don't want you traveling with your bow and arrows, knife, or weapons of any kind. Make or buy what you can when you get to your destination," the Huntsman exclaimed. "My job is done. I'll leave you now to prepare," he continued. "But I'll be back in a couple of days before you depart."

Parsons embraced the Huntsman again. "I thank the High One above. You've been a real blessing."

"You've been a blessing to me as well. Thank you for allowing me to be a part of his training." The Huntsman directed his attention to Nila. "Soul hunter, or should I say spirit tracker, I'll send a message to a friend of mine as well. Godspeed."

The church van transporting Nila to the city was now out of sight. The Huntsman was ready to walk away before Parsons held him back. "I still don't understand why we didn't tell Nila he has a little brother, or why Sogundu wouldn't let his mother mention it in her letters?" Parson inquired.

"Nila would've been hesitant to leave, if at all. The miracle of his mother at her age to have a son, and then to name him after her husband, we didn't want to risk him getting sentimental and not going on this campaign."

"Campaign? You make it sound like he's going off to war."

"What he does from this point on will have an invisible impact on a greater war unseen by men. I'll check in on Nila's mother and little brother and see how they're doing," the Huntsman said as he picked up his oversized backpack, slung it onto his back and walked away.

THE SOUL READER

I n the middle of a desolate landscape where the hot, dry wind blew stood a white adobe-faced temple structure. Erected on the flat barren plains of a white sands desert, located deep in Baja California, Mexico, was the four-sided pyramidal edifice made of adobe bricks. Standing almost eight stories high, built in successive recessed terraced levels, it resembled an Aztec or Mayan temple. Molded and formed up, the entire forward-facing side of the structure ascended to balcony landings on each level. At the summit were a prayer meditation room and an observation chamber.

One-story dormitories, a storage warehouse, and a kitchen and dining facility, all made of adobe, stood throughout the courtyard of the sanctuary building. A two-story high adobe battlement encircled all the structures of the compound. On top of the battlement stood tall white poles lashed with white flags, equally spaced from one another; the arid wind caressed each standard. The compound's main portico was a tad under the length of a football field from the landing of the stairs.

A late middle-aged and wise sage, named Orland, peered out from a small balcony on the top terrace level at an approaching male clothed in a sandy-beige colored, Bedouin type outfit covering his full body. Only his green eyes were visible, outlined by his copper skin tone derived from his Shoshoni Indian mother and Caucasian father. The sage knew the man. His name was Chrishav, an outcast from his tribe. He was an outcast not for his mixed-race parentage, and having the blood of the ancestors tainted as some of his tribe derided, but because those who practiced the art of shamanism that still existed on his former reservation feared and loathed him.

Chrishav was a man able to see into the hearts of men, to see the seeds of inspiration for their hopes and dreams, their motivations, and their discouragements. He understood those who were contentious and spiteful, yet saw through them when they cloaked it with the façade of kindness. He could sense the vile one felt towards others, even though they strove to cover it, wearing a mask of friendship, deceiving themselves of the austere emotions. Chrishav was also the type of man who sensed the edifices of binding friendship yet undiscovered between two unassuming acquaintances, knowing their struggles would forge lifelong companionship.

It was because of these abilities that Chrishav's mentor and patriarch sage, Orland, considered him a soul reader. However, he could not narrate the souls of all men, only those in severe turmoil or themselves who had the ability, sometimes unknowingly, to perceive eccentricities beyond the earthly realm. Chrishav could also breach, albeit for a quick peek, the psyche of one attuned to the ethereal plane of existence.

Welles, another temple vicar, joined his peer, Orland the sage, who was the same age, but with skin less aged and cracked. Even though Orland was sixty years old, many considered him to be in his mid-forties.

"Is he returning from another one of his walk-abouts?" Orland asked as he repositioned himself on the balcony, moving closer to the doorway.

"Yes, he says it helps to clear the symphony of emotions that overwhelm him from time to time while he's here in the temple complex."

"His emotions overwhelm him?"

"He claims they're of those who head in a direction many are afraid to travel, yet a road we all travel. They come upon him and then fleet away as if into the empty eons of eternity."

"Do you feel he's gifted?" Orland asked, adjusting the sleeve edge of his frock top.

"He's something," Welles answered.

"What do you mean?"

"I can't explain it, but all the time he's been here, the others, they're both in awe of what he can do, and fear him. I think more so, though, they're threatened," Welles responded. "But then again, I haven't been here that long myself."

"Threatened? Why are they threatened? Each individual needs to be confident upon their own foundation of faith and ability, and not worry about the gifts of others given by grace."

Welles stepped past Orland and returned inside after watching Chrishav ascend the stairs on the front of the temple structure. "Easier said than done," he noted, leaving his companion still standing on the balcony.

Orland followed Welles inside. "Go on." Orland directed.

"One student remembers talking to Chrishav about his faith. He would help him through all testing and failures. This student was reconciling how he performed in his ordination rites. Not even a minute later, a fellow student came and told his peer his sage was prepared to discuss the decision."

Orland interrupted. "I know this situation. Chrishav's somehow discerned the sage's intentions, and the student's sentiments."

"You know of this situation?" Welles asked.

"Yes, it was I who experienced the unexpected manifestation of his ability. It has gotten to be more pronounced."

"You didn't expect as much?"

"No. I assumed he was perceptive in understanding simple mannerisms, body, and voice inflections, with maybe a hint of spiritual insight. But he's shown over the last several weeks a propensity to read the spiritual psyche of others," Orland said.

This alarmed Welles. "You're saying he can read men's souls?"

"No, not of all men, only those themselves able to discern the supernatural. I also believe more than that he's able to perceive those entities that come onto this plane."

Welles didn't feel relieved. "Wait a minute, now you're trying to say he can discern daemons and guardians?"

"That's exactly what I'm saying. He is a true soul reader."

"I didn't know such men existed."

"Nor I; I'm not even sure if he's aware of the full potential he possesses."

Welles returned to the miniature balcony, peering down the vacant front stairway to find Chrishav had entered the temple.

"Why is a soul reader revealed unto us now?" Welles expressed.

"I've been contacted by a colleague of mine. He's a missionary in Africa. A darkness has come upon the earth," Orland said. "It attempts through the minutest of maneuvering to undo everything of the Great Creator we believe in. What fortune unfolds for what is ahead, we don't know. All I know is what I've been told of an elusive malevolence. Have Chrishav meet me in the prayer room after his evening meal."

"Yes, High One, I will."

Orland wanted to make sure he didn't mention too much to Welles. There was more to Chrishav's ability he had wanted to obscure, if not conceal altogether. He could read a person's true soul name, something considered fantasy or lore. The first time Orland met Chrishav, Chrishav called him by a name he had never heard before, but the name that caused Orland to stand frigid. It confused Chrishav why Orland was icy towards him; Orland knew otherwise. There was a deep compulsion to obey Chrishav's every word, as if what he spoke were a puppeteer's string. Moments later, the emotions passed.

Chrishav returned to his dorm room and removed the off-white cloth wrappings that protected his body during the desert walk. No matter how tight and secure the wrappings, dust and dirt still invaded his clothing, necessitating a body wash. There was a knock on the door.

"Who is it?" Chrishav asked, suspecting it was Friar Welles.

"It's Welles."

"It's open, brother."

Welles entered the room and stood by the doorway. "Afternoon, Chrishav; how was your walkabout?"

"Fine."

"Why do you like to go on so many walks?"

"The clarity it brings is hard to explain."

"And why away from the town? Nuevo Chahalua is only a little less than ten kilometers away, and yet you seem to head to the outback." Welles glanced down at the floor where Chrishav had piled his outfit, which sat next to the water camel pack he had removed from his back.

Chrishav sensed dimness and obscurity from Welles, but not a darkness originating from within, but as if he empathized with an emotional heaviness weighted to his soul. "Orland has weighed you down with an unrevealed burden."

How does he do that? "How do you know it was Orland?" Welles asked.

"I saw you two talking as I ascended the temple to undertake my daily prayers."

Wells rolled his eyes. "Of course you did. Did you also know that Orland would send me here to request for you to visit him after your dinner meal?"

"No, but then again, I can't foretell the future, which is why you're so interested in wondering if I'm able to."

How'd he know? "You'll have to forgive me. It seems there's so much to you. Your abilities intrigue Orland, the other monks, and me."

Chrishav stopped pulling off the lower portion of his outer garments, revealing light beige khaki pants. "What's so hard to understand?"

"I don't know if it's a matter of understanding, or a matter of accepting is what I'm trying to say. What you have is extraordinary. Men today are not capable of such things, and yet, to hear you and Orland, it almost seems commonplace for you."

Chrishav rolled his dusty outer garments into a ball and stuffed them into a laundry bag already filled. "I've been here a year, and you're still confused?"

Chrishav sensed a bit of jealousy from Welles about why he wouldn't be Orland's favorite. Welles considered himself an astute cleric, serving most of his life for the Order. Having arrived at the monastery six months prior, after years of missionary work, Welles was confident the Order's hierarchy would exalt him into the leadership within the temple's clergy higher echelons. Yet Orland relegated him to a simple presbyter. Orland had noted that positions of humility in this life yield greater glory in the next. Orland's insight didn't remove Welles' envy.

"Don't forget, I've been here a few months before you." Welles noted. "How did you end up here?"

"I can't say, only why I left my reservation. The Shamans were antagonistic towards me."

Welles knew of Chrishav's self-imposed exile, but not of the reason. "Did you have to leave? Was it because they didn't like you since you're half black and half Native American?"

"No, the Shamans considered me something of an outcast because of my abilities."

Chrishav had sensed other identities within the Shamans' personas. When he learned about daemons, he realized it was they, minor daemons, who dwelt within the Shamans. It was these voices that had supplanted the pure voices that once filled their consciousness, and to Chrishav, unnerving. He considered the guiding spirits of the Shamans' wayward entities leading the tribes astray. Chrishav was confident that the spiritual leaders embedded with malevolent entities were subtle instigators to the lawlessness persistent on the reservation.

Crime, lack of personal motivation, lethargy, and carnality soared on the tribe's territories and in the local communities as the native religious leaders usurped the political and missionary influences attempting to bring in change. Sullenness tainted the psyche of his people. The

Shamans would say the ghosts of the innocent, those killed during the 1864 massacre, cursed the land. The Shamans reprimanded Chrishav with severe antagonism when he tried to present the truth of what he experienced; an inky presence embodied their souls.

During a major federal initiative to reduce violent crime on several of the largest and crime-ridden reservations, Chrishav's nation, the Shoshone, saw an increase in violent crime as compared to the other Indian nations. A tribal advocate for the federal government attempting to reform the tribes on the reservation told Chrishav, "this place has always had gloom here, but because they see me as a mere weak squaw, I'm not a threat to their way of life." She warned him the leaders had cast a vote for his spiritual purging and cleansing from the land of the living to appease the ancestors. Chrishav knew it to be cryptic for something malicious planned against him. It was best to leave.

"Was there anything else?" Chrishav asked, standing in the center of the room in a yellowed unbleached T-shirt, khaki pants, and hard-soled desert sandals. "I'd like my privacy so that I can finish getting cleaned up before dinner." Chrishav didn't want to discuss his gifts or arrival to anyone in the monastery anymore.

"Sorry bout that, didn't mean to take up so much of your time." Chrishav knew Welles wasn't genuine.

In leaving, Welles left the door open, which irked Chrishav.

Chrishav entered a hexagon-shaped room, each wall made of clear and colored glass fragments mosaicked into the wall, and reflecting the light from a hundred candles placed in ten separate five-foot candelabras positioned around the room. Orland, his mentor, sat in the middle of the room on the gray, unpainted concrete floor, getting up from lying prostrate.

"How are your studies of the scriptures?" Orland asked.

"They're going well."

"Good, now do you know why I called you here?"

Chrishav didn't and remained quiet. He knew something had unsettled Orland.

Orland gestured for Chrishav to sit down and join him on the floor. "You have a unique ability. You're aware of that, aren't you?"

"You've told me many times before," Chrishav responded.

"I received a disturbing message today—a very disturbing message. It was from a friend of mine that I used to accomplish missionary work with years ago in Africa. He's retired over there now, but he still volunteers for the Order. We were keeping each other abreast of our recent endeavors and encounters. He's been keeping me up to date on someone with unique abilities, in some ways similar to yours."

Chrishav's eyes exploded wide open. "There's another soul reader?"

"No, not a soul reader, but someone who can pierce beyond our world, perceive those entities that are at enmity towards men, and can track and dispatch them."

"I don't follow."

"You know that there are daemons running around, causing mischief, mayhem, and other pandemonium?" Orland questioned. "But you haven't had experience with encountering one firsthand, have you?"

"No." Chrishav's time at the monastery led him to live an insular life for the last three years. "My last experience with anything like that was with the indwelling of shamans in my tribe."

Orland continued. "There's a class of daemons called Destroyers, each one having a unique ability and purpose. Men many times are not sure of their purpose, only that they are powerful. They can be overt, or act with subtly and discretion."

Chrishav was apprehensive about Orland's intentions. "What does this have to do with me?"

"The young charge of my friend is heading to northern California, a town called Elysium. Join him in hunting down and expelling the destroyer daemon, one more enigmatic than most. This one entered our world under the guise of a minor daemon."

"That's such an undertaking, what is it I could do?"

"You'll find out. Ensure you remain on the path of light."

"And what of resources?"

"The order will pay for your trip and his, plus any supplies, gear, and needed weapons."

"Weapons?"

"Not for you, but for the spirit tracker. Never has our Order had to send those unaware of what is before them."

"And why Northern California?" Chrishav asked.

"One never knows the logistical providence for our personal destiny. My friend relayed he discovered this is where you are to travel. No more questions, and may the Great Creator's blessings be with you."

REMINISCING OF SISTER

Randall estimated he had played close to twenty games of solitaire, attempting to suppress his grief, before he had started his drinking binge. He didn't want to believe his sister was dead. His languishing mind overflowed with drunken induced reveries of playing tag with her and the neighborhood kids, chasing fireflies at night, or watching shooting stars during their summer evening camp outs, Randall treasured the memories of their fun times playing together in the fields on the outskirt of the town when he was ten, she was eleven.

Wearing paint-stained jeans and a sweat stained, yellowed t-shirt, Randall sat on the side of the motel room bed with his face buried in his hands. No matter how hard he tried to remove the mournful memories of his sister from his mind, his tears, like a waterfall, flowed from his eyes; sniffling their trustworthy companion. With the onslaught of sorrow re-assaulting his emotions, Randall remembered his mother would tell him men don't cry. He worked to regain his composure. When he finished smothering his unintentional outburst, he poured another shot of Scotch from the bottle on the nightstand into one of the complimentary clear plastic tumblers; he held it up in the light and stared at the amber colored liquid.

"Sherry, you were the best sister in the world," Randall slurred. He gulped the contents of the tumbler and poured another shot.

The next morning was unforgiving. Suffering a throbbing headache, and feeling dizzy, Randall looked over at the motel room entrance; one of his work boots rested at the threshold, with a large scuff mark on the door. Then he remembered he had thrown his boot to chase out the maid, whom he didn't hear knock and enter, asking if he wanted her to clean the room. She retreated outside, spewing verbal obscenities from what he could make out based on his limited vocabulary of Spanish.

The clock displayed "10:21 AM." The odorous smell of vomit assaulted his nose. With his broad hands, he pushed himself off the bed top. A small amount of dried puke decorated his shirt and the bedcover.

The maid's going to be upset when she comes back. Randall finished getting himself out of the bed and into the bathroom, witnessing the result of missing the toilet during one of his heave runs in the middle of the night. *She's not going to be* upset; *she's gonna be pissed.*

He stared at the nightstand. It came back to him why he felt so miserable. A fifth of Scotch lay on top on its side. A dribble of liquid remained. Why wasn't he in an alcoholic coma? His six-foot-two, 265-pound, muscular frame had experienced similar alcohol binges while bar hopping, playing pool, or watching football games at the local sports bar with his friends. Last night was different—he'd consumed shots of the spirits in rapid succession until he passed out. Even if he ended up in a coma, or died, Randall didn't care. His sister was dead.

Randall sat on the side of the bed and stared at the wall, reminiscing. He believed Sherry was the one individual who understood him, and in some ways, made him act as a more responsible person. Randall was the type who ridiculed or intimidated others, especially those whom he considered weaker than him. The last time he and Sherry were together at home in Chicago a couple of years back, he went to the mall with his best friend. Driving home leaving the freeway while on the off-ramp, a vagrant with a long unkempt beard streaked with gray and dirt splotched skin, was holding up a sign made with a piece of wrinkled cardboard ripped along the edges, and read "Homeless and Hungry-Anything Will Help."

Randall pulled out a five-dollar bill from his wallet. He rolled down his window and drove up to the vagrant layered in soiled and faded clothing. Randall made sure no one was in front of his car as he extended his hand out the car window, holding the money.

"Hey buddy, hope this helps," Randall said.

Just as the indigent peddler reached for the donation, Randall snatched his arm back into the car. "Psyche!" he yelled as he pressed his foot hard on the accelerator.

Wheels screeched. Randall was lucky and avoided a collision, turning onto the main road, not noticing a small four-door Toyota sedan traversing through the intersection. Randall and his best friend laughed until they returned to his mother's house. Sherry wondered what was so funny. While Randall went to use the bathroom, his friend detailed what they considered a humorous incident.

An icy shiver rippled along Randall's back in the middle of his taking a leak. Reflexively, he turned to look over his shoulder, almost missing the toilet bowl mid-flow. He couldn't explain it. No one was there, but he sensed Sherry was mad. When Randall returned to the living room, his sister greeted him with an icy stare, crossed arms, and a rapidly tapping foot. Randall's friend scurried to the front door, excusing himself, envisioning the impending confrontation.

Coward. Randall thought. "What!?" he said, attempting to stand up to his sister.

"Don't play stupid; you know what?" Sherry acknowledged, with a scolding voice.

Randall shrugged his shoulders and remained quiet, feigning ignorance.

"You're going back there and giving that man twice what you had planned to give him," Sherry directed.

"Bullcrap," Randall replied, annoyed. "Most of those guys are faking it, anyway. You saw that investigative news report. How much you want to bet he's suckering money from idiot saps that drive by? I bet that guy drives a nice SUV or BMW or something."

"That doesn't give you the right to act like an asshole. The world is full of them; my brother doesn't need to be another one. You know better than that, and what if that man needed that money?"

"What the..."

"Ssshhh," Sherry said as she grabbed her purse sitting on the coffee table. "Don't let me go around saying I'm ashamed of my brother."

That's all she needed to say. Hearing Sherry make that comment was the same as if from his mother. Randall dropped his head and apologized.

They drove around for fifteen minutes. Finding the beggar, Randall gave him ten dollars.

Randall reminisced about other fond memories of his sister until they collided with the present day. He was sitting on the side of a bed in a budget motel in the middle of Nebraska, driving back from her funeral, heading to his mom's home.

Still feeling the effects of the alcohol, he changed his shirt, washed his face with a damp rag and skipped taking a shower. He had opted to get back on the road instead of getting something to eat, but while at the front desk checking out, intense hunger pangs arose. Arriving at the Flying J truck stop and walking from his car in the parking lot to the restaurant, a thin, freckled-faced red-headed young man approached, holding a set of small pamphlets. The man flaunted immaculately cut ruddy hair parted down the center of his head. He wore blue jeans pressed with a perfect crease down the front, and a wrinkle free starched dark blue polo shirt.

"Sir, can I interest you in a tract and tell you of the wonderful work God our Great Creator did through his..."

"Leave me alone!" Randall interrupted. "Where was your God when my sister died?"

"Umm, umm," the young redhead said, stunned, unable to find any words to say.

"Thought so," Randall retorted as he continued towards the restaurant.

Waiting for his meal, Randall replayed in his mind the conversation at the funeral with Bethany, Sherry's best friend. She told him they were on a girl's get away traveling up the coast to San Francisco, and then driving on to Seattle. Almost two and a half hours north of Sacramento as they traveled on the Interstate Five freeway, they explored some of the nearby small towns hoping to find out of the way antique shops or undertake a quick hike. They drove into the small city of Redding and discovered a road leading into the mountains, as told by a stranger. The road led to a town that didn't appear on any maps or on their navigational system. The local antique hunters in Redding considered the small mountain town an antique haven.

Nothing led Bethany to believe anything had been plaguing Sherry for her to take her own life. And as far as she knew, they were having a wonderful trip, staying there for a week and a half longer than planned. It was as if time stood still in the town.

Randall's breakfast arrived. He finished only half of his plate of runny scrambled eggs, overcooked hash browns, sausage links, bowl of lumpy grits, and toast. He considered finishing everything, but thinking of Sherry, an onrush of nausea hit. Pushing the plate with his half-eaten meal away, he sat back in the booth and stared listlessly out the window.

Randall's cell phone rang, breaking his brooding. By the chime, he knew it was his mother. He plopped thirteen dollars on the table to cover the meal and tip, and stepped outside to answer the call.

"Hey Mom."

"Hi son, when do you think you'll be home? When you get here, we can start going through your sister's belongings and close out her affairs."

This was something Randall didn't want to be concerned with right now. He drove cross-country to attend his sister's funeral, allowing time for his mind to clear on the return trip, especially before having to deal with her business matters and personal affairs in Los

Angeles and Chicago. Finding out she had killed herself made little sense to him. Sherry didn't act distressed. She handled her personal life well, making sure her friends and acquaintances were above reproach. And she managed her money well, even looking forward to opening up her own boutique in Santa Monica during the next year.

"Mom, I don't wanna talk about this right now," Randall pleaded.

"You're going to have to talk about it sometime. You were so closed up at the funeral."

"I know, but now's not the time. I want to take some time getting back and get my head back on straight, to come to grips with this."

"Come to grips with this?" Randall's mother questioned, as her voice cracked. "I don't know if I ever can. It's not right. I don't know why your sister would've done something like that. I feel like something is wrong with all of this."

Randall sensed the lament building in his mother's voice the more she spoke. This was foreign to him. She was consistent in showing emotional strength, regardless of the situation. Since when he was a young child and a car accident killed his father and older brother, she didn't show any emotions in public to help maintain a tough front for him and his sister. He remembered in the middle of one night when he was eight; he awoke to grab a drink of water; he heard muffled crying coming from behind the closed doors of her bedroom.

Over the years as he and Sherry grew up, his mother was both mother and father, nurturing, but also strong when needed. She was a traditionalist and believed women should be sensitive and caring. She treated Sherry as if she were a little princess or heiress adorned with privilege. With Randall, she was firm and hard-nosed, wanting him to learn how to handle his own problems. When he was nine years old, he came home from playing outside with some of the neighborhood kids, crying because another boy had hit him. His mother's response was, "Did you hit him back?"

She sent him back outside and threatened him with no dinner if he didn't even out the situation. He returned ten minutes later with tussled hair, a black eye, and a wide beaming grin. He asked his mom if the boy he had been in a fight with could come over for dinner. The two became best friends. Many of Randall's fights later in life wouldn't be as fruitful, garnering him a couple of permanent scars on his face.

Throughout his life, with his mother many times holding back her affection, Sherry had been there to help comfort and nurture him. As he got older, his mother set him straight if he misbehaved.

"Mom, it's gonna be okay," Randall said, trying to prevent her from crying on the phone, something he didn't want to deal with.

"I know, but I miss her. It's not the same as knowing she was in California. To do what she did in some small town in the middle of nowhere, I don't understand."

"I don't think any of us do. Mom, can I call you back later? I'm getting ready to hit the road again."

"Yeah, call me later to make sure everything's alright."

"Ok mom, will do. Love you." Randall disconnected the call on his cellphone. He and his mother had this same conversation in Los Angeles at the funeral. Sherry loved the city and told her friend Bethany she wanted to be buried out there if anything ever happened. Bethany didn't think it would be so soon after they had discussed it.

The angst of thinking over what happened to his sister, the funeral, and the emotional fragility of his mother stressed Randall and inflamed the jock itch in his groin. It became uncomfortable and irritating. He needed to apply more of his prescription cream, but ignored the discomfort.

As much as he tried to keep from replaying the same conversations with his mother, he wondered the same thing. Why did Sherry commit suicide when everything seemed to go right in her life?

Randall decided that when he got back to Chicago, he would help his mother and then fly back out west to the town where she took her life. There's no way she would have committed suicide.

RENDEZVOUS

N ila, his first time flying, and assigned a window seat, was enjoy-
ing his trans-Atlantic intercontinental trip. Watching the earth
below pass filled him with awe. As they flew over the Atlantic, he never
comprehended the wide expanse of the ocean. His hometown did rest
by the seashore, but he had no reason before now to consider the
distance between the continents. And during one leg of the trip, the
setting sun with the evening twilight revealing a sky full of flourishing
stars impressed him of the cosmos's beauty.

Nila attempted to sleep. As soon as his eyes shut and he drifted
into unconsciousness, the plane shuddered, jarring him awake. He had
never experienced turbulence before. The pilot instructing the crew
to secure the cabin and all passengers to fasten their seatbelts didn't
comfort him. Outside, the sky appeared clear, until he saw off into
the distance the semblance of a dark splotch of an orange, gray, and
white cloud forming. It was familiar. It reminded him of the same
mysterious clouds that had formed in the sky the same day his father
died.

The airplane banked. The imbued light from the sunset-filled horizon flared into Nila's vision. He didn't notice what appeared to be
a tear in the clouds. From the darkness of the sky, Nila caught sight
of what he assumed was the spiraling manifestation of a small smoky
orb hastening towards the plane. Peering harder off into the distance,
it disappeared. Then something caught his eye; the orb approached
from the lower quadrant of his view. It closed in on the plane's un-
derbelly.

Nila lost sight of the enigmatic object. The aircraft jolted, throwing
a flight attendant to the floor as she tried to confirm everyone's seatbelt
was secure. He expected something else to occur. Craning his head
and viewing the cabin, some passengers showed nervousness, react-

ing to the intensity of the turbulence. One man whipped his head back and forth, trying to look out the window to determine if the weather outside could cause additional instability. A few passengers slept through the jostling; others read magazines, e-books, worked on their computers, or sat not finding anything interesting on the inflight entertainment system.

The turbulence abated, with the remainder of the flight uneventful. Yet the knot in Nila's stomach made him sense something was amiss.

Chrishav wasn't happy with the information given to him about who he was supposed to meet. When asked for a description, Orland responded, your spirit will guide you. Chrishav wondered was the person he was to pick up was male or female, white, black, Asian, Hispanic. He didn't know. He also didn't know Orland wanted Chrishav to exercise his abilities in an unfamiliar environment.

Orland told him to keep an eye out for someone coming from a distant land who looked lost. Since the airline for the terminal supported international flights, most of the arriving passengers were from distant lands. More so, many of the passengers and their companions picking them up at the airport appeared lost. Families and friends searched through the sea of bodies, attempting to find one another.

A river of faces cascaded down the escalator leading into the baggage claim area. Caucasians, blacks, Hispanics, Asians, Middle Easterners, wave after wave, a deluge of humanity crested from the top of the movable stairs. Chrishav speculated about what this person may look like; what you expect in your mind never matches reality. Soon, the volume of passengers from the gates on the escalator dwindled before the next wave appeared.

Amid the next flood of arrivals, a young, tall, black, older teen male with a weather-worn face and very short afro stood out. He examined the young man intently, focusing on him as he floated down the escalator. A name pounced into Chrishav's mind: Daynell. Chrishav knew this name wasn't his given birth name, but took this to be his spiritual name. A soul name would present itself for another man able to pierce the natural world in subtle ways. He found his assigned ward.

Chrishav had been wrong before in attempting to peruse someone. This influenced his standing with the Council of Shamans to act against him when he still lived on the reservation in Wyoming. At first, the shamans believed the gods had blessed Chrishav. He entreated they renounce the spirits of the Shamans, sensing they were malevolent; the Shamans instead ostracized Chrishav. Later, the inky veil of malfeasance within the tribe's spiritual leaders that hid deep behind their individual psyches cemented unease and distrust in his soul as a young adult that they would try to harm him.

Chrishav snaked his way through the crowd over to the tall African teen. Nila saw the approaching man staring at him with a focused gaze and determined he was the one to meet.

Chrishav extended his hand to greet the young man. "My name is Chrishav. Yours?"

Nila accepted the handshake, sensing he could trust the stranger, and smiled. "My name is Nila."

"Do you have any luggage?" Chrishav asked, noticing Nila carrying nothing more than a small backpack.

"Yes, one piece."

"Let's find out which carousel it's on."

Reviewing the monitor and cross-referencing with Nila's flight number, they found their way to the assigned luggage carousel. Waiting with the throngs of other passengers for the conveyor system to come to life, Chrishav pursued other questions.

"So where are you from?"

"I'm from a small town on the west coast of Africa. And you?"

"A monastery down in Mexico, although I'm not from Mexico. I'm part Shoshone Indian. I grew up in Wyoming. I don't know if you know where Wyoming is."

Nila smirked and raised an eyebrow. "Yes, I know where Wyoming is. I studied it in school," he said.

"Sorry, I didn't mean to offend you."

"Do you know where we're supposed to go from here?" Nila asked.

"A town a bit of a ways outside of Redding, California. What's odd is I can't find it on a map. I'm not even sure if it exists, and providence is playing tricks on us. I have to rely that the instructions on how to get there that my mentor gave me are accurate."

Nila chuckled.

"Why do you find that amusing?" Chrishav asked.

"They say the same about my town in Africa. Many say they can't find it on a map, yet it exists."

The two arrived at the assigned baggage carousel. A large roll-up door opened next to the portal of the luggage conveyor system. Two airline employees struggled to transport an animal carrier into the pickup area. The container violently jerked as they lifted it from the transition opening. The caged dog's snarling inflicted uneasy emotions within everyone who was within earshot. Several passengers experienced goosebumps or as if the hairs on their arms raised. The incessant and sinister growling stifled the conversations of a multitude of passengers and guests. A couple of nearby children, more sensitive to the unnatural non-corporal source within the beast, moved behind their parents and clenched their hands for security.

Each time the dog barked was like discordant clawing on Chrishav's soul; goosebumps danced on his forearms. Nila winced; his body shivered as if cold for a quick instant. Something was awry hearing the canine's unnatural guttural outburst-each bark bore impassionate ravenous hatred. The Huntsman had warned him-these emotions and feelings could be significant.

"Chrishav, there's something unnatural about that dog," Nila said.

"I sense it to, but what are we supposed to do?"

Nila scanned the area, having no weapon and feeling inadequate. The environment differed from his native land. "We have to do something."

The dog rammed his head into the wire cage door, causing the carrier's center of gravity to shift for the two workers. They struggled to maintain a secured hold.

"Think there's gotta be something we can do," Chrishav said. "I don't think this could turn well."

Nila spotted an unattended cleaning bucket and mop by the entrance of a nearby men's room. *Good, a wood handle. I may need to use that*, he thought, as Chrishav's earlier comment reminded him of the Huntsman training.

The dog again rammed its head against the wire-framed door. With the carrier becoming harder to grip because of the shifting weight, the luggage crew placed it on the floor.

The waiting area went silent.

"Damn, they didn't say this dog was this mean on the shipping papers," one of the airline workers said. He scanned the area, hoping the owner was nearby to claim the container.

The dog butted its head once again; the wire grid door bent and loosened the locking mechanism. The worker nearest the carrier's front, noticing the impending escape, reached down, and attempted to secure the door. It was too late; the dog withdrew back onto all fours, gathering a surge of strength and lunged forward with full force. The door swung open; an adult Pit Bull-Rottweiler mix found itself free. The snarling canine stood still next to the luggage conveyor belt, acclimating to its freedom.

Panic erupted in the crowd. Many screamed and shrieked, most backing away from the ferocious creature.

Nila darted over to the men's room entrance, grabbing the unattended mop from the bucket. He rested the mildew scented, stringed mop head on the floor. Then he placed the handle at an angle to the wall and kicked the wood handle above the mop head. He broke the shaft, creating a jagged end that fashioned an improvised spear. With his makeshift weapon, Nila rushed after the dog. Chrishav hurried to follow and catch up.

The growling beast found its objective after searching through the multitude of panicked onlookers—a man in the terminal's baggage claim area. He had arrived on a flight from Chicago. The man was broad and had a rugged face containing two large scars. It was Randall Steiner.

The dog charged, nipping at the calf of a twelve-year-old boy, unable to back away fast enough. His father attempted to fend off the creature. It then bit the leg of another man wearing sweatpants in its way. Witnessing the canine's aggression towards the man and the child terrified all the other bystanders. The crowd un-zipped, creating an unencumbered path allowing the dog to charge towards its prey. Randall, witnessing the attacking hound charging, turned to run. A businessman trying to move out of the way failed to shift his rolling carryon suitcase out of Randall's path. Randall tripped over the luggage and fell to the floor.

The Pit Bull-Rottweiler mix pounced and found itself on top of its target, standing on Randall's torso. Now face to face, Randall was now staring into its yellow-brown eyes; the hot, rancid breath expelled from the snout blasted onto his face. Intermixed with the dog's growl, Randall heard it speak and say, "You will be ours."

Randall's muscles paralyzed with fear. At any other time, he would have attempted to evict the beast from his body with force. Imagining hearing the beast speak caused him to become petrified. The dog arched its head back as saliva dripped from its jowls; it readied to lunge down and bite at his neck.

Chrishav yelled, "Sun-Ithobah," as he and Nila ran up to Randall; the canine's muscles seized and tightened, suspended as if time froze; the barking and growling ceased.

"Nila, now!" Chrishav yelled again.

With fluid-like agility, Nila took several more steps, and with his makeshift spear, focused his thrust on the creature's rib cage, impaling the Pit Bull-Rottweiler mix in its side. Blood flowed from the wound.

An eerie, piercing wail reverberated through the terminal. Passengers and terminal employees in the vicinity all cringed at the unnatural death moans. The animal fell limp onto the floor. Randall exhaled in relief. Nila and Chrishav witnessed a wisp of green smoke extruding from the dead beast's nose. Nila wondered if the same outcome would occur to him as it did his father. According to Sogundu, the exorcised daemon had enveloped and killed him.

The green emanation dissipated.

At first, Nila was relieved, then a wave of guilt hit. Did he just kill an innocent dog that was simply super aggressive?

Randall lay on the ground and expelled a large breath, relieved. "Thanks, whoever you are," he said, rolling over to the side, pushing the lifeless carcass onto the waxed tiled floor.

"You're welcome," Nila answered.

Chrishav sensed though Randall was appreciative, he grappled with the suppression of an inner turmoil.

A crowd mulled around the three men, some mystified, viewing the lifeless canine. For someone to kill one of God's creatures horrified and angered a few, regardless of its ferocity and attack on Randall.

Chrishav and Nila helped Randall to stand up as the airport police surrounded all three men, guns drawn. The dog's owner worked his way through the crowd, yelling at Nila and Chrishav. Obscenities weaved every other word with repeating references he would sue for losing his pet.

Separated and questioned for several hours, then released, Chrishav and Nila sat together in the security holding area reception room.

Nila was eager to ask a question, still overwhelmed by the earlier incident, dismissing his lengthy interrogation. "What was that you said to cause the dog to stop like that?"

"It was the spiritual name of the daemon possessing the dog."

"It's spiritual name?"

"Every person, every spirit, has a unique spiritual name. If you learn the true name of someone and say it before using their given name, for an instant, you bind the soul. Otherwise, the name is nothing more than a name." Chrishav didn't tell Nila it would work with others who could touch the spiritual world, such as himself and Nila, but not all men.

"I'm not sure I follow."

Chrishav peered into Nila's eyes. "Daynell."

Nila believed Chrishav had gone crazy. "Who or what is Daynell?"

Chrishav chuckled. "Oh nothing. By the way, smart idea with that broomstick. How'd you come up with that?"

"I don't know. I looked around and the idea came to mind," Nila answered; he didn't know how to explain that he almost forgot his training by the Huntsman to be ready, especially if you have to craft a weapon.

"I have another question," Chrishav queried.

"What's that?"

"How is it you're here, coming to the United States?"

"It's something I have to do, something I was trained to do," Nila answered with boldness.

"Trained to do? That doesn't answer my question?"

"I am hunting down the daemon that killed my father."

Chrishav's blank expression showed he was confused. "You know what? Do you think the entity possessing the dog was the Destroyer?"

Nila's eyes widened. "I don't think... how would we know?" Nila wondered if he'd be able to react if he faced a Destroyer infused creature. His stomach turned.

"It's not like the daemon is going to say, Hey, I'm the Destroyer, the one you're looking for," Chrishav said. "The daemon in the dog may have been nothing more than a minor one. You saw how it evaporated and returned to its original realm in a whimper."

A senior TSA officer wearing dress pants, a white shirt, and a purple striped tie approached the two men. "Well, it looks like the two of you can go. Talking to several witnesses and reviewing the video, you two weren't the cause of the incident. As a matter of fact, you may have saved quite a few of the passengers from any potential injury. But that doesn't stop the dog's owner from contacting you about compensation."

Chrishav grinned. "We're free to go?"

"You're free to go. We don't need any more weirdness around here. We got your information in case we need to contact you."

Randall sat alone at the gate for the flight to Redding, waiting in the connected hard plastic seats at the boarding area for the commuter jets. Seeing Nila and Chrishav heading his way caused a surge of panic to flood his emotions. *This is great. Now what*?

"Why are you two here? It's bad enough I get attacked by a wild dog, and then questioned by the airport police only to miss my plane. Now I gotta wait here to see how the airline is gonna get me up to where I'm going, and you two pop up."

"We're supposed to be heading on this flight up to Redding," Chrishav responded.

"Redding? That's where I'm headed," Randall said, as he arched an eyebrow, not expecting to hear the city name. "Actually, I'm heading to a town called Elysium," he added, hoping the information would segregate any further similarities between himself and the two travelers. Randall noticed both men didn't expect to hear the name of that town, yet by the reaction of their eyes popping wide open, he suspected they were traveling to the same destination. "Don't tell me you're heading up there?"

"Yes, we are," Nila answered as he and Chrishav sat a couple of seats over from Randall.

All three remained quiet, not having anything to say to one another. After a few minutes, Randall broke the silence stalemate. "Since we're gonna be stuck together for a while, why are you two going up there?"

"We're on a spiritual journey and quest, I guess you can say," Chrishav answered.

Chrishav's response irritated Randall. "Wonderful, I have to be here with a couple of religious nuts," he said as he rolled his eyes.

Chrishav sensed growing antagonism within Randall; he needed to help diffuse the situation. "Look, I understand you may not be religious, but we're not here to bother you. We'll leave you be; we know you have your own personal reasons for going up to where we're going," he replied in a reconciliatory tone.

"Sorry, gentlemen," the gate agent interrupted, walking up to the three men. "With all that happened in the terminal today, a lot of folks missed their flights. The last commuter flight of the day had already left earlier this evening. You'll have to stay here tonight, but the city is gonna take care of your accommodations since they were, in part, the ones responsible for keeping you for so long. We'll be able to book you on the first available flight with seats leaving tomorrow morning. It'll be a few more minutes before we complete all your arrangements."

The gate agent walked away.

"This is f'in wonderful. Now I'm stuck here with you two until tomorrow," Randall said. "No offense," he added, not sounding conciliatory.

"None taken," Chrishav acknowledged as Randall got up to sit further away to await his new travel arrangements.

The next morning, Randall approached the gate where Chrishav and Nila were already waiting amongst the other passengers. They presented him with polite smiles, a hand wave, and then continued their personal conversation.

Randall's stomach sank thinking of his sister, now remorseful for the way he had acted towards the two the day prior; she would not have been proud of him. He strolled over to Chrishav and Nila.

"Hey, I'm sorry about yesterday," Randall mumbled loudly. "I've been going through a lot lately. I lost someone who meant a lot to… that's not important. Anyway, sorry."

"Not a problem," Chrishav responded, presenting a comforting smile.

"I'm going up to Elysium and try to tie up some loose ends, and I'm on edge. I'm not sure what to expect."

Chrishav and Nila knew Randall was genuine with his apology.

After an uneasy pause in the conversation, Nila said, "I'm sorry for your loss. I understand. I'd be lying to you if I were to tell you I knew what you were going through, but I don't. I lost my father a while ago. I still miss him, but I know it's not the same."

Chrishav, surprised by the openness of Nila's response, sensed Randall appreciated the comment. He sat next to the two men.

"Sorry about your father," Randall said. "I lost mine too when I was young, but I didn't know him like you did. It sucks, doesn't it?"

"What sucks?" Nila asked.

Randall and Chrishav chuckled.

"No, I mean that it's no fun losing our fathers," Randall said. "That's what I mean by it sucks."

"Oh yes, it sucks," Nila responded.

ARRIVAL

E lysium, a small town near the center of the Shasta-Trinity National Forest, rested in a sweeping valley amongst the Coast Ranges in Northern California. The intense heat of the hot, dry summer traumatized the sparse, rain-starved forests blanketing the mountains. However, luscious and vibrant ponderosa pine trees, hearty oaks, expansive shrubbery, berry bushes, and other woodland vegetation surrounded the town.

Over 6500 souls lived in the village. If you include the active hunting seasons, the population swelled another forty to fifty deer and boar hunters any week. Some tourists found the hidden mecca by accident. Many enjoyed antique hunting, window-shopping, gawking at many of the local handmade crafts, hiking on trails yielding panoramic views to the east of town, or driving through while on a family outing. There were other passersby; most residents and visitors in town weren't aware of; they didn't pass through for leisure, travel, or hunting. Elysium was a waypoint onto their final destination.

The town comprised a variety of old-fashioned brick buildings, most two or three stories - an old hardware store, a bakery, a drugstore, antique shops, a diner, and a motel. The newest retailer was the game and sports store. The theater on the main street even premiered first-run movies. The construction of many of the structures comprised old bricks, some unpainted, others painted ivory white or a dull blue. Awnings painted with the store's name adorned a few of the establishments.

Two roads led into Elysium. From the east was a winding one-way thoroughfare that originated from a side street in Redding. Most of the residents and visitors used the two-lane highway heading south. Only certain passersby could travel north or west beyond the forest boundary. North was the preferred direction.

Nila and Chrishav met Randall for a late breakfast in the pastoral and antique hotel lobby adorned with wood beams on the low ceiling, wood columns, and country style furnishings. They were starving, not having eaten much during their early morning trip up from Los Angeles. Randall was at ease starting his excursion in town with someone he knew, even if they were new acquaintances. He would've liked to strike out on his own, but still had a hard time processing the bizarre incident that occurred at LAX the day prior. And if his sister were alive, she would have liked both men.

Randall also wanted to later search for a drugstore in town to fill his prescription for the special antifungal cream to help with his jock itch. He'd forgotten to get it filled before leaving Chicago and hoped they had it on hand. He hoped they didn't have to special order it since they were so far away from the larger city of Redding.

A beautiful, thin redhead woman approached the three, escorted by a five-foot ten uniformed deputy sheriff with a dark cinnamon complexion, muscular body, short afro, and weather-worn face with a strong jawline. Chrishav experienced the sensation of mutual attraction between the two, yet in her repressed heartfelt regret, in him, forgiveness. As soon as the surge of emotions cascaded through him, they washed away.

"Hi there, my name's Chantrelle, and this is my husband Carlson. I work over at the town hall, and he's the deputy here," the young woman said. Her greeting effervesced with pride. "What are your names? Where are you from?"

Chrishav answered first. "I'm Chrishav. I was born in Wyoming, a member of the Shoshoni Indian tribe, but now I live in Northern Mexico."

"I'm Randall, ma'am. I'm from Chicago."

"They call me Nila. I come from Africa."

"You're all the way from Africa?" Chantrelle inquired of Nila with glee. "Your English seems so proper. I'd thought you'd speak in broken English or with a thick accent."

Nila didn't mind responding to her comment, already having had a similar discussion with Randall while they waited for their flight at the airport in Los Angeles. He explained that English was the common trade language, allowing the various ethnic groups and distinct dialects to communicate with one another in his and neighboring countries.

Chantrelle continued her inquiry. "I've never met anyone from Africa before."

Nila wasn't sure how to respond, since the deputy glared down at his wife in disbelief.

Chantrelle sensed her husband's annoyance. "Last I remember, you were born in Atlanta."

"But my ancestors were born over there."

"And how long ago was that?" She replied. Nila assumed she was serious. He didn't understand her sarcasm and waited for an answer from the deputy. Chantrelle turned her attention back towards the three guests. "What brings you to visit our quaint little town? Sight-seeing? Antique hunting? Hunting?"

Nila didn't have an answer. He was apprehensive of what to say, or if he should talk to anyone, wondering if they were to be of help with searching for the Destroyer. He knew you don't ask, "Excuse me, but have you seen a destroyer daemon running around here? I'm here to hunt it down and dispatch it back to its ethereal realm."

Chrishav remained quiet, still a bit unsettled over the short barrage of emotions he experienced.

Randall responded before his two companions planned any type of answer. "I was hoping to talk to you about my sister, Deputy."

Deputy Rutherford raised an eyebrow. "Not sure if I know your sister. About what?"

"I don't know if you remember a Sherry Steiner?"

Deputy Rutherford tilted his head, looking upwards, and scrunched his face as he attempted to recall the name. "Sorry, the name doesn't ring a bell."

"She was believed to have committed suicide about three weeks ago."

The incident reignited Deputy Rutherford's memory. He didn't know why he couldn't recall the name since the suicide was the first one to occur in town. "I don't remember the name, but I remember your sister. She came into town with a friend of hers. They wanted to stay for a couple of days to go antique hunting and hiking in the nearby woods, but ended up staying a little longer. I believe they found her in a car on the edge of town. According to the M.E., she overdosed on pills and alcohol."

"That can't be right; she'd never do anything like that. Are you sure?" Randall responded.

"Are you calling the county M.E. a liar?" Deputy Rutherford replied, puffing out his chest as the nostrils of his bulbous nose above his small trimmed mustache flared.

"Whoa, whoa, whoa, I'm not calling anybody anything," Randall responded.

"Hun, calm down," Chantrelle interjected while stroking Deputy Rutherford's muscular arm. "I'm sure he didn't mean anything by it; he lost his sister, after all."

Deputy Rutherford's wife's gentle massaging soothed the cauldron of his boiling emotions.

"Deputy, we didn't mean to insult you," Chrishav said.

"No problem," Deputy Rutherford replied, relaxing his shoulders.

Randall's appetite suppressed his wanting to ask more about his sister and provided the opportunity for the deputy to calm down. "Deputy, I didn't mean to come off sounding so standoffish. I'm starved, but after I get something to eat, any problem if I come talk to you or someone about my sister's death?"

"Not a problem," Deputy Rutherford conceded, responding to Randall's conciliatory tone. "You can talk to me or the sheriff. We should be at the police station down the block, but if it can wait until tomorrow morning. The Sheriff has some errands to run, and I'll be ending my shift soon."

Chantrelle interjected, wanting to change the conversation. "Oh, before I forget, you three must join us for a barbecue. One of our local celebrities, Barclay, is hosting."

Nila perceived this irritated her husband by his facial reaction. Randall and Chrishav didn't notice and didn't care; they were focusing on getting something to eat, hoping the discussion would end.

"You just can't invite anyone over to Barclay's house," Deputy Rutherford said.

"He won't mind. You know how he has unexpected guests showing up anyway; two or three more won't make a difference. What time was it supposed to start, hun?"

Deputy Rutherford placed his hand on the butt of his gun and dropped his head down, waving it back and forth. "God, I don't believe you sometimes."

"But you still love me."

"Excuse me, ma'am, but we're all starving," Randall said. He wanted to hurry and eat so he could start talking to the residents before visiting the sheriff or deputy.

Chantrelle's grin widened, exposing a full set of white teeth. "Of course you are. Hearing there're real visitors here who are going to stay for a few days, and not pass through or do some hunting or antique shopping, I had to come and welcome you. I'm with the local Chamber of Commerce and Visitors Bureau."

"You are the Chamber of Commerce and Visitor's Bureau," Deputy Rutherford said.

"I still need to do my job, hun," Chantrelle countered.

"Excuse us, but we're wanting to go get some food," Randall said, a bit exasperated.

"Oh, I'm so sorry," Chantrelle said. "The restaurant here at the hotel is quite good."

"Sammi's is quite good too," Deputy Rutherford added.

"That place is almost good enough for the locals," Chantrelle continued. "I think it's one step up from a truck stop."

"Ouch, that's a little harsh, don't you think?" Deputy Rutherford said, "I like what you call truck stop food. Sammi's has character."

"I like truck stop food too," Randall added.

The deputy smiled.

"So, why are you young men here?" Chantrelle asked, changing the subject. Randall, Chrishav, and Nila agreed it was ironic she called them young. She appeared young herself. Nila estimated in her late twenties.

Chrishav responded first. "We're each here for different reasons. I'm here on a sabbatical from my monastery."

"Monastery, are you a monk?"

"Of sorts, I guess you can say."

"How interesting."

"The old man of my village sent me after my father died," Nila said.

Chantrelle expelled a quick gasp, not expecting that answer. "I'm so sorry to hear that. How did he die? And why come here?"

"That's kinda odd," Deputy Rutherford said. "Coming out here all the way from Africa because your father died. Did he die near here or something?"

"He's with me," Chrishav responded. "I guess you can say I'm his mentor. We're traveling on a spiritual journey to resolve some issues, his father's death being one of them."

Randall became impatient, wanting to escape from the conversation, as opposed to Chrishav and Nila, both accommodating of Chantrelle's pestering. He had scouted the lobby and discovered the restaurant entrance in the corner opposite the bellhop station. He nudged his two companions and pointed out their destination. "Excuse us, but we're going to get something to eat over in the restaurant."

"It was nice meeting you," Chrishav said.

"Likewise, it was nice meeting you three," Chantrelle said, "and don't forget, join us this evening at Barclay's house for the barbecue. I'll leave the directions for you at the front desk."

The three men excused themselves, proceeding across the lobby to the hotel restaurant.

"They seem so nice," Chantrelle said.

"Yeah, and it's a good thing they're staying a while. You know what happens to those who are passing through?" Carlson responded.

"I know, so you don't think they're passersby?"

"Not my job to worry about that, and if they are or aren't. That's the mayor and sheriff's problem."

Arriving at Barclay's party in the early evening, Deputy Rutherford and his wife expected a fraction of the massive number of guests in actual attendance. A few were friends and townies were mulling around gossiping about family affairs, arguing over their favorite football teams, or bragging about the exceptional mediocrity of their children graduating kindergarten, fifth, or eighth grade. The rest of the guests comprised passerby strangers. Deputy Rutherford didn't recall Barclay hosting a party this large since he moved to Elysium. After a bit of chitchat, the deputy and his wife navigated through the maze of people to the outside patio deck, where they noticed Barclay had laid teriyaki marinated, Korean style short ribs on the grill. They were burning.

"How come Barclay isn't out here watching this? It's gonna burn," Deputy Rutherford said as he grabbed the extra-long barbecue pincers and flipped over the meat. Their host was busy in the root cellar gathering potatoes and onions to work on making additional side dishes.

"I'll go see if I can find him," his wife said.

A couple of hours passed. The guests in the house swelled to over forty-five. As fast as a batch of boneless country style ribs, shish kabobs, bratwursts, hamburgers, or hot dogs were finished, Deputy Rutherford slammed them onto a serving dish. Chantrelle then carried the platter to the kitchen with another serving of meat flung onto the grill.

"Why is it I'm barbecuing? I thought we were the guests?" Carlson inquired of his wife, who waited for the next batch of meat to finish cooking.

"Don't worry about that. I bet Barclay is inside somewhere with his guests, trying to keep his head above water. Just be glad we got here when we did. He wouldn't have been able to cook all of this and work inside if we didn't help."

"We? I didn't see you over here helping flip this meat," Deputy Rutherford said, as he assaulted the flare-ups with a spray bottle filled with water threatening to scorch the batch of Teriyaki marinated Korean style short ribs.

"You know men are better at barbecuing than us females," Chantrelle said, jesting with her husband.

Deputy Rutherford stopped flipping the meat on the grill, giving his wife a sardonic stare; his mustache-topped lips pursed to one corner. "Very funny."

"Hey, I've been running the meat inside for you, making sure everyone is getting some of your wonderfully cooked food." Chantrelle smiled. "You know though, I swear, it seems so many of the guests are eating as if this is their last meal on earth."

"Speaking of everyone, did your uninvited trio ever show up? I haven't seen them around. Of course, I've been stuck out here cooking."

Chantrelle rubbernecked around her husband to sneak glimpses of guests through the large glass patio doors, peering into the house to spot the three new town guests. "I don't see them. But Barclay is in the kitchen now."

"Now that I think about it, would those three even be allowed in the house?" Carlson asked. "I mean, apart from the town's residents, aren't those awaiting transport west supposed to be in here?"

"I don't make the rules about this place. Like you always say, that's the mayor and sheriff's problem," Chantrelle answered. She placed the meat platter on the all-weather wicker table near the grill before heading inside, concentrating on finding out if Nila, Chrishav, and Randall had arrived.

"Don't leave me," Carlson requested of his wife. "The next batch of meat is about ready."

Chantrelle ignored her husband and continued inside. "Hold on, I'll be right back."

Chantrelle mulled through the multitude of people, not finding her intended guests. She came across the town's mayor, Mayor Corbett, as she searched through the living room. He himself appeared muddled by the inordinate amount of activity.

"Mayor, I didn't expect you here this evening."

Mayor Corbett was relieved to see someone he knew. Other town residents tried their best to avoid him. "Chantrelle, you're attending another one of these?"

"Carlson and I enjoy getting out from time to time. Nothing much else in town."

"What are all these people doing here?" the mayor interrupted, not interested in Chantrelle's response. Around the room, amongst the crowd, he saw a young man holding a baby girl, and several elderly men and women walking around making small talk with anyone who would listen. A Latino family of five huddled around the couch. A boy, six or seven years old, sat in the corner playing jacks.

Babies and children aren't supposed to be here; *this has gotta be fixed*. A middle-aged married couple stood arguing by the table of food in the dining room, with other guests milling about ignoring the two.

"Where's Barclay?" the mayor questioned aloud.

"I saw him in the kitchen a minute ago cooking," Chantrelle answered.

The mayor failed to excuse himself and darted straight towards the kitchen. Accustomed to the mayor's rudeness, she ignored the slight and continued her search for the three recent visitors to town, concluding they must have decided not to attend; she rejoined her husband.

Mayor Corbett found Barclay peeling and chopping potatoes, placing them into a large pot on the stove. The mayor presented Barclay with a scornful stare.

"Why do you have all these people here?" The mayor inquired.

"What do you mean, me?" Barclay replied in a response laced with ire. "It's not as if I invited them all here. I didn't expect all these people. It's all I can do to keep their faces stuffed before they're picked up. You never told me I'd have to host this many passersby as part of my agreement. I thought it was supposed to be a couple, if any at all."

Barclay slammed the knife down hard, slicing through a raw potato, almost embedding the blade into the wood cutting board.

The mayor raised an eyebrow. "You need to keep up with your part of the agreement, unless you want to head west early," he said. Each word the mayor enunciated sounded stressed, with a hiss.

Barclay froze. The unyielding and stern expression on the mayor's face showed he was serious. Barclay dropped his head, sighed, and continued prepping the potatoes.

The mayor scanned the crowd in the house. "Do you know how messed up this is? I need to go take care of some things."

"So, no help with any of this?" Barclay asked.

The mayor gave Barclay a wry grin. "Why, you have a pool game to play."

The comment was the emotional equivalent to a gut punch. Barclay enjoyed playing pool, but hadn't done so in a long while. He also liked to play for high stakes while making wagers on the side. Most times, he won. When he did lose, it would be big. During one major tournament, he lost so much money, he almost lost his home, and his wife threatened to leave with the children. Barclay promised he would control his gambling on the games.

Barclay met Mayor Corbett during a consequent tournament, who sponsored him. Barclay won most all his matches over the next two years and climbed in the standings, becoming one a top ranked players in the northwest United States. He once again made side bets against the tournament association rules. Barclay became overconfident because of his recent winning streak. Ranked as a top seed, he then bet all his savings and previous earnings on his semi-finals match during a regional tournament in San Francisco. He lost.

An anonymous individual had informed the tournament association of Barclay's illicit wagering. The association banned Barclay from playing professional pool. He tried hustling, playing in sordid pool hall taverns, but continued to lose more than win. Barclay's wife, frustrated by his playing and high-risk gambling, took the children and moved back east to Indiana. She filed for divorce and full custody.

Barclay was moments from taking his life when the mayor mysteriously showed up and offered him a place of temporary refuge to rebuild his life. Barclay moved to Elysium, living at one of the mayor's homes to host special guests, called "spoiled packages" destined to head on the road west. Barclay didn't realize the mayor was the one who had informed the tournament association of his illicit wagering.

"I haven't played in a long time. I made my ranking like you promised, but then that all went to hell, didn't it? I just want my family back and to play some serious pool again."

The mayor smiled. "Don't worry, you'll play again, I promise."

THE SHERIFF

C larissa, the office assistant for the small police house, was already at work sitting at her desk working on the computer when Sheriff Knight arrived. Her hair color today–dark burgundy, cut short, and feathered on the side, high and spiked on top. The sheriff had become comfortable with the previous shade of dirty blonde she had maintained for two weeks. It was one of her longer periods of keeping a color. Before this stretch, she would dye her hair or change its spiked style every three or four days. Even though Clarissa was thirty-five years old, her petite smooth face, tiny blue eyes, and thin frame gave the impression she was an older teenager, a detail she wouldn't correct when meeting someone new who would mistake her age.

"How's Rory and the girls?" Sheriff Knight asked as he walked around behind her desk to the key cabinet that hung on the wall.

Clarissa's expression dulled as her head tilted to the side, forehead furrowed, and eyes glared over with disbelief. "I thought you knew. I got tired of his crap and kicked him out last night."

The sheriff glanced at Clarissa as he pulled his work keys from the cabinet. "Really? Hmph."

The revelation didn't surprise Sheriff Knight. Clarissa had ping-ponged between her two ex-husbands, Dugan and Rory, over the last six years. After separating from one of the two, she would say she'd have nothing to do with men until she got her life squared-away for herself and her three girls. Then she returned to the other ex-husband within a week or two.

The sheriff knew both men well. Rory slept off his periodic drunken spells from time to time in the jail cell. His most recent confinement excursion occurred two nights prior, while he and Clarissa were seeing one another. The sheriff also formally arrested Dugan twice for causing a public disturbance and destruction of private property. The most recent incident was when he and Clarissa were last seeing each other a couple of months back; he had gone into a rage in the town's diner, trying to track down Clarissa, furious, thinking she was sleeping with Rory behind his back. Dugan was insecure, thinking she wanted to be with Rory. Rory bottled the same insecurities towards Dugan.

Many of the townspeople believed Clarissa didn't enjoy being alone and played the men against each other. Sheriff Knight assumed differently. He considered Dugan and Rory to be two negative emotional stones tied to Clarissa's soul, weighing her down, knowing she depended on their attention. Ironically, the two were excellent fathers and never put the girls in danger during their tirades.

The sheriff wandered into his office, sat, and kicked his feet on top of the desk. "What happened this time?" He asked, afraid he'd receive a response.

"I'd rather not talk about it," Clarissa responded.

Sheriff Knight was relieved, not wanting to contend with listening to what he considered her self-inflicted emotional turmoil, and not able to feign concern much longer. Minutes later, she stood in the doorway, leaning against the doorjamb with her thin arms crossed and sporting an angry face.

"You know what that a-hole told me?" Clarissa yapped.

"Language," the Sheriff interjected, remembering to show patience and concern.

"Sorry, but he told me he slept with some woman a short while back. It was someone passing through, but regretted it and broke it off. Can you believe him? He was so concerned about me having an affair, and he goes and sleeps with some out-of-town floosy."

Sheriff Knight didn't expect to hear that Rory had committed that type of indiscretion. "Really?"

"Yeah, he claims he didn't know what came over him. He said it was like he was possessed, wanting to be with her."

"Sorry to hear that," Sheriff Knight said, attempting to console her.

"Thanks for listening, sheriff." Clarissa returned to her desk, comforted by the Sheriff's response and able to get that off her chest.

The Sheriff expected her to continue and wax on. It was now that he noticed three sheets of paper stacked on top of his desk. They weren't there when he left work the day prior. Reaching over, grabbing, and reading the pages, he became concerned.

"Clarissa, did you put these on my desk?"

"You mean the transfer lists?" Clarissa answered, yelling from the front reception area.

"Yes, the transfer lists?"

"Yeah, the mayor was upset and wanted to make sure you stopped by and talked to him 'bout those."

Sheriff Knight perused the paperwork, reaching the last sheet. On a normal day, he wouldn't have to review any documents, but the lengthy list of names caused concern. In analyzing the content, the situation wasn't as disconcerting as he believed. Crumpling the papers into a ball, he tossed it towards the small circular trashcan next to his desk. The wad of parchment flung from his hand towards the receptacle opening; it combusted into a blue orb of flames that streaked through the air like a miniature shooting star, leaving no ash or airborne residue.

"Did Carlson report in yet?" The sheriff asked.

"Yeah, he did. He went over to Sammi's. He heard she was having a breakfast special this morning."

Hmph, should have known. He loves to eat. "Any calls this morning?"

"Nope, it's been pretty dead around here."

Sheriff Knight propped his feet up on the desk and sat back in his light brown, high back, bonded leather chair. Studying the room, as he did every morning since his assignment to the town, were red brick walls, a forty-five-year-old office desk, a bookcase, a gray five-drawer filing cabinet, and a few pictures of trees on the wall; it was all drone. He was already bored.

"Think I'll go down and join Carlson," the Sheriff said to Clarissa as he passed her desk, leaving the station house.

"What about the mayor?" Clarissa asked, with the Sheriff almost out the door.

"He'll be fine. I'll catch up with him later. If anything happens, you know where I'll be."

The sheriff strolled down the main street occupied with a traditional old movie theater and active marquee, boutiques, and antique stores. There was also an outdoorsman and game store, a couple of bars, a pool hall, and office fronts, all living in buildings with aging Victorian and New England style décor. Rooster, one of the town's newest citizens, was sitting in front of the one bakery in the hamlet. Many considered Rooster and his elderly compact frame frail and weak. He walked an average of three to four miles each morning, tended his own garden, and until a couple of months prior, farmed a couple of pigs and chickens on his plot of land. At least that was what they were told. However, none of the residents could recall when he arrived in town, except for the Sheriff.

"Morning, Rooster, how ya doing?" the Sheriff asked, passing by.

"Doin' fines Sheriff. How 'bout you?"

"Just fine. How's the traffic today?"

As soon as the Sheriff made the comment, a tractor trailer followed by a dark blue SUV worked their way down the main street. At the roundabout, they both headed down a narrow road north. No other traffic followed. The only cars on the street were parked in front of the outdoorsman shop and boutiques.

"I would say bout the same, sheriff; last two or three weeks though, it's a little heavier than normal. Lots of stuff headin's north past Barclay's; been a few headin' west past the roundabout, too," Rooster said.

"Thanks for the traffic report." The sheriff would have liked to hear traffic was light, meaning only antique hunters, seasonal hunters, or the occasional visitor were in town. Heavy traffic heading west or north meant he needed to keep an eye out.

Arriving at the diner, the sheriff spotted his colleague making himself comfortable at their regular table near the front window.

"Morning, Carlson," Sheriff Knight greeted.

"Morning Sheriff," Deputy Rutherford replied, placing the newspaper he had been reading on the table. "Sammi, can we get a cup of coffee for the sheriff?" Deputy Rutherford requested of the diner's owner.

"Don't worry, Carlson, I'm good."

Sammi worked her way over to the table. "Did you want anything to eat, sheriff? I got Duke working on some breakfast specials. Want one?"

The sheriff flashed Sammi a beaming smile with his straight and snow-white teeth. "No thanks. I already had my manna for the day."

"By the way, sheriff, there's three recent visitors new in town. Thought you oughtta know," Deputy Rutherford said.

"Visitor visitors, or passerby visitors? More been comin' through lately."

Clarissa rushed into the diner, distressed, with tears forming in her eyes, and carrying a small post-it note. Scouting out the dining area, she saw the Sheriff and rushed over to him, handing him the small salmon colored slip. "I'm so sorry, sheriff! I forgot to mention you had a call on your special line."

Grabbing and reading the note, Sheriff Knight's eyebrow arched. "Thanks Clarissa. Says here to expect a couple of visitors; I wonder if that's them."

"You're not mad that I forgot to give that to you earlier, are you, sheriff?"

"Don't worry about it."

"I'm so sorry about. The call came in on Friday after you left for the weekend. I forgot all about it when I came in this morning. If I would've seen it earlier, you would have gotten it that much sooner."

"Clarissa, it's alright."

Relieved, Clarissa withdrew.

"You say there were three of them?" The sheriff asked of his deputy.

"Yeah."

"Maybe those aren't the two, since I should look out for a couple of men coming to town."

"I don't know, sheriff. I think one of them isn't with the other two. He's here about that girl who committed suicide 'bout three weeks back. I think he's trying to figure out what happened."

"I don't know what I could tell him. If Doc Williams says it's a suicide, it's a suicide," the Sheriff asserted.

"Don't look now, but your favorite mayor is coming in," Deputy Rutherford said.

The Sheriff turned around to see a five-foot six, olive-skinned man with craggy features, and thin set eyes, entering the diner. The mayor worked his way through the tables over to the sheriff and Deputy Rutherford, exhibiting an irritable disposition weaving through the diners, not apologizing to a young couple after bumping into the table as they were eating, causing the coffee in their cups to spill

"Morning, Mayor Corbett," Deputy Rutherford greeted.

The sheriff remained quiet, keeping his back to the mayor.

"Sheriff, did you see the paperwork I had Clarissa leave on your desk?" Mayor Corbett asked.

The sheriff reached over and grabbed the newspaper resting on the table. "Yeah, I saw it."

"Well?"

"What do you mean, well?" Sheriff Knight replied, flipping through the pages.

"What are you going to do about it?" Mayor Corbett asked.

"There's nothing to do. Everything balanced out in the end, so I signed off on it."

"Sheriff, I was out at Barclay's last night, and if I didn't know better, there were a lot of spoiled packages. You were there, deputy, tell him," the mayor said.

A spoiled package was the mayor's euphemism for rejected passersby that went up the road north. The term amused the sheriff.

"Not my problem," the sheriff said. "Rejected passersby are your concern."

"What do you mean, not your problem?" the mayor hollered, the diner becoming quiet. "You represent the law here, and I'm not gonna have someone @#$% around with things."

Sheriff Knight became incensed and turned around in his chair. "Whoa, whoa, whoa, whoa. First, I don't know how many times I have to scold you—don't use that type of language around me. Second, if the transfer balances even out, then no foul, and your boss and my boss are happy. How do you know something's wrong anyway?"

"Maybe because I got word a lot of processing had to be adjusted for those heading on the north road," the mayor snapped back.

The sheriff turned away from the mayor. "Still not my problem."

"Damn it, sheriff, you need to look into this."

The sheriff continued to ignore him. The mayor's neck veins throbbed, and he clenched his teeth, constraining himself from giving any type of outburst. With no response from the sheriff, he stormed out of the diner.

The sheriff knew Mayor Corbett was right regarding the increase in the spoiled package count. There was no reason for it to flag as an issue. Not at this time anyway, everything balanced out. "So, what about that party, Carlson?"

"There were a lot of guests there, not the normal townies. They could've been passersby, but I haven't seen them here in town before. However, that's not my department," Deputy Carlson replied. "Since they were at Barclay's though, that's not good, is it?"

"Not really, for them anyway. Anything else weird?"

"If you call me spending most of my time barbecuing meat, and Chantrelle serving food weird, then that's about it."

The sheriff chuckled. "How'd you end up cooking?"

"Barclay was so busy trying to keep up with the sides and appetizers, he forgot about the meat he threw on the grill. I jumped in to help, for what I thought would be a few minutes, but he didn't come back out until the end of the night when the passersby were picked up to go west."

"None stayed on the road north?"

"Nope, I think they all went west, minus the kids after everything got worked out."

The sheriff drummed his fingers on the tabletop. "And there were quite a few people at the party?"

"Yeah, few of the townies or friends of Barclay's."

"And kids too?"

"Yeah, the mayor knew they should've been allowed north with no problems. They must've got mixed in with the others."

"Hmmm, that is strange. Maybe we should keep an eye out for something strange."

Back at his office, walking into the small police station, Clarissa assailed the Sheriff with a ream of paperwork.

"Sheriff, you need to sign all of this. The mayor is concerned."

The sheriff grabbed the heap of papers, taking them back into his office. Resting that stack on his desktop, he flipped through the sheets to each one containing his signature block. The sheriff would glide his finger above the line on the sheet, his signature emblazoned on the paper. He did this for thirty sheets, straightened the stack, and took them back to Clarissa's desk.

"Done already? I'm amazed at how you can do that so fast."

"Think I'll go patrol around town. The deer hunting season will start soon, so maybe I'll check out how things are at the lodges. We had a lot of drunk troublemakers last season."

THE TOWN

The Hotel Metropolis stood at the east end of Main Street in Elysium. This is where Randall, Nila, and Chrishav started their day together. Each purposed a different destination. Randall was determined to talk to the sheriff concerning his sister. Nila considered this the perfect time to purchase a bow and set of arrows. He was concerned about how to ask the front desk clerk for a place in town to buy the type of gear he needed. He was relieved to find out that hunting was one of the major attractions of Elysium. A new game and sporting goods store called *Granger's* opened two days prior to his arrival in town. With the season opening for black-tail deer and the near year-round perpetual wild boar hunts, his request shouldn't seem out of the ordinary. Chrishav wanted to explore the town. He was considering taking an extended stroll through the side streets, starting past the round-about at the end of Main Street on the west side of the drag.

The three men passed Sammi's. Rooster sat in front of the bakery, propped up on the rear legs of an old wooden chair, sitting next to a dark green, three-shelf wire-frame newspaper holder.

"Paper gentlemen?" Rooster asked.

"No thanks, old man," Randall answered.

"Name is Rooster, not old man, young man. But I's suppose yous have a name too, and I shouldn't call you young man," Rooster replied, followed with a playful grin.

Randall stopped, not expecting the mild sarcastic rebuke. "Sorry, name is Randall." He avoided looking Rooster in the eye.

Chrishav sensed this was not typical of Randall. "My name is Chrishav," Chrishav interjected, attempting to deflect Randall's embarrassment.

Rooster stared at Nila. "And you, young man?"

The hairs on Nila's arms stood for a moment; a chill ran down his back. For a moment, Nila thought he knew the old man. "I'm Nila."

"You three jus' passin' through, or jus' visitin'?" Rooster asked.

"Just visiting, hoping to take care of some business, and then head home," Chrishav answered.

Rooster hurried and pulled the newspaper back, placing it on the stack. "Oh, thens you don't wants to be reading the paper."

"Why not?" Chrishav asked.

Randall peeked at the headline– "Red Corvette Involved in Fata..." With the paper folded, he could not read the rest of the headline.

"It's for passersby in case they're interested in finding out why they're passing through."

"You're the newspaper salesman, I take it?" Randall asked, overcoming his remorse.

"Ain't no salesman."

"You're out here selling papers, aren't you?" Randall retorted.

"Did I say I was selling?" Rooster asked.

"What else are you doing with them?" Randall replied in a snarky tone.

"Givin' them away to passersby."

"What's the difference?" Chrishav asked.

Rooster's cracked face rendered a small grin. "Difference is if yous gets a paper or not?"

"Just forget it, old man," Randall said. Irritated, he plodded down the sidewalk to the sheriff's office.

"You'll have to forgive our friend; he's been through quite a bit recently," Chrishav said.

"No reason to 'pologize for him, although he looks mighty familiar. You three be visitin."

No sooner than Rooster finished his comment, a candy apple red Corvette pulled up to the curb. A pockmarked teenager, the same age as Nila, got out of the car, leaving it running, walked up onto the sidewalk, having a glassy-eyes stare.

"Excuse me, where am I? I was racing along with a friend of mine, and then somehow, I ended up lost, and next thing you know, I was on a road heading up here."

Rooster reached into the wireframe stand, grabbed the top newspaper, and passed it to the teen. "Here you go, son. Maybe this'll help."

The teen scanned the paper, then back to Rooster; the appearance of confusion fleeted away from the young man's face. Rooster nodded his head. Chrishav experienced an intense sense of peace had enveloped the teen.

"You go down to the roundabout, turns right going north. You'lls find what you're looking for," Rooster said.

"Thanks," the teen responded. "How much do I owe you for this?"

"Where you's goin', the price is already paid."

"You're being gracious."

"The grace is not mine," Rooster replied.

The teen returned to his car, driving in the direction instructed by Rooster.

Chrishav grabbed a newspaper sitting on the top ledge and read the name *The Elysium Chronicles*. The headline displayed "New Game and Sports Store Celebrating Grand Opening," with the accompanying article covering a third of the front page. Other printed story fragments were a pageantry of smaller stories and bylines of a cat in a tree, a local civic meeting, a quilting party planned at one of the resident's homes, and the Bridge Club moving to a new location, another resident's home. They all looked out of placed compared to the teen's reaction.

"What the...none of this seems to have anything to do with that kid," Chrishav said, while placing the paper back on the rack.

Rooster smiled. "Both of you's have a good day," he said, sitting back in his chair. He resumed watching what little traffic that flowed on the road, ignoring Chrishav and Nila, acting as if they had left.

Wanting to find a simple bow and arrow set, and overcome with the large array of merchandise the Sports and Game store in the small town held, Nila never imagined there would be so many types of bows. There were plastic molded variations, fiberglass composite models, and traditional wood bows.

Holding, sizing, and testing the draw on each, he found it difficult to select one. He decided against the aluminum compound bows considering their design to breakdown and fold too complicated to use effectively. It was contrary to the simple techniques his father and the Huntsman taught him. For many other forms, their unique styling, ornate grips, and fancy tips deterred him from selecting from the wider array of choices. Nila selected an inch fiberglass basic recurve bow. The grip set and form fitting to his hand, accommodated a long draw length because of his extended reach stemming from his seventy-inch height. Now it was a matter of determining what type of arrowhead he needed. He selected a dozen bullet-point arrows to use for practice. Would he choose a narrow three blade, 100 grain broadhead, or a wider three blade, 125 grain broadhead barbed heads if the need for confronting a daemon possessed beast arose? Nila didn't know which one to choose.

"What do you like to hunt—deer, or boar?" the salesman asked, observing Nila's confused look. "Then you'll know what type of head you need."

Nila hesitated, awed by the array of weaponry, and not sure of the question. He didn't think about the local game. "Sorry?"

"What do you like to hunt? Deer or boar?"

Again, Nila hesitated, but answered, thinking of the animals reminiscent of what he had hunted at home. "Boar."

The salesman attempted to cover up his suspicion ignited by Nila's delay. "They're running in the night these days. Damn smart animals. They know the weather's been getting better and more hunters coming out. Not as many bagged in the daytime lately."

"Thanks, that's good to know."

Nila browsed through several medium and high-quality crafted quivers and arrows, selecting a lower cost quiver, high-quality wood shaft arrows, and a hunting knife. After paying for the entire collection, he discovered he could have the equipment delivered to his hotel. The salesman was again concerned, believing Nila to be staying where many of the hunts occurred, at one of the local hunting lodges on the southern edge of town to allow for butchering and temporary storage of the carcasses.

Randall entered the lobby of the sheriff's station house, captivated by Clarissa's attractiveness. Her whirlpool blue eyes complemented her cute, petite framed face. He almost forgot the reason for coming to visit the sheriff.

"May I help you?" Clarissa asked, displaying a small smile.

"I guess I'm here to see the sheriff. I was told he could help me out."

"Sheriff, you have a visitor," Clarissa yelled.

"Tell whoever it is I'm not here," a voice returned from the rear office.

"Very funny, boss."

"Go ahead and send him back," the sheriff said.

Randall walked into the sheriff's office to see him sitting back in his chair with his feet up on the desk. The sheriff swung himself around in his swivel chair, stood, and reached out to shake Randall's hand. "I'm Sheriff Knight. What can I do for you?"

Randall accepted the handshake. "I'm Randall Steiner, and I'm here about."

The sheriff interrupted. "You're here about Sherry Steiner's suicide?"

Hearing his sister's name mentioned in the suicide reignited his uneasiness at having to confront the incident. He had pushed the uncomfortable emotions to the hindmost regions of his psyche. "Yeah, how did you know?"

"My deputy mentioned he talked to you when you arrived here in town with your friends."

"Friends, Nila and Chrishav? They're not my friends. They helped me out down in Los Angeles, and we ended coming the same way up here."

"Not your friends, huh?"

"No, but Sheriff, about my sister."

"What about her?"

"I can't believe she committed suicide. She's not the type." It surprised Randall to still consider his sister in the present tense. "I mean, she wasn't the type."

"We can pull out the police report and take a look."

The sheriff walked into the main anteroom area, stopping at Clarissa's desk. "Clarissa, pull out the case file for Sherry Steiner, please?"

"Sure, sheriff." Clarissa rummaged through the file cabinets, returning to her desk empty-handed.

"Sorry, sheriff, they must've been transferred over to the records section at Town Hall for archiving."

Randall was perturbed. "Wouldn't you already have known that?" he noted sardonically.

Clarissa's complexion reddened.

"There's no reason to be obstinate, Mr. Steiner. A little humility can go a long way," the Sheriff replied. His easy-going response and calm demeanor aided in soothing Clarissa's building irritation.

"You can head over to the Town Hall and see for yourself," Clarissa said, wanting to snap at Randall.

"I think I will." Randall turned around to storm out the front door. About to step outside, he turned back around. "Uhmmm, where's the Town Hall?" he asked in a meek and soft timbre.

A tiny smile formed on the sheriff's face. "When you go outside, make a right to the roundabout, go left and it'll be about half a block on the left-hand side of the road."

"Thanks."

"Why'd you tell him which way to go?" Clarissa asked of the Sheriff after Randall left. "I would have told him to find it himself, or sent his butt around the block the long way for being such a pain."

"It's not in my nature," the Sheriff responded, as he strolled back into his office.

The town hall was much closer than Randall expected. He scanned the directory on the wall for the Records and Archives Department. Heading down to the end of the hall, he passed the first open door and peeked in. He recognized the young lady behind the desk. It was the deputy's wife. She recognized Randall.

"How are you doing?" Chantrelle said, disembarking from behind her desk to join Randall in the hallway. "What are you doing here in the town hall?"

Randall obligated stopping. "I'm here to see if I can find out anything 'bout my sister."

"Oh, I'm so sorry. I remember you mentioning that she killed herself. But the Sheriff isn't here," Chantrelle said.

"I already went there, but he wasn't much help at all. He thought I might find something in the town's records department."

"Destiny can help. She's the mayor's aide and in charge of the town's records. I'll take you down."

Chantrelle led Randall through a doorway prior to a set of double doors labeled Meeting Hall. Standing behind the counter was an attractive, slender woman with long curly brunette hair that flowed midway down her back. Light rouge and blush accentuated her pale complexion.

"Hi Destiny," Chantrelle said. "Could you help our friend?" Chantrelle's cheeks blushed. "I'm so sorry. I forgot your name."

"Randall."

"Please help our friend Randall here?"

Attracted by Randall's muscular build and roughen, handsome face, Destiny flashed a seductive grin more than a warm greeting. "Of course I can. What can I do to you, I mean, for you?"

Destiny's actions caught Chantrelle off guard; she had never experienced her acting flirtatious. Randall didn't notice the advance, preoccupied with believing he was one-step closer to finding out additional information concerning his sister.

"Umm, he's here to find out information about his poor sister, who committed suicide a short while back," Chantrelle said.

Destiny blushed as embarrassment exploded onto her face. "I didn't realize."

"I'm going to leave you two now. I have work to get back to," Chantrelle said as she left.

"What can I help you with?"

"I talked to the sheriff, and he thinks a lot of the information about my sister's death may be filed away over here."

"What was her name?" Destiny asked, grabbing a small notepad and pen.

"Sherry Steiner."

"Can you spell that?"

Randall spelled out the last name.

"Her date of birth?" Destiny continued.

Randall gave her the date.

"I remember this case. Hold on." Stepping away and peering into the columns of shelving units and filing cabinets, Destiny returned with a couple of small manila folders, deflating Randall's hope for the retrieval of something substantial.

"I'm sorry, Randall, all I could find is a small newspaper snippet and paperwork from the sheriff's office. It's a statement from the witness who found your sister, and the initial investigation report. I shouldn't do this, but you seem nice. You gotta promise not to tell anyone. The article is fair game, but the police paperwork isn't. Besides, I think the other paperwork, like the autopsy and test results, are all still in the county seat."

Destiny eased the paperwork to Randall across the countertop. He thanked her and accepted the offertory. Reading the article and police reports while trying to reign in his emotions, it hit him that his sister was gone. Her funeral was supposed to provide closure. He wondered if he'd ever come to accept the loss of his sister.

Randall wondered why the news story comprised one short paragraph. He assumed that, for a small town, someone committing suicide would be a headline story and major gossip for the townspeople. Yet, the sheriff, the deputy, Clarissa, Chantrelle, and Destiny didn't see it as out of the ordinary.

"There's nothing else?" Randall asked.

Destiny retrieved the article and sheets of paper from Randall. "Sorry, that's all. Like I said, since the county seat has the filing for the death certificate, the M.E. will file everything there."

The hallway door swinging open took Destiny and Randall by surprise. It was Mayor Corbett sticking his head in. "Destiny, I need you to shut down here and help upstairs. Seems like there's a bunch of spoiled packages passing through town. Who's this?" The mayor asked, taking notice of Randall.

"He's researching information on the death of his sister, who killed herself here in town, about two to three weeks back."

"Whatever. When you finish taking care of him, come upstairs."

"I can't help you much more with this," Destiny continued after the mayor departed, "but if you'd like, this is a small town and a lot goes on that many of us don't already know about. I can find out something, and maybe we can discuss it over a beer later."

Randall wasn't sure of Destiny's intentions; he simply wanted to find out more information. "That'll be cool. Where and when?"

"Lake Alice Billiards at seven tonight. It's around the corner on the main drag."

Reaching the roundabout, Chrishav stared north. Compared to the other roads extruding out from the remaining directions, this one was narrow. It inclined into the forest bordering the village's north side. There wouldn't be much to explore if he went in that direction. Chrishav estimated there was a mile, maybe two, to the tree line past a couple of homes scattered along the way, with the largest an archetypal multistory log cabin home sitting off the road. While standing on the corner debating whether to continue heading west or south into the array of neighborhoods, a bright green semi pulling a faded white tractor-trailer traveled from behind him down the main street of town. It navigated the turn and journeyed up the narrow road north. A couple of cars followed, one traveling straight through the traffic circle and proceeding westward, past the long block of homes and into the distant woods. The next car turned north. Chrishav didn't know why, but when the two cars passed, he sensed emotional distress from both. The first aired a ravenous anger, as if the source of consternation would never resolve. The second car, the one turning north, conveyed emotional sorrow. Chrishav focused hard, not wanting to be consumed by the negative feelings.

Strolling westward, houses of various architectural styles adorned the tree-lined street, as if they were from a Norman Rockwell style small town Americana picture. Each had large, expansive front yards with meticulously manicured lawns. Several houses along the block contained a driveway heading to an adjacent garage. It was a contrast from where he grew up while he lived on the reservation–faded paint, weather worn trailer homes and small, dilapidated houses, some burned out and layered in graffiti, most all with dirt and weed patched yards. Black Velvet whiskey, vodka bottles, and discarded painkiller prescription containers littered the roadsides.

Strolling past a large brown brick, colonial revival style home with a huge front porch containing a swing set, was a middle-aged Hispanic woman. She wore a pair of faded blue jeans, a pink sweat top, a lavender colored gardening smock, and a straw sun hat. She noticed Chrishav while working on all fours with a small spade tending to the soil around her rose bush garden in front of the raised porch.

"Hello young man," the lady said, calling out in Chrishav's direction.

Chrishav turned his head to the left and right, wondering if she was addressing someone else on the street. He was alone and returned the wave.

"Now is that all you're gonna do, young man?" The woman responded. She stood and brushed fertile black soil from the knees of her jeans. "You get over here and give me a proper hello." She then presented Chrishav with a warm smile.

Chrishav, disarmed by her smile, didn't know why she was being cordial. Not feeling threatened, he strolled down the concrete pathway leading from the main sidewalk. As he neared the unfamiliar woman, she opened her arms wide and greeted him with a hearty hug.

"Now there, young man, that's a proper hello. It's nice to hug someone when you say hello to let the world know you're alive." She released him.

The woman's embrace comforted Chrishav. He didn't know why the earlier two vehicles had distressed him.

"I don't think we've met before. You're not from here, are you?" The lady asked.

"No, I'm not."

"Are you passing through or visiting?"

"Visiting."

"Good, because if you were passing through and heading west as you were, I'd be worried."

The remark took Chrishav aback. "Sorry, I don't understand."

"No need to worry. How long you been in town?"

"Got here yesterday."

"Oh, who did you meet so far?"

"Deputy Rutherford and his wife."

The lady's face beamed with a broad smile. "Oh, I love those two. They're so wonderful. And what about the sheriff? He's such an angel. The town is blessed to have him."

"I haven't had a chance to meet him yet."

"Such a shame. You really must. So what are you doing out this way?"

"Just taking a walk around town to see what it's like."

"I don't want to hold you up. I'm going to get back to my gardening. I like to make sure those heading west have something beautiful to look at before the end of their journey." The lady hugged Chrishav again, returned to her garden, kneeled, and tilled the earth around her rose bushes.

Chrishav strolled back up to the road from the house and continued west. After another block, the row of homes ended. The last ones on each side of the road sat next to a small field buttressing the forest boundary. He turned around and walked back towards the town center on the opposite side of the road. Continuing eastward towards the town's roundabout, several more cars were heading opposite him, westward. In between those two, another one headed south and parked at the Town Hall. The rumbling of a diesel engine attracted his attention. From the north, a tractor-trailer maneuvered through the roundabout, turning right and heading westward. Chrishav recognized it was the same tractor-trailer he had witnessed earlier heading north on the road.

Maybe he got lost. Chrishav didn't see many places up the road if the truck had picked up or dropped off a load. Suddenly, a surge of multiple emotions, ranging from sadness and despair to anger and contempt, flooded Chrishav's psyche, originating from the semi-truck trailer.

Another car, this time an SUV, traveled westward. Another thought came to Chrishav. During his walk up to this time, all the traffic he witnessed headed in one direction-westward. Not at any time did a vehicle come from the east into the town. From the north on the narrow road, except for the tractor-trailer, the same was true.

Chrishav continued his excursion south from the roundabout. Past the smoke shop and a couple of antique stores was the Town Hall. Made of dark maroon bricks, with beautiful white trimmed quarter pane windows, was a small set of six stairs that adorned the front. Atop the landing of the stairs, two broad columned posts supported the portico overhang, covering the threshold of the white double doors. Continuing, he wandered into neighborhoods with quaint homes. Deeper in town, he found a couple of gas stations, small convenience stores, one or two strip malls, and a school. In the neighborhoods he visited, the scenery of home after home was becoming monotonous. Journeying through what he believed to be most of the town, he realized the main street didn't run through the dead center of town, but at the northern end. Turning around from the longest extent of his jaunt, Chrishav returned to the road that passed the quaint two-story town hall building. Deputy Rutherford was exiting, giving his wife a tender kiss on the lips before she entered back in.

"Hold up," the deputy requested of Chrishav.

Chrishav was awash with the emotions emanating from the deputy, best described as absolution. "What can I do for you, deputy?" He asked.

"I was curious why you and your friends are here in Elysium?"

"For me, it's more of a sabbatical. I'd say the same for Nila since the death of his father. With Randall, you learned he wants to find out about the death of his sister. Why is something wrong?"

"It seems strange for your friend to come all the way from Africa for a sabbatical, and then to find out he purchased some expensive archery gear."

"Not sure I understand you, deputy? I know he enjoys hunting."

"Really? You sure he's not working with your friend Randall, maybe to help him carry out some sort of weird revenge for his sister?"

Chrishav smirked. "Trust me, deputy, Nila is not that type of person." Chrishav knew now was the time to exploit the subtle emotions exuded by the deputy. "Nila doesn't seem to believe in revenge. I'm certain he would forgive, even those he wasn't familiar with who wronged him, or those he was very fond of."

Chrishav sensed the comment affected the deputy as if an emotional brick had hit him.

"I'm wondering and being careful, that's all." Deputy Rutherford responded, his voice a little shaky, not wanting to carry on any further. "You have a good day."

As the deputy turned around to head back into the Town Hall, Chrishav had a question. "If you don't mind my asking, how did you and your wife end up here?" The swirling emotions of love, regret, loss, and forgiveness that Chrishav sensed earlier puzzled him.

Deputy Rutherford raised an eyebrow. "What brought that up?"

"I guess I'm curious. This place seems so out of the ordinary for you to end up here."

Deputy Rutherford was cynical about Chrishav's question, but answered. "I used to be a deputy sheriff outside of Atlanta. Chantrelle and I were leaving on a trip to visit her parents, who live in Portland, Oregon. On our last leg of the trip, it was getting late, but we pushed it. I was getting a little sleepy, and Chantrelle said she felt fine enough to drive. I fell asleep, and along the way, I woke up as she was driving and we ended up here in Elysium. We fell in love with it; well, Chantrelle did anyway. I don't mind it. So, this was the end of our journey."

Chrishav didn't need to probe to hear the subtle heartbreak in the deputy's voice, contradictory to the story he presented. "So, you both came back down here after Portland?"

Deputy Rutherford tilted his head with an inquisitive stare. "Curious, huh? We never made it up to Portland. We keep saying we're going to make our way up there. We love it here too much. Time goes by so fast that it seems like we got here yesterday."

"How long have you been here?"

"None of your business. I need to get back to work."

"Thanks for your time."

"Not a problem."

Deputy Rutherford turned to head into the building before Chrishav interrupted him again.

"By the way, deputy, something else I noticed—most of the traffic seems to head out of town either west or north, except for a semi hauling a trailer. It went north and then turned around and headed west."

Deputy Rutherford arched an eyebrow. "You said you saw a tractor trailer come from the north and then head west?"

"Yeah," Chrishav answered. He assumed this alarmed the deputy from his tone.

"Thanks," Deputy Rutherford said, rushing off down the street back to the station house to go find the Sheriff.

THE POOL GAME

Deputy Rutherford tracked down Sheriff Knight coming out of *Granger's Game and Sports* store.

"What's going on, Sheriff?"

"Just following up on that Nila character. I think he and his friends are the ones the note Clarissa gave me referenced. If they are, that's a good thing."

The troubled look on Deputy Rutherford's face alarmed the Sheriff. "Is something is eating at your craw."

It amazed Deputy Rutherford at how the Sheriff seemed to know when something bothered him. "It's about those two new fellas. I spoke to the one called Chrishav. Weird fellow, but he mentioned something odd. He saw a tractor-trailer go north, and then head back and west out of town."

"Just the semi?" The sheriff asked.

"That's all he mentioned."

"I wonder if it had a load? If it did, that's a lot of spoiled packages." There was deep mourning in the sheriff's voice.

"Great, another batch the mayor's gonna be upset about."

"He'll get over it. It seems, though, that Hannibal and I've been at this battle for eons. But I have to admit, this time something's not quite right. Earlier, Rooster mentioned there's been more traffic lately. Let's go talk to him."

Both traveled down the block, crossed the street, approached Rooster, who sat in front of the bakery, kicked back in his chair resting on the two rear legs, propped by the building's sandstone brick wall. Seeing the two law enforcement officers, Rooster leaned forward, placing the two front legs of his chair on the sidewalk.

"Rooster, how's it going?" Deputy Rutherford asked.

"Gentlemen, seeing you's two together means you got's a question for me?"

"As a matter of fact, we do." Sheriff Knight replied. "Remember, you believed that the traffic seemed to get a little heavier lately? Do you remember when it started?"

"I do; abouts the same times that pretty little lady dun killed herself."

"Wait a minute. You don't think it was when our three recent visitors arrived in town?"

"Ah, heck no, it was rights before Rory wents and broke up his little affair with her."

Sheriff Knight and Deputy Rutherford's eyes widened. Neither expected to hear news about the affair with Rory.

"How come we didn't hear any of that gossip?" Deputy Rutherford asked.

"Carlson is right," the sheriff said. "I just found out earlier that Rory had an affair. I didn't know it was her. How come we didn't hear about any of this?"

"If you asks me sheriff, and you' find out why the traffic is getting heavier, maybe you'lls find out who would keeps you in the dark about all of this."

"You think something's going on?" Sheriff Knight asked.

"Yeah, why's it when I looks down the street at the turnabout, I've seen a couples of those who went north, but comes back and then heads west."

"More than normal?" The Sheriff asked.

"More than I've seens before," Rooster responded. "Use to be none before I gots here in town."

"Carlson, go see if you can track down Rory and bring him to the station. I got a couple of questions floating in my mind about that suicide now."

Sheriff Knight addressed Carlson with a forcefulness he had never experienced from his boss the entire time he'd been in Elysium.

A clerk dropped off more pages of documentation to review, even before the mayor finished going through the pages placed on his desk several minutes prior. As soon as the clerk stepped out of the office, Destiny entered, carrying more paperwork. Searching through the documents on his desk turned out to be simple town administration paperwork he'd already reviewed. He wasn't sure why he was receiving copies of the same documents again.

"I already took care of most of this. Did everyone lose their minds around here?"

Destiny perused the paperwork. They were duplicates of documents she had requested for the clerks to catalog and file. "You're right, we already took care of this," she said, ripping the sheets of paper. Taking the remaining documents, she placed them in front of the mayor one by one. They were brief biographies of eleven different individuals.

"Don't tell me these are more spoiled packages?"

"Afraid so, your honor. Maybe you should call you know where to find out," Destiny said.

"What? Are you being an idiot? You know I can't let my ruling potentate down there know about this. Are you trying to get me in trouble?"

"Just making a suggestion, that's all."

The mayor wasn't appreciative of the comment. "Is that the last of the paperwork?" he asked, as Destiny placed the last sheet for the mayor to sign.

"Yes, your honor."

In reading the sheet, the mayor noticed several typos. "Destiny, what are these?" He asked, pointing out the glaring mistakes and obvious spelling errors. Having worked with her for years, he knew her to be meticulous.

"Sorry about that," she responded apologetically, taking the paper and heading out of the office. "Let me take care of these, and I'll be right back."

Almost three minutes later, she returned with the corrected sheet. "Here you go."

The mayor reviewed the changes; it was good to go. Swiping his finger over the signature block, his name, Hannibal Rebus, materialized in black as the characters released miniature whiffs of smoke. "Let's go get something to eat."

On the way to Sammi's, neither had anything to say to one another. This was normal for the two of them whenever they headed out to lunch or dinner while they were working. Rooster, seeing the two approaching, more so because of the mayor, wanted to dart inside the bakery and hide. It was too late; they both saw him.

"Rooster," Destiny greeted as they came upon Rooster.

"Miss Destiny."

"Rooster," the mayor followed.

Rooster at first pursed his lips and crossed his arms, but opted to show some courtesy. "How's it going, Mayor?" he asked, emotionless.

The mayor remained quiet. Rooster didn't mind.

As the mayor and Destiny walked by, Nila walked out of the hotel down the street. Destiny's pulse raced and skin complexion flushed witnessing his thin, muscular frame in new gym shorts and spandex armor muscle shirt he had purchased at *Granger's*. He started jogging opposite their direction.

Destiny reached over and grabbed the mayor's lower arm, causing him to stop walking. Her long fingernails dug deep into his skin. "Who's that Nubian prince?" She asked with a squeal in her voice.

The mayor grabbed Destiny's hand and flung it from his arm in annoyance. "What's wrong with you?" The mayor asked.

"Not yourself today, are you, Destiny?" Rooster said, more in a mocking tone than asking a question. Her glazed over green eyes scarcely blinked; he knew something was out of the ordinary.

The mayor wondered the same. All the years he has known her, she possessed a mild-mannered disposition. He didn't expect her to be open and forward.

"He cames with those other two fellas," Rooster said.

"What two fellows?" The mayor asked.

"The one's figurin' out what happened to his sister and the other ones don't know much about him, but he's here for a reason."

"You know, mayor," Destiny said, "one of them, the one you saw me with earlier in the records room. He was trying to see if we had any information about his sister, who had committed suicide. I'm supposed to meet him later at Lake Alice's Pub and Pool Hall."

"Lake Alice's, huh? What time?"

Destiny knew the mayor was concocting some sort of scheme. She had other intentions. "Around nine thirty. Maybe play a couple games of pool." She lied.

"Pool, huh? I need to get Barclay over there. If I plan it right, I can seal the deal with what he owes me and send his butt westward." Mayor Corbett intended for Barclay to lose the next high-stakes game of pool, securing the last payment. That would facilitate his being able to get out of being assigned in Elysium, and from having to deal with Sheriff Knight for what seemed like an eternity.

Chrishav, Randall, and Nila enjoyed an early dinner of meatloaf, mashed potatoes, peas, corn on the cob, and garlic toast at Sammi's. Nila completed a little less than half of his plate. The brick-sized slice of meatloaf and mountainous portions of sides were too much for him to complete. He never experienced what he equated with three or four meals served on a single plate for one sitting.

As they finished, Randall placed his silverware down, napkin on his plate, and then leaned back in his chair. "Damn, that meal was good," he said, followed by a rumbling burp.

Nila and Chrishav stared at him, expecting an apology for the manners infraction. A response didn't come.

"It was good, very good," Chrishav said, realizing Randall would say nothing regarding his etiquette breach. He stared out the window, observing the tourists and townspeople strolling along the main road.

Stepping outside after paying at the front counter, they sauntered westward, wanting to burn calories and work off the heavy meal. A handful of townspeople were lining up outside the Main Street theater across the street from the bakery where Rooster sat in his usual spot. Randall recognized the marquee displayed the title for a first-run movie, was amazed it would show in a small town.

"Evenin' gentlemens," Rooster greeted. Randall picked up a newspaper in the wireframe stand next to Rooster. Snatching a glimpse of the headline, it read, "Gray Ford SUV in Single Fatal Car Accident." The story detailed the events occurring in southern Nevada on I-15, on the outskirts of Las Vegas.

Why would this small town be interested in what goes on down in Nevada? Randall dismissed the article and placed the newspaper back on the stand.

"Well, gentlemen," he said, "I'm gonna skip on the walk and head back to my room and brush my teeth, and then wait around. I'm supposed to meet up with someone who may know what happened to my sister. Just as well, I tried asking a cute pharmacist out earlier while filling my prescriptions. I need to remember never to ask out the person who fills out your prescription for that special cream for that special itch. I didn't think that one through."

Chrishav and Rooster chuckled. Nila didn't understand, raising one eyebrow and tilting his head. After Chrishav explained it to him, he and Rooster laughed harder at seeing the expression of illumination on Nila's face. Randall joined in.

"Night guys," Randall said, walking away from the three, still chuckling.

Chrishav and Nila agreed to head back to their rooms. Rooster whistled as he sat back in his chair, wishing the two men good evening. After they entered the lobby of their hotel, a gray Ford SUV with Nevada plates drove onto the main strip and pulled in front of Rooster. The driver got out and stepped up to him.

"Beens waiting for you," Rooster said to the young male driver wearing sunglasses while handing him a newspaper.

The driver read the headline. "Which direction do I go?" he asked.

"Gotta finish readings the article. Each man's story's d'ffent, I'm's just a old man passin' out newspapers."

Randall was prompt in arriving at the tavern. Five pool tables occupied the open area in the middle of the room. A handful of small tables with multicolored geometric shape-painted tops sat in an outcropping in the corner opposite the main entrance. Wood tables lacquered in faded, cracked varnish lined both sides of the pub and were surrounded by booths shrouded with dried, cracked, green pleather seat cushions and dark red seat-back cushions.

Destiny sat waiting in a booth next to the massive picture window facing out onto the street, drinking a beer from a frosted glass. As soon as Randall sat, the waitress brought him a glass with what appeared to be two shots of an amber colored liquid.

Randall took a sniff. "Is this Scotch?"

Destiny smiled. "It is."

"How'd you know I like Scotch?"

"You seem like a Scotch person. I don't know what it is, but lately, I can read people a lot better than they can understand themselves, it seems."

"Okay, that's not weird. Thanks a lot, though." Randall downed the shots.

"What do you do for a living?"

"I'm part owner of a general contracting company."

"That's interesting. What type of projects have you worked on?"

Randall was steamed. "I was hoping you would tell me more about what happened with my sister?"

"There's time for that later. Let's talk about us."

Randall raised an eyebrow. "I prefer to talk about my sister."

"I promise we'll discuss her. I want to…"

Randall presented Destiny with an uncompromising gaze. "Look, tell me about my sister or I'm leaving."

Destiny capitulated. "Alright, here it is. I learned she was having an affair with a local man. It got serious in a short amount of time. However, he called it off because he felt not like himself falling for someone new, but wanted to get back together with his ex. For him, it was too late. He wrecked any chance of getting back together with her."

"I don't care about whoever it was my sister was supposed to have been with. What about her?"

"Your sister fell for him hard, and was devastated by the breakup, saying it was the most intense relationships she's ever experienced."

Randall didn't remember his sister's best friend Bethany mentioning any of this. It didn't seem like Sherry; she was the one more reserved of the two. Bethany had eluded that she didn't know of the liaison until the last couple of days of the relationship. Randall wondered how Sherry could have kept something like that from her best friend for over a week in a small town.

Randall downed another shot that Destiny had ordered. For the next ten minutes, no matter how many ways Randall tried to extract a more definitive answer as to what happened, he encountered the same responses from Destiny, apart from finding out a couple of hikers came across Sherry's body on the outskirts of town in her car. The autopsy report revealed a combination of alcohol and sleeping pills.

"Destiny, where's the mayor?" a male voice interrupted. "I thought you said he wanted to see me?"

Barclay stood at the end of their table. Randall, irritated by the interruption, didn't recognize him and wanted him to leave.

"He'll be here soon enough," Destiny replied. "By the way, have you met Randall here? He's passing through."

"Just passing through, huh? Not visiting?" Barclay asked.

"Yep, he's passing through," Destiny continued. "Plus, I heard he's an excellent pool player."

Randall didn't know why Destiny would blurt out the unrelated comment. Plus, how did she know? He never told her he was a pool player. Randall wanted Destiny to refocus attention back on their initial conversation. "All I want to do is finish finding out more about my sister. Who was she having this affair with?" *I want to kick his ass, maybe even kill him*. Randall deduced the man was the reason for his sister's fatal decision.

"You're a pretty good pool player, huh?" Barclay asked.

Randall moaned under his voice before he responded. "I don't give a damn about pool right now."

"He wants to know who his sister was having an affair with," Destiny said. "She was the one who killed herself about three weeks back, but I've been trying to tell him I don't know who it was with."

"How 'bout this? We play pool and I'll tell you the guy's name?" Barclay asked.

Randall rocketed out of his seat, grabbing the collar of Barclay's red and blue plaid shirt. "Don't play games; tell me."

The conversations in the pool house silenced; a Bob Dylan song playing on the jukebox and the low rumble of air blowing through the vents bellowed in the background.

Barclay responded by staring into Randall's eyes, showing he wasn't backing down. "Play me for the name."

"And what if I beat your butt right here?" Randall responded.

The bartender, Hispanic, bald with a muscular build near the same as Randall, approached the two men carrying a baseball bat. "Do we have a problem here, gentlemen?"

"Nothing that a couple games of pool wouldn't solve, Ricardo," Barclay replied.

Randall released Barclay's collar and mimicked dusting it off. "There's no problem here."

Ricardo stared at both men for a minute and then withdrew back to the bar.

"We can take this outside, and I can make you tell me," Randall said, attempting to sound menacing by talking in a subdued and threatening voice.

Barclay's brown eyes stared into Randall's. "There's nothing you can do to force me to tell you. I have nothing to lose, and everything to gain."

The intensity of Barclay's gaze disturbed Randall. Barclay showed he wasn't stepping down.

"Why do you want to play so badly?" Randall asked.

"Let's say I have a vested interest in playing."

Barclay glanced over at Destiny, who sat in the booth unbothered by the two men's alpha male showdown. "Destiny, is the mayor supposed to show up anytime soon?"

"Not for a while."

Barclay grinned. "Good. Destiny will officiate and validate our play. If you win, I'll tell you the guy's name."

"And what if you win?" Randall asked. "I don't have much money on me."

"I don't care about money. We'll play as if our souls were on the line."

"What the..." Randall didn't know how to take the comment.

"Here's the deal, I like to play pool."

Destiny eased herself out of the booth, standing behind and to the right of Randall. "I know you don't feel like playing, but for your sister's sake, what've you got to lose?"

Randall pondered Destiny's comment. "I'm pretty good," Randall said. "I'm top ranked back where I come from."

"Know what, so am I." Barclay smiled, revealing a top and bottom row of yellow crooked teeth. "Let's go a couple of rounds."

"Games are on me," Destiny said. She rummaged in her small clutch purse and pulled out a handful of quarters. "This looks like it'll be fun to watch."

Barclay grabbed the coins and stepped over to the pool tables. Destiny leaned over to Randall's ear. "Barclay had been a tournament class player, but he's all washed up. That's why he's up here, hiding out here in Elysium."

Randall puffed up, confident of an easy win. He didn't know that Barclay wanted to play for greater stakes, and was not interested in information for Randall. This was Barclay's chance not to be under the mayor's servitude, having to host "Spoiled Packages" parties. Heading over to the nearest pool table, Barclay laid a row of four quarter stacks on the ledge above the coin slot.

"Let's say eight ball, best of eleven," Barclay said.

"Sounds fine to me."

Randall and Barclay selected their pool cues from the house offerings, confident of their choice. Now preparing to shoot to lag for the break, they each gathered a ball, placed it on the billiard top, and shot towards the far rail. The balls traversed up, hit the rail, and rolled back atop the slate. Barclay won.

Randall was concerned. The Newtonian reaction resulted in the sinking of the one ball. Shot after shot, the balls dropped into their intended pockets with ease. The flawless English applied to the cue ball astonished Randall. If Barclay wanted it to spin back a bit and to the right, setting up to line the next shot, it found its spot. In no time, the game ended. Randall knew he would have to step up his game. He also tried to impair Barclay's playing after finding out Barclay wanted a drink. Randall set up a tab and ordered the next three rounds.

Games flip-flopped between the two men. Best of eleven changed to the best of thirteen once they finished the eighth game–both worried they could lose. Randall also wondered how Barclay continued to play without losing his edge. Guzzling five shots and two beers, Barclay played as if he were sober. Randall didn't know that the more Barclay drank, the more relaxed he became. Barclay was a functional drunk and needed to consume more shots before the alcohol had a negative effect on his coordination. Barclay hoped that the same strategy with the drinks Randall consumed would worsen his gameplay.

Twelve games played, six wins between each, Barclay won the thirteenth. Randall retreated to the booth they had since claimed; Destiny, watching the competition, gauged Randall's loss penetrated him negatively by gauging his expression.

"Sorry, Randall, seems like things didn't go your way," she said.

"Thanks for the obvious," he snarled. "You wouldn't do something decent and tell me, anyway?" Focusing his question to Barclay.

Barclay ignored him and pranced around the bar, ecstatic. "See you Ricardo, I'll be out of here." At each of the booths and tables, he gave the occupants different departure tirades: "See ya suckers," "I'm outta here," or "You won't see my butt around here anymore; this place can go to hell."

After disturbing the last patron, Barclay danced out of the bar.

"Don't worry," Destiny said. "I'm sure there's someone else in town who can help you with what you need to find out. There are those who know the town's gossip."

"You better be right," Randall said, accompanying Destiny out of the tavern.

"You wanna head back to my place?" Randall asked once they stepped out onto the sidewalk.

Destiny flashed a quick, seductive smile. "You know what, I'll like that. I'll catch up with you. I have to take care of something at the office first." She brushed her hand against his and then walked off towards the town hall.

It was nine in the evening. The mayor arrived at Lake Alice's searching for Destiny and Randall. Scanning the crowd, they weren't there. *Where are they?* He went to the bar thinking Ricardo, the bartender, would know.

Ricardo finished fulfilling an order for the waitress when he acknowledged the mayor, who stood waiting at the bar. "What can I get for you, your honor?"

"Just a glass of water."

Ricardo's efficiency promptly placed a glass of ice water in the mayor's hand.

"Destiny get here yet?" The mayor asked. He took a sip and placed the glass on the granite bar top, still holding on to it.

"She came and went."

A scowl flashed on the mayor's face. "What do you mean, came and went?"

"She left with the new guy in town after he lost a set of pool games with Barclay."

"What the?" the mayor bellowed. "They played pool?"

"Yeah, they got here around sixty thirty or seven, drank, and started playing. Then they left about an hour or so later. Barclay was happy as a clam, though. They didn't play for money, if that's what you're worried about."

"What do you mean, Barclay was happy? Happy about what, and play what for money?"

"Pool, Barclay, and the new guy in town played pool. Then, that new guy and Destiny left together kinda chummy."

The mayor's jaw clenched; the tall glass he held frosted; the ice crystals migrated from the glass exterior onto the bar top. Seconds later, the liquid solidified, and the un-tempered glass cracked from the expanding frozen water.

"Mayor," Ricardo said, "you're doing it again."

The mayor released his hand from the unintended ice sculpture and hurried out of the tavern. He trudged over to the Hotel Metropolis, charging up to the front desk. He pounded on the wood countertop with his hand balled into a fist.

"What room is that visitor Randall staying in?" the mayor hollered.

"You know I can't give you that information, Mayor," the clerk defiantly answered.

"I need to talk to that Randall character and Destiny, who came in with him."

"Destiny didn't come here with anyone," the clerk noted.

"Bullcrap. I was told they left Lake Alice together."

"And I'm telling you, he came in here by himself."

"Maybe she came in when you weren't looking?" the mayor said. "She had to have gone by you somehow without you knowing."

"The only persons to go by here were a couple of guests going to their room and that half Indian fella. Said he was goin' out for an evening stroll."

"She had to have come in; call up to his room. I want to speak to him."

"If he said she didn't come in Hannibal," a tenor voice said behind the mayor, "then she didn't come in. Whatever it is bothering you can wait until the morning."

The mayor turned around, stunned to see the sheriff standing there. The hotel desk clerk didn't notice Sheriff Knight walk up either.

"Damn it, I hate when you do that," the mayor said. "Sheriff, someone around here is doing their best to mess things up."

"Language," the Sheriff said.

"You know what, Sheriff, you can blow it out your…"

Sheriff Knight snapped his fingers; the mayor's voice muted while he mouthed a flurry of words. Every other one resembled profanity. When the mayor ended his inaudible tirade, the Sheriff snapped his fingers again. "Finished?"

"Yes."

"Good. We'll talk about all this in the morning, Hannibal."

"Damn it, I need to talk to that man now."

"Don't say anymore. It's settled. We'll talk about this tomorrow. I need to go on patrol now."

The mayor returned an icy stare; the sheriff remained stone-faced. The mayor relented and stormed out of the hotel lobby.

SEDUCTION

The night was clear. Victorian style faux-gas street lamps illuminated the silent street. Rooster's chair and wireframe newspaper stand stood empty. Further down the street, Chrishav passed opposite Lake Alice's Pool Hall. Gazing through the large picture window, it framed a few bodies playing pool, carousing around a couple of booths, or occupying stools at the bar.

On the road heading north away from the main street roundabout, Chrishav came up to a couple of homes. The first had the dancing flicker of a television display muddled by the living room curtains. The second, across the street from the first, was a lifeless, unilluminated husk of wood and glass. No one was home, or they all may have already gone to bed. The further north Chrishav walked, the road ahead faded into a veil of darkness. Car headlights of a vehicle coming from behind him lit up the road ahead. It passed on the narrow road and continued past the large log cabin multi-story home on the right, inclining up into the tree line of the forest before the pitch of night swallowed it.

The ebony of the evening sky, now with the gentle offset from the glowing moonrise, didn't conceal from Chrishav the celestial residents' orientation that seemed out of the ordinary, almost as if he was viewing the constellations from the opposite side of a mirror. He'd become familiar with the evening constellations while observing them during his evening walkabouts down in Mexico. The moon and accompanying stars seemed out of place. The Big Dipper's orientation was backwards for this time of year. Even though he was in Northern California, being in the same hemisphere as the monastery in Mexico, the two stars that aligned comprised the side of the bowl, Merak and Dubhe and, if extended, did point to Polaris. Polaris should be up and to the right. The two stars in the sky pointed up and to the left. The Little Dipper was also out of place. Chrishav didn't know how to account for the discrepancy. This was something else out of the ordinary for this town that concerned him.

Maybe he was overthinking everything. Overwhelmed was the best way to describe how he felt. The short time in town, sensing a plethora of souls, had assaulted him. Whether residents or passersby, he had snatched inklings of their emotions. Then it hit him. He sensed that those whom he encountered differed from those before he arrived. Outside of Elysium, he read the souls of those themselves attuned to the souls of others. As a result, the general populace was an empty book in his readings. In this town, with most everyone he met, he sensed distinct soul-based emotions or spiritual conflicts. That had never happened before on such a large scale.

Chrishav stopped in his tracks, yards from a log cabin style house where it seemed as if someone were hosting a party. Yet most inside emoted despondency, rejection, forlorn. Clearing his mind and focusing on his reason for arriving in town, he recalled that he and Nila were there to seek a destroyer daemon. Chrishav continued north.

A set of car headlights approached from the forest on the narrow road. Getting closer, Chrishav made out a red and blue light bar atop the vehicle. The ambient light from the rising moon unveiled writing on the side. It read Sheriff spelled out in large block letters below Elysium painted in small cursive penmanship. The tinted letters reflected a blue tint. The sheriff's car slowed and came to a stop. Expecting to see Deputy Rutherford, the driver was unfamiliar. The light from the dashboard's instrumentation-mobile radio, and installed tablet system illuminated the unknown face. The patrol car driver's flawless appearance made Chrishav consider he resembled a lifelike mannequin. He possessed the rugged features of a chiseled square jaw, well-defined brow line, straight nose, unblemished skin, and combed hair where a single strand was not out of place. A sense of awe and constrained power flooded Chrishav's emotions.

"Evening," the uniformed driver said. "Don't think we met. I'm Sheriff Knight. You are?"

The wave of emotions passed before Chrishav answered. "Chrishav."

"Ah, you're the one my deputy mentioned he met earlier. Kinda late to be taking a walk, isn't it?"

"No, I don't think it's that late at all," Chrishav responded.

"Hmmm. So, what brings you here to our small town?"

"Sightseeing."

"I think you'd be better off and head back to town. Nothing much up that way except maybe wolves and bears."

"No lions and tigers?" Chrishav cracked a small smile. The sheriff was unaffected.

"I think I'll be okay, Sheriff," Chrishav said.

"If you say so. You know, I have a feeling your friend may need your help pretty soon."

What did he mean by that? It wasn't as if the Sheriff was threatening with his comment. It came across as infused with thoughtfulness. "Excuse me, sheriff? I'm not sure I understand."

"Sometimes strange things can happen in this town, and I want to make sure our tourists and visitors are safe."

"Strange things like what?" Chrishav asked.

"All I can say is, of all the years I've been in this town, it seems like an eternity."

The name Cammael popped into Chrishav's mind, followed by his thoughts slamming into a mental wall. The Sheriff winked, waved his finger back and forth, and smiled, displaying straight and fluorescent bright-white teeth, almost as if they were self-illuminating.

"Just be careful and don't head off north into the forest. And like I said, you might want to head back to town. I think your friend is going to need your help." The sheriff drove off.

Chrishav shuttered. Disquieted, he sensed the Sheriff was right. He needed to get back right away.

Someone knocking on the hotel room door startled Nila. He wasn't expecting anyone, and knew Chrishav to be out for an evening walk. Chrishav noted that after dinner and his evening stroll, he would turn in and call it an early evening. Putting on a tee shirt and securing the drawstrings on his pajama bottoms, Nila walked over and opened the solid wood door. Destiny stood leaning against the doorsill. The subtle scent of a rosewater-based perfume satiated his nose. She wore a skintight, maroon, short length and strapless, one shoulder evening dress with a sloping neckline. It revealed a hint of cleavage; the right side of her dress at the upper end of the slope was a long sleeve made of lace. The form fitting dress revealed her slender yet slightly busty figure. Her naturally wavy hair flowed down her back like a brunette waterfall, reflecting a diffused sheen from the hallway light. Nila had met no one dressed in a provocative outfit before.

Destiny presented Nila with an impish smile. "Hello Nila," she whispered in a seductive tone.

Nila didn't know how to respond. *Who is she, and why is she here?* "Do I know you?"

Destiny inched in closer. "You don't know me, but I would sure like to get to know you."

"Who are you?" Nila replied. His voice wavered.

Destiny continued to encroach on his personal space. Her intoxicating perfume befuddled his ability to maintain concentration. She took her small, delicate hand, placed it on the upper half of his chest, and slid her fingertips down his chest over the tee shirt. "I'm Destiny," she purred.

Destiny then took her fingertips and glided upward from Nila's toned torso, over his chest, and ended at the base of his neck. Nila blushed, despite his sable skin tone. He knew he should back away, but her sensual hand gestures captivated him.

"You know we don't have to stay here in the doorway," Destiny said, moving in closer, their faces almost fusing together in a kiss. Nila sensed the heat radiating from her body as she pressed her body against his. It was difficult for him to concentrate as the scent of Destiny's floral perfume saturated his nostrils. He didn't know what to do, but noticed heightened emerging urges he hadn't experienced before. He had affections for a young woman in Parsons' village before he was to leave, but the most they ever engaged in was holding hands and a simple kiss. Once Parsons had learned of the relationship, he pressured Nila to separate from her and concentrate on his training.

Nila was ignorant of how to respond. No woman had ever seduced him before. He became excited.

"Have you ever had a moment of magic with a woman, Nila?" Destiny whispered.

"I'm not sure I understand what 'moment of magic' means?"

"You have to have some idea of what I mean," she responded, her hand again sliding down his toned abdomen.

"I'm not sure what it is you want," Nila whispered with a nervous shakiness in his voice. He wanted to reach out and embrace her.

"Isn't that cute?" Destiny whispered, moving in closer, their lips inches apart. "I'll tell you what I want, I want to…"

"Nila!" Chrishav hollered as he entered the hallway exiting from the stairwell.

Nila and Destiny snapped their heads towards the boisterous voice coming from down the corridor.

Destiny pulled back, appearing confused, turned back towards Nila, then back to Chrishav. Chrishav for a quick instant sensed an ink-black personage to her soul; then it wiped away, as if a heavy veil went up. Her psyche went from one borne of hostility and rage to the emergence of befuddlement, then unease, disorientation, and then embarrassment. She stepped further back from Nila.

"I think you should leave," Chrishav demanded of Destiny when he approached the couple.

Destiny sashayed past him, gazing into his eyes with displeasure. She dashed into the same stairwell Chrishav had entered.

"Damn it, wake up. Don't you see what's happening?" Chrishav asked, making sure the auto-closed door to the stairwell shut.

"I am awake."

"That's not what I'm talking about. Can't you see there was something strange about her, something dark and ominous?"

"I didn't have time to find out," Nila responded, snapping back in anger.

"I'd guess not with you almost getting your wick wet, but I'd say her soul is polluted. Let her go."

Nila wasn't sure what Chrishav meant by the "wick wet" comment, but had a good idea of its context. "Polluted because she wants to be with me? We almost...you know...I wanted to. How come you didn't leave us alone?"

Chrishav mustered as close to a stern father-like stare as possible. "Remember why we're here. You don't have time to go chasing after pretty girls."

Nila, taught to respect his elders and the authority of those in charge, and with his service to God coming first, humbled himself. "I'm sorry, you're right," Nila said, dropping his head momentarily. He still held resentment towards Chrishav for interrupting his chance of being with a woman. If he hadn't shown up, Nila knew he would have yielded to Destiny's advances.

"Good, now go get a good night's sleep. I have a feeling tomorrow will be busy for us."

Nila retreated into his room, knowing Chrishav was correct, but wishing he hadn't shown up.

Sammi's became the de facto meeting space for Chrishav, Randall, and Nila. The three met in the lobby and walked over for breakfast, considering the familiarity they developed amongst one another, and still not feeling comfortable in town.

"What did you do last night?" Chrishav asked Randall as they strolled down the street.

"Man, I really thought I was gonna get to tap this hot babe who talked me into playing some games of pool. If I won, she led me to believe that it was possible to find out something about what happened with my sister," Randall answered.

Chrishav detected Randall was deceiving himself, as if nothing was wrong, but maintained and internalized profound despondency.

"What do you mean, tap this?" Nila asked.

Chrishav blushed. "I'm not sure if we should explain this to you. You're young and innocent of these types of things."

"Damn it, tell him," Randall said, and then explained the term to Nila. He was blunt, upsetting Chrishav.

"I don't think you should have done that?" Chrishav said.

"Oh, you mean like what I almost got to do with this woman who came to my room last night," Nila said, still angry towards his companion.

"Really?" Randall exclaimed. "You almost got lucky? What happened?"

"Chrishav showed up and decided I shouldn't."

"Decided you shouldn't? What is he—your father? And dude, you blocked your buddy here?" Randall said, giving Chrishav a look of disbelief. Nila didn't recognize or comprehend the idiomatic expletive Randall used, but guessed by its context.

"It was for his best," Chrishav responded, defending his actions. "Besides, there was something odd about her."

"Not cool, man, not cool."

"Finish what you were about to say about your pool game," Chrishav said, wanting to deflect Randall's aggressiveness.

"Anyway, I lost, but afterwards, this chick said she'd make it up to me. She stood me up, though," Randall continued.

Seeing a tour bus approaching, Chrishav experienced a weighted, heavy feeling with a tinge of nausea.

"Something's strange about that bus coming this way," Chrishav said, feeling uncomfortable — more so than with the other traffic he'd been observing since they arrived.

Nila and Randall, also about to enter the diner, stared at the large white tour bus, noticing not anything odd. Adorned with red and gold stripes down its side and the name Golden State Tours, it traveled past the diner, approached the bakery, pulled over and stopped.

"The only strange thing I notice," Randall responded, "is that the letter n was peeling off."

"I feel weird. There's something strange about that bus," Chrishav said.

The tour bus door opened, with the driver stepping out. He wore a pressed white shirt, gray pants with a red strip down the side of the legs, and black oxford shoes with a mirrored spit-shine. He stepped over to Rooster, who handed him a newspaper. The driver read the headline, and then waved for everyone on the bus to disembark. One by one, the passengers got off and received a newspaper from Rooster. When the last passenger re-boarded the tour bus, the door closed, and they pulled out, heading westward.

"All of this stuff is a bit too weird for me," Randall said, as he stepped inside of Sammi's, leaving his companions in the doorway watching the tour bus. Once it arrived at the roundabout, it stopped, letting off what Chrishav and Nila counted to be twenty-one passengers. The bus then turned right and continued north, while the twenty-one passengers meandered west. Both men's keen eyesight noted most to be sobbing or weeping, two others groaning. Chrishav's emotions flooded with dread and trepidation.

"I wonder if they live down that road?" Nila said.

"I don't think so. There's nothing much down there but homes on a couple of blocks before you leave town. The road passes a field and then goes into the forest from there."

"Then where are they walking to?" Nila asked.

Chrishav shrugged his shoulders. "No idea."

The bus proceeded out of sight; Chrishav and Nila rejoined Randall, who was seated at a booth along the side wall of the restaurant with his back to the window. Ordering and waiting for their meal, the men were quiet. Randall read his emails on his mobile phone, surprised that his smartphone had full signal strength since the time they arrived in town. He recalled driving on the way up a couple of miles before entering the town that his phone displayed unrecognizable icons and unintelligible gibberish characters. Powering his device down and then back up, it wouldn't reset. When he entered town, his phone worked properly.

The bus encounter still disturbed Chrishav. He wanted to resolve the chorus of soul emotions he couldn't explain. After a few moments, the uncomfortable feelings faded. Nila concentrated on taking the archery gear he purchased to a practice-range the store clerk recommended on the south side of town.

Their meals arrived. Chrishav started a conversation to dismiss thinking about the tour bus. "Randall, I've noticed since we've been here, you haven't talked much about your sister. I get the impression she was important to you?"

Randall wasn't sure how or if he wanted to respond. He opened up. "My sister was an all-around good person. Know what I mean?"

"How's that?"

"She was there for me. Because of her, she made me do the right thing a lot of times. Sometimes my anger got the best of me. If I got into trouble, she bailed me out. She watched out for me the best she could. And she was the type of person who did what she said she would do and stood by her friends."

"Sounds like she meant a lot to you."

"She did. If there's a special place in heaven, she'd be the first in line," Randall boasted.

"I take it she was a believer in the Great Creator?"

"You don't have to be a believer. We never went to church and grew up with that religious crap, but my sister was an all-around good person. I don't think you have to believe to get to the good side once you die. Me, I can understand if I don't make it. I lived a crappy life, but her."

Nila eyed a disheveled, but pretty woman, walk by outside on the sidewalk. Seeing her distracted him from listening to Randall and Chrishav's conversation. He almost didn't recognize that it was Destiny until she walked into the diner. She wore glasses and no makeup, with her wavy hair tangled and crudely combed. She went to the register counter and ordered a cup of coffee to go.

"That's the woman who came to my room last night," Nila said, interrupting his companions' conversation on the verge of becoming tenuous to Randall because of its religious components. Chrishav and Randall turned to garner a view. They both recognized Destiny.

"What the hell?" Randall muttered under his voice. He shot up from his chair like a bottle rocket and dashed over to Destiny. "What happened to you last night? I thought you said you were gonna come up to my room?" he said harshly.

Destiny's facial response displayed both confusion and appall by Randall's allegation. "I was going to do what?"

"Come up to my room. You and me were...I ended up crashing."

Destiny shook her head. "I'm sorry, but I don't know why you would think something like that."

"Don't mess with me," Randall said, loud enough to capture the attention of the diner's patrons and staff, his outburst quieting all the conversations. "It was after those pool games I played you talked me into," he continued

Destiny's face became panic stricken. "I don't remember any of that. I need to get to work." Destiny turned back towards the counter. "Shirley, I'll be back later for my cup of coffee."

Destiny attempted to leave, but Randall stepped in front of her. She trembled.

"Don't you at least owe me to help find out what happened to my sister?" Randall gruffly asked. "It was because of you I got into that damn pool game. You blew the one lead I had."

Chrishav had walked up to the pair.

"I'm sorry. I do not know what you're talking about. I need to get to work. I'm already late as it is." Distress filled Destiny's voice.

Chrishav detected Destiny wasn't the same individual as the night prior in the hotel hallway. Today, he perceived a scared and confused woman, lost to the morning. "Randall, let her go. I think she's telling you the truth."

Destiny flashed Chrishav a thankful glance while sidestepping her way around Randall's wide-shouldered frame and hurried to the exit.

"What are you, some sort of mind reader? You weren't even there last night. I may have had a few drinks, but I remember what she did."

"She seemed genuine. Are you sure?"

Randall became furious; Chrishav worried he would erupt in physical violence.

"Yeah, I'm sure." Randall stepped around Chrishav. "Screw this. She's gotta know something," he snarled.

He followed Destiny, with Chrishav glancing at Nila, nodding his head to the side, before going after Randall. Nila understood Chrishav's signal, knowing he was asking for help. He trailed the two out the door.

Outside, Destiny was halfway across the street, with Randall ready to race up to her until Rooster yelled out from his chair. "She ain't gonna remember you's from last night. Destiny's back to her old self."

"What are you talking about, old man?" Randall said, walking over to Rooster.

"I says young man, Destiny's back to her old self. She's not goin' be much help to you now."

"Could you please explain?" Nila asked Rooster in a conciliatory tone, attempting to diffuse the tension Randall had ignited.

Rooster ignored Nila's question. "You sure we's haven't met before, fella?" he asked, his attention directly on Randall.

"We met yesterday. Don't tell me you're getting senile, old man?"

Rooster flashed a broad smile. "It'll come to me." The smile pacified Randall, who wanted to stay angry.

"I'm gonna go back inside and finish my breakfast," Randall snapped. "I gotta find that Barclay guy. He said he knew something about my sister."

Randall went back into the diner; Chrishav and Nila followed—none of the three heard Rooster make the comment, "Nows I remembers why he's looks so familiar; his sister went west."

THE GRAY WOLVES

A misty breeze accompanied the morning sunrise to meet Nila at an archery practice range in an expansive field near Omega Lodging Ranch located outside the southern edge of town. The Omega was a favorite among recurrent hunters during their excursions. The fragrance of pine and damp earth loitered in the cool air, saturated with dew. This was far different from his homeland. During the rainy season, hot and humid mornings set the framework for the rest of the day. In the dry season, it was the arid air.

No one else occupied the grassy pasture. This was a good time to practice with his new bow and arrow equipment he purchased from *Granger's*. Finding a small outcropping of trees by the forest edge, the arrowhead pierced trunks showed previous archers had used them for practice. Attaching a target to a lead tree, Nila paced off the number of steps to estimate the distance he had practiced when in his homeland. Setting his excess tackle on the ground, and leaving his quiver strapped to his back, he extracted an arrow, inserted it onto the bowstring, and pulled. He let the bolt loose. The arrow was high and right of the target's center.

The Huntsman wouldn't be happy.

Having made a mental note now that he was accustomed to the pull tension of his bow, he fired another arrow. Off center again. He slotted another arrow onto the bowstring, adjusted, and released. Bull's-eye. Letting loose three more arrows, Nila grouped his shots in a tight pattern.

The Huntsman would be proud.

Nila, meticulous and careful, attempted to remove each arrow from the tree, whereas not to damage the heads. The first three, he withdrew intact. Nila pulled too hard on the fourth, overconfident by not rocking it with gentle up and down pressure to loosen it. The head remained embedded. The fifth pulled out with no resistance. Abandoning the fragmented arrowhead, he walked back to his gear.

Nila sensed someone, or something, with malice was watching him. The gentle, refreshing breezes blowing across the field receded. An unwelcoming fog rolled through the trees, halting at the forest edge. The air grew sour, rank, and pungent, now filled with odors that reminded him of musky wild animals. The hair on his arm stood up.

Three spurious shadowy shapes appeared within the heavy mist as if rising from the ground, from as best he could estimate, human in physique, with unfurled wings folding in onto each of their backs. They advanced, piercing through the fog and mist onto the field. The silhouetted figures, obscured by the morning sun's light scattering through the towering trees, transformed into four-legged shadows resembling dog-like creatures.

Three hulking gray wolves strode onto the dew-covered grass. Nila estimated their height from the paw to the shoulder was the same distance as from his hips to the ground. He didn't know wolves could reach that size. One was bulkier than the other two, covered with gray fur mixed with brown speckles. Light chocolate brown and blonde fur covered the other two, interspersed with the gray. White fur shrouded the undersides of all three. The canines, now snarling, exposed pointed yellowed teeth within their snouts.

Nila reached behind his back, extracting an arrow from his quiver. He forced himself to settle his trembling hand. He inserted the shaft's slotted tail onto the bowstring's nocking point. The wolves charged. Nila said a quick prayer, *Great Creator, guide my arrow*. Focusing on the one closest to him, he aimed and released. He struck the wolf in the upper shoulder near its neck; it rolled on the ground.

A lucky shot, but I'll take it.

The dog's momentum stopped; it vaporized into gray dust. The distraction of not expecting the wolf to disappear made Nila realize he lost valuable seconds. The distance between him and the two remaining animals shrank.

Nila hurriedly charged his bow. Taking aim, pulling the bowstring back, he focused on the wolf on the left and loosed. When he released his fingers, Nila knew he pulled back a bit too far. The arrow overshot. It grazed the top of the wolf's head and impaled into the ground. Firing two more arrows would be tough. In haste, he placed another one on the bowstring, recalled his breath control and took aim; he fired. The arrow found its target. The wolf vanished in the same way as the first, evaporating into a similar cloud of gray dust. There was enough time to unsheathe another arrow from the case.

Nila inserted it onto the bowstring, drew and aimed. The final beast halted yards away. This was odd. Nila didn't understand why he was reluctant to release the arrow. The wolf fixated its intense stare with its greenish-yellow eyes. It circled Nila, who rotated with the canine, keeping the charged arrow aimed at its torso.

"Who are you, that you can dispatch my companions to their temporary abeyance?" The wolf said and then snarled as it took a sniff.

Nila almost dropped his aim at hearing the wolf speak. "What is this sorcery?"

"Sorcery is not involved with what comes natural to me," the wolf responded.

Nila remained quiet.

"Who are you that you can do what no natural man can do?" the wolf asked, as it took slow and methodical steps, eyeing Nila.

"I'm called a spirit tracker. I'm in search of a destroyer daemon."

"So, the spirit tracker thinks he'll find and dispatch a destroyer?" The wolf said. "Without the soul reader, you're impotent."

"It is not Chrishav where I derive my strength." Nila wondered how the wolf knew of his companion.

"You're weak. You don't even have the courage to sleep with a beautiful woman. You can't even call yourself a man."

"How is courage determined from that? You spout nothing more than simple insults." Nila now wondered how the wolf knew about the situation with Destiny.

"I know your father didn't show courage when he died," the wolf said.

Nila re-exerted his strength by pulling on the bowstring and taking greater focus on his target. "You must be the Destroyer?"

"Silly boy, if I were the Destroyer, I'm sure you'd be dead already."

"Then who or what are you?"

"I am a sentry of Elysium. My brethren and I ensure that those who attempt to forsake their determined destiny do not escape."

"I don't understand."

"Nor should you." The wolf said as it circled Nila. Nila kept his arrow trained on his target. The wolf took two hearty sniffs. "You're nothing more than a visitor to this border realm town. You're not spoiled."

Spoiled? Nila, confused by the comment, dropped his aim again. "What do you mean, spoiled?"

"That is not my place to tell you."

Nila focused on another question that came to mind. "Tell me about the Destroyer?"

"No."

The wolf turned away and ran back towards the fog entrenched trees. Arriving at the forest edge, the previous two wolves took shape as if appearing from the air. The pack of three regrouped and sprinted into the woods. The fog dissipated.

Nila secured his gear and rushed to hurry back so he could describe the encounter to Chrishav.

THE MAYOR'S TUMULT

The mayor glanced at his watch - twenty past eight in the morning, and there was still no sign of Destiny. She'd never been this late before, yet he wasn't upset about her tardiness. The one thing on his mind was how to discipline her for undermining his machinations concerning the forlorn pool player Barclay. He had wanted the joy of squeezing the last inkling of hope from him. In the end, the mayor couldn't have Destiny receive the penalty he orchestrated for Barclay. The sheriff wouldn't allow it. She, like many other residents in town, was his pet, although they never went as wayward before.

For the Sheriff, the law was binding. The mayor was happy about that fact. Barclay tried to play his way out of his agreement. The mayor made sure there were stipulations that slanted the contract in his favor. Even though the intercession of the Guardians' superior forced him to provide a loophole, most rejected or ignored the covenant clause, focusing on immediate material gains or physical gratification. Whenever someone who the mayor considered ignorant mortal meat bags ratified an agreement with him or his peers in other realm boundary towns, they never escaped the finality of their contract.

Strolling into the records department, the lights were off, the computer workstation display dark, and the file cabinets locked, with no sign that Destiny had checked into work. Going throughout all the town hall, she wasn't in the building. When the mayor returned to his desk and sat, she burst into the office wearing a wrinkled blouse and rumpled skirt. A panicked expression of confusion shrouded her face, revealing a flushed complexion and uncombed curly brunette hair.

"Where've you been?" the mayor bellowed.

"I'm so sorry. I somehow woke up late this morning. I don't know what happened."

"What was that crap with Barclay last night? What gives you the right you can go around and renegotiate any changes to my agreements?"

"What are you talking about? I did nothing of the sort?"

"Bull crap, Ricardo at Lake Alice's said you were there last night. You instigated a game between Barclay and one of those recent visitors."

"Like hell I did. I don't remember doing such a thing. I swear everyone is going crazy around here."

The mayor arose and walked around his desk to stand in front of Destiny. With his small but muscular hand, he took off her glasses. With his other hand, he grabbed her throat, applying pressure like a miniature vice grip and pulling her face down to his. Even though he was five foot six, she was three inches taller. The mayor's daunting and staunch expression as he stared deep into Destiny's eyes made her feel as if he were a giant. The building heat in his fingertips added to the discomfort of his grasp.

"You're saying you don't remember a damn thing about last night?" the mayor asked, focusing on Destiny's eyes, watching for the minutest change in her pupils.

"No, as a matter of fact, the last day or so seems like a dream. It was like I wasn't even in my body."

Analyzing her eyes, he pushed her back. Destiny almost lost her balance. The mayor was upset that her autonomous reactions broadcasted she wasn't lying.

"Then what in the sam-what happened to you?"

"I don't know."

"And you don't remember any of that b.s. that you pulled?"

"No, I don't."

Destiny's voice inflections, muscle twitches, breathing, and direct answers showed she was telling the truth, or at least what she believed to be the truth. The mayor walked back to his red, high back Corinthian leather office chair behind his desk. The mayor knew the mouth may lie; the body doesn't. He was a master of reading simple twitches, jerks, and eye movements to know a person's body language will reveal the truth, even when someone lies to themselves.

"What is going on around here? Spoiled packages showing up left and right, you losing your mind; I swear someone is trying to muck up things around here."

"Did you need me to take care of anything?" Destiny asked in an insecure voice.

"No, just get your butt to work."

Leaning back and resting his feet on top of his desk, the mayor was at a loss. He'd had to reconcile an abhorrent amount of recent paperwork. The Sheriff also needed to sign off on the reconciliation to validate the correct persons passed north or west. Then there was the disturbing observation from the other night, finding children at Barclay's mixed in with the other spoiled packages.

Children were supposed to have immediate passage north whenever they accompanied a group passing through town. Many times, young adults as old as twenty or twenty-one years of age were granted immediate passage. The mayor didn't agree with the law, but the sheriff was there to enforce it.

Damn it, maybe I should talk to the sheriff about all this strange crap. As much as the mayor dreaded having to deal with him, he proceeded over to the station house.

The mayor left unannounced. Normally, he told one of his junior staff members, or Destiny, if he was heading out and where he could be found if they needed to get in touch with him. He didn't find it necessary to carry a cell phone, not having a need for one in the small town.

Walking up to the round-about, the mayor watched a bright red BMW approach from the north, drive right of the sandstone brick walled circle filled with small lilies and marigolds, then head west. He wasn't too happy observing the car. *Another spoiled package. No one should ever drive from the north, yet it's happening more frequently.* Once you pass Barclay's, the road, one way. None of the town's residents except the sheriff should drive north and then back into town.

The mayor entered the sheriff's station. The first thing that caught his attention was Clarissa's hair color. Today, a bright artificial sun-blond color adorned her hair, styled in a semi-spiked fashion.

"Blonde doesn't do you any favors," the mayor said with revulsion. "It clashes with your natural skin tone. It makes you look weird, especially for someone your age. Your boss in?"

"He's back there," Clarissa answered, attempting to conceal being upset after the mayor's customary blunt and uncompassionate comment. She expected it, but today, it wrenched her emotions with a deeper impact. After the mayor walked away from her desk, she cried.

Sheriff Knight waved his hand as if batting a fly after Mayor Corbett entered his office; the door closed.

"First off, when you leave, apologize to Clarissa. Now, what was it you were so upset about last night, Hannibal?"

"Damn it, sheriff, you have to fix whatever is going on around here."

"And what is going on?"

"You know what's going on. You've gotta sign off on the paperwork, too. All these damn spoiled packages. I saw another one come back from the north as I was walking over here."

The sheriff sat up straight in his chair. "How come I haven't seen the paperwork on that one?"

"Now you know why I'm perturbed." The mayor was eager to use a stronger expletive, but refrained himself.

"Hmmm, I may have to make another run up past Barclay's."

"And that's the other thing, Barclay. I wanted to warn you he tried to circumvent the contract I have with him. He ended up playing pool with one of those visitors and won. He's up at the house now, attempting to pack to go back into the world. You know I can't let him leave."

"If he met the conditions of payment, and won against a tournament class player, I don't think there's anything you can do?"

"Wrong answer, sheriff. Small print on his contract, game has to be facilitated by me."

"But your aide Destiny was there, and you said she's able to represent you on most matters here in Elysium."

"But I didn't expect it to be used against me," the mayor said.

"Not my problem. But if Barclay leaves, who's going to host the parties at the house?"

The mayor stared up at the ceiling for a minute, contemplating a response. "I'll figure something out."

"There's your answer. Nothing much I can do for you. Figure it out or let him go."

"Thanks for nothing," the mayor said.

The mayor opened the sheriff's office door and was about to leave when there stood Randall, ready to knock.

"Who the are you?" The mayor asked, wanting to garner more information about Randall, recalling seeing him with Destiny in the Records Office at the Town Hall.

"Randall Steiner. Who are you?" Randall retorted, not appreciating the mayor's abrasive tone.

"I'm the mayor of this glorious hellhole." The mayor said.

Randall brushed aside the mayor, finding him to be an irritant, and entered the sheriff's office.

"Sheriff, you gotta help me find some guy called Barclay," Randall demanded.

"Now, why would I want to do that?" the Sheriff responded.

Randall's comment intrigued the mayor. He stayed to listen.

"I played pool with him last night. One of your city workers, I think her name is Destiny, set up the game, and if I won, Barclay was gonna tell me who my sister had an affair with."

"And what if he won?" the Sheriff asked.

"He mentioned something about he was playing as if his soul depended on it."

"I take it he won?"

"Yeah, but I want to find him to see what it would take to get him to tell me about whatever a-hole it was that my sister was with."

"Watch it, mister. I don't appreciate any unwholesome language in my presence," the Sheriff said. "Besides, I understand he may leave here pretty soon."

"Not if I have anything to say about it," the mayor interjected.

Randall wondered why the mayor had made the comment.

"Where can I find him?" Randall asked.

"You're not going to find him here."

"Sheriff, you gotta help me," Randall implored.

"What if I could help you?" the mayor asked again, interrupting, stroking his pudgy chin.

"How can you help me?"

"Hannibal, don't go there. You're not going to pull any of your cursed agreements in here. As for you," Sheriff Knight mentioned, focusing his attention back to Randall, "don't go around trying to find out what happened to your sister. Unequivocally, as God in heaven in my witness, your sister committed suicide." Randall didn't notice the mayor cringe and shrug his shoulders when the Sheriff made the comment "God in Heaven."

"Sheriff," Randall tried to continue, but the sheriff cut him off.

"That's all I'm going to say about it. Have a good day." The sheriff's resolute, stoned face expression told Randall the discussion was over.

Both men left the sheriff's office and stood by the station house's main entrance out of earshot of the sheriff.

The mayor gazed at Randall. "I might be able to help. We just might see each other again," the mayor concluded, while reaching for the doorknob, preparing to leave the building.

"Wait a minute," Randall tried to plea in keeping the mayor from stepping out the now open door. "Can't you help me now?"

"Just head back to your room. I have to take care of a couple of things first."

Nila returned from the practice range to his room to store his tackle, bow, and arrow. He discovered his quiver was short four arrows. He recalled the one he had damaged when attempting to remove it from the tree. The other three used against the wolves could still be imbedded in the ground at the practice range. Excited by the oddity of the mysterious creatures, he overlooked retrieving the expensive arrows and didn't want to consider them lost. Maybe later he would try to retrieve them, if they were still there and another archer or hunter didn't recover them.

Nila changed and went to knock on Chrishav's door. There was no answer. He presumed he might have gone down to Sammi's for a cup of coffee. Rushing out onto the street, heading to the diner, he could see Randall was walking back from the sheriff's office. Chrishav surprised Nila by not coming out of Sammi's, but the neighboring bakery as Randall was passing Rooster, where all three men congregated.

Rooster took a hard look at Randall. Randall noticed.

"What's up, old man?" Randall asked.

"You haves a picture of your sister?"

Randall, a bit peeved, wondered why Rooster had made the strange request. "Yeah, why?"

Rooster's stare unnerved Randall. Randall wanted to resist. He tried bringing up a picture on his phone; it didn't work. He pulled a miniature picture from his wallet and presented it to the old man.

"Thoughts so—looks like you. So many passin' through here, hard to 'member faces."

"What do you mean, looks like me?"

"She's head'd up the road 'bout three, maybes four weeks ago."

Randall lunged towards Rooster. Nila and Chrishav's quick reflexes grabbed him by his arms, keeping him from pouncing on the old man. The tussle caused Chrishav to bump and knock the wireframe newspaper holder onto its side.

"Why're you mad? Only tellin's you what I saw," Rooster said.

"Damn you, old man, you know my sister's dead. I went to her funeral."

Chrishav and Nila found it hard to hold Randall back, even though he didn't exert his full strength to escape his restrainer's grip. Randall became aware he acted on his impulses, almost attacking an old man.

He calmed down, in part because Rooster didn't react to the physical outburst.

"I knows she killed herself, but I also knew went and walks west," Rooster said.

He reached down and grabbed the newspaper lying next to him on the stand. He folded it in such a way that the front-page headline and photo were prominent. He then presented it to Randall and Chrishav. It was a picture of a white tour bus with red and gold stripes along the side and read "Golden State Tours." The headline read, "Tour Bus Crash on Road to Big Bear Mountain." The subheading stated, "All 48 Aboard Died," followed by a picture of the driver.

"Familiar?" Rooster quizzed.

The three men froze. They remembered the bus and the driver from the day prior. It had traveled through the town center and turned right at the roundabout, heading north after dropping off some passengers. His curiosity squelching his anger, Randall resisted attempting to assault Rooster before reaching out and snatching the newspaper.

"It can't be," Randall said. "It can't be."

Nila glanced at what could be interesting to the two men. "It looks like the same bus as the one we saw yesterday." He tried to come up with an alternative. "That company has got to have several buses, wouldn't it?"

"I don't think you understand," Chrishav said. "Notice the letter n. It's peeled in the same way as the one we saw yesterday."

"Then the accident didn't cause what we see in the picture, did it?" Nila asked.

"No, all the more reason to be concerned," Chrishav continued. "Looking at the date and time of the accident, there's no way that bus could have been down in Southern California and up here in a matter of minutes when we saw it. Could it?"

It dazed Randall, trying to comprehend Chrishav's comment. "What's going on here? How's it possible for us to see that same bus here in town if it's the same bus as the one that crashed?"

"Mista, do you know where you'res at?" Rooster said, handing the small picture to Nila. "Here, gives this back to your friend."

Nila sneaked a quick peek at the image of Randall's sister, viewing a female face having long blonde hair and hazel eyes. He was about to pass on the picture, then realized he'd recognized the face. He'd met her before, but she had short brunette hair.

"This is your sister? When did you say she passed?" Nila asked, staring at the photograph.

"Three weeks ago."

Chrishav sensed a tsunami of emotions flood through Nila. He trembled; his dark-skinned complexion flushed. Something had disturbed him.

Randall also witnessed Nila's reaction. He grabbed the photograph of his sister. "This is too much for me. I'm going back to my room."

Chrishav sensed Randall felt defeated and waited until he was out of hearing distance. "Nila, what's wrong? You seemed bothered by something."

"Randall's sister. I saw her before."

"What do you mean, you saw her before?" Chrishav asked. "Where?"

"It was in my country in a place called the River Purgo in the Hinnom Valley, just before coming here. How could she be there when she was to have passed away? That meant that she was already... and then you count the incident with the bus...Rooster, what's going on here?"

"You gotta talk to the sheriff 'bout that. I can't help you. Maybe he can lets you know about all the weird stuff arounds here," Rooster said.

It was now that Nila remembered the incident with the gray wolves during his archery practice earlier in the morning. "Chrishav, I need to tell you something."

Chrishav fixated on the tour bus and Randall's sister, oblivious to everyone around him.

"Chrishav," Nila called out again, working to get his companion's attention. "Chrishav."

"What is it, Nila?" Chrishav snapped, perturbed that Nila had broken his concentration.

"This morning, on the outskirts of town, I came across three gray wolves. One of them spoke to me."

Chrishav's eyes widened. "A wolf spoke to you? Did you dispatch it? Was it the Destroyer?"

"No, but they said it was behind what's going on, and then they folded into the fog."

Rooster chuckled. "You mets the wolves who guards the town."

"Guard the town from what?" Nila asked.

"They keep those who tries to not go on the road west, from goin' the south or east. They be's sentinels of Elysium."

"What's wrong with going west? Why wouldn't anybody want to go west?" Chrishav queried.

"Alls I can say is that there's a question for the Sheriff."

SHEPHERDING THE LOST

W alking up the road north from the roundabout, the mayor was euphoric. There was no traffic heading south from Barclay's place. It was a good sign all the vehicles and periodic pedestrians were heading in one direction. If everything was going well, no one was to be rejected from going north and having to go west or having to wait at Barclay's home. Distraught at not being able to go north, some wouldn't wait until a transport came to haul them to the lost realms. They walked to delay the inevitable.

Maybe everything was getting back to normal. The mayor was tired of trying to explain the large number of discrepancies to his superiors, and with the threat of his recall for incompetence. Barclay's residence looked quiet enough. There wasn't the same activity level as when he had last visited, and the house was full of spoiled packages. Walking up the quick jaunt of steps onto the porch, the mayor barged through the front door without knocking.

Barclay sat in the living room on the leather couch. "It's about damn time. I was expecting you sooner than this."

"And why's that?" Mayor Corbett replied, pretending to be coy.

Barclay knew better. "Don't play me for a fool, Mayor. I know you know about the pool game."

The mayor displayed a wry smile. "That I do."

"I guess this is you coming to say goodbye?"

"You think so?" The mayor responded. "You don't think you're going anywhere, do you?"

Barclay jumped up off the couch. "Bet your sweet butt I am. I'm outta here."

The mayor smiled. "I don't think so."

Barclay approached the mayor in disbelief. The mayor's impish grin told Barclay he should be worried; the mayor had tricked him before.

"What do you mean you don't think so?" Barclay questioned.

"I mean that your game doesn't make up as being official per our agreement."

"Oh, no you don't, you slimy son of a b. Everyone in town knows that Destiny is your assistant and represents you with a lot of crap around here."

The mayor chuckled. "That she does, but it wasn't her at the pool game."

"You know that's a bunch of bull." Barclay said.

"I've strong reason to believe she may've been possessed. And if that's the case, I can't hold her responsible for her actions."

"I can't believe you'd make up something so silly just to get out of keeping the contract."

Barclay gasped for air, trying to grab at an unseen heated lasso force constricted around his neck.

"Don't think of me trying to be silly. I don't joke around."

It was as if a vice grip was closing and tightening around Barclay's neck; an unperceivable downward pressure forced him to drop onto his knees. He attempted to pull at the invisible garrote cord, wheezing for air.

"Now listen to me, you little piece of human filth," the mayor said as he bent over his vassal. "Don't think that you can circumvent your way out of your contract around here. Do you know who you're dealing with or who I serve?"

The mayor waved his hand, restoring Barclay's breathing, and stepped over to the front door. "I should send your meatbag butt across the river Purgo to the chasm, but unlike you, I believe in keeping my obligations."

Barclay expelled a couple of coughs. "When it suits you."

The mayor's nostrils flared; his dark brown eyes transformed to a bright fiery yellow. "Unlike you human vermin, I don't go trying to weasel out of my agreements. It wouldn't be good business for me if I didn't keep to my contracts, now, would it?"

"No, I guess not," Barclay replied, relieved the choking sensation subsided.

"My next question, have any of the spoiled packages passing through mentioned anything weird at the parties?" the mayor asked.

"Like what?"

"Like maybe why they're spoiled?"

"Most of them are surprised to be back here. They thought for sure they were good enough to go north without being turned back."

"At least no one's here now," the mayor said. He wanted to celebrate seeing the empty house.

Barclay glanced out the lodge's large picture window facing north to see what he estimated twenty people traversing down the road approaching the house. Most displayed a disillusioned countenance; others appeared traumatized. All looked to be weeping, a couple of others as if they were gnashing their jaws and grinding their teeth.

"I wouldn't get too happy, mayor," Barclay noted. "Look."

The mayor wanted to burst into an explosive fit when he glanced out the window, but knew Barclay wasn't to blame for what he was observing. "What the...you know what, don't let them stay; send their asses on to walk westward before the transport gets here. Maybe that'll screw up whoever's trying to mess things up around here."

Nila didn't expect anyone to be knocking on his door. The last time it led to an uncomfortable encounter with one of the towns' people. It could be Chrishav. They separated from one another half-an-hour prior after the incident with Rooster and Randall. There was no reason for Randall to visit him.

Grabbing the doorknob, Nila was reluctant to answer. "Who is it?" He yelled through the door.

"Chrishav."

Relieved, Nila opened the door. "Chrishav, thank goodness it's you. I was concerned it may be someone else again."

"Can I come in?"

Nila gestured for his companion to enter and presented him with a chair in the room. Chrishav accepted, sat, and sighed.

"You know, Nila, since we've been here, I don't know if we made any progress," Chrishav said.

Nila was relieved. "I too felt the same. Nothing has led us to find the Destroyer. Yet we know it's nearby based on what happened."

"I know, I sense it, but I don't know where we go from here. They sent me to help you, and we're nowhere closer to finding the daemon."

"One thing I learned while hunting, even though we may feel like we're getting nowhere, we need to be patient and wait out wait prey. The tracks will present themselves as long as we keep looking."

"Keep looking where?"

"I'm not sure."

Chrishav waited a few minutes before continuing. "Do you know what we're looking for, at least? I mean, you're the hunter. You must've done this before."

Nila appeared nervous. He was unsure of their next move, and who or what to be searching for, even how to attack his supposed prey. "I never hunted a daemon before."

Chrishav expelled a large huff, almost forgetting how to breathe. "What? This is your first time?" Chrishav didn't know how to take hearing this. He rebuked himself for not bringing it up before. "How are we supposed to know how, or what to do if we track it down?"

"My father and a Huntsman taught me everything I needed to know. Besides, I put my faith in the Great Creator."

"I do too, but I also put faith in practicality," Chrishav countered. "We have to be surefooted in our ways to ensure we're successful. We can't go chasing after daemons in the dark. It's like the blind leading the blind."

"We won't be that blind; you've done this before, haven't you?"

Chrishav tilted his head down for an instant, regretting he had scolded Nila for not having any experience. "Ummm, I have to admit, I've done nothing like this before, either." He waited for a scolding or snide comment, which didn't come.

Nila presented Chrishav with a small grin. "I'm sure what we need to know will be revealed to us."

Chrishav's embarrassment lifted. "I hope you're right. This is a small town; I don't see how so much could be hidden."

"Yet it is in the darkness of souls where daemons sometimes like to hide. They may be before us, and we do not even realize it. I remember that's what the Huntsman once told me. We mustn't give up so easily. I also remember my father teaching me to be patient when hunting clever prey," Nila said, wanting to present some of what he had learned so as not to appear ignorant of their circumstances.

"But your prey may not be where you expect it," Chrishav countered.

"I've learned that beasts can be territorial."

"We're not talking about natural beasts, are we? We're talking about daemons," Chrishav responded.

"And daemons are sometimes territorial in ways we may not understand. They mainly act upon their nature, and that is by instinct to undermine what is good and righteous."

Chrishav's soul became disquieted, overcome by a surge of rage, aggressiveness, and hostility. It wasn't Nila that had caused emotional change, but he didn't know why; it occurred since their current discussion was at worst - indifferent. Chrishav perceived a familiar foreboding of malevolence like when he grew up on the reservation; it reminded him of the shamans in his tribe. Concentrating on calming down his emotions, the disturbing feelings weren't rooted in any distinct person, but as if ethereal. They originated outside, growing in intensity. Chrishav glanced out the window to see a light, frothy mist rolling in. He rushed over to the room's antique framed glass and gazed down the two stories. Nila joined him, curious about what had distracted Chrishav's attention from their conversation. Down below, a fog comprising a luminous, slightly green tincture saturated the air. It rolled over the street and sidewalk like the waves of the ocean onto shore.

"This doesn't feel natural," Chrishav said. "We should check this out."

Nila agreed.

The two men made their way downstairs and out the hotel's front entrance, where the desk manager and neighboring store owners had already stepped outside to observe the growing mist. Nila thought no one had ever seen fog before, as if it were an unnatural phenomenon. Then, an oddity of the fog hit him; the moist air turned warm, foul, and damp, reminiscent of a dog's breath, suspending within it a putrid and rotting meat odor. Howling and barking, followed by the sounds of running footsteps accompanying the moans and wails from disembodied voices, echoed from down the street to the east. The noise was getting louder. Everyone emotionally shivered.

"Don't steps onto the road. Nobodys be able to help you then," Rooster said to make sure anyone within hearing distance got the message.

"What are you talking about, Rooster?" Chrishav asked.

A couple of other visible town's people were already standing back up against the front of the hotel, bakery, Sammi's, and other storefronts. The fog got thicker. Chrishav and Nila couldn't tell if others along the cloaked street.

Ominous moaning and the sounds of vicious snarling mix with howling now interweaved with weeping and sobbing streamed past the bystanders. The noise faded into the west. Nila, although unsettled. Chrishav's stomach turned nauseous. The fog rolled westward, trailing the haunting sounds. The aroma of pine and flora replaced the fading foul stench in the air.

"Rooster, what was that?" Chrishav asked, noticing the local townspeople returning to their previous activities. Visitors and tourists were attempting to comprehend the bizarre incident.

"Kinda thoughts that would happen, seeing all them folks tryin' to run to the south where they shouldn'ts 'stead of goin' west from the round-about," Rooster said.

"What are you talking about?" Chrishav asked.

"You two ain't notice, if anyone comes from the road north, theys suppose to go west, but no other direction. The problem lately, befores you two gots here, ain't no one ever supposed to come from the north, least not as much as the last several days. Ain't good for the town."

The slamming of car doors down the street interrupted the three men, followed by the screeching of tires and blaring of sirens from the sheriff's and deputy's vehicles in front of the station house taking off. One cruiser navigated the roundabout, then drove south. The deputy executed a U-turn, proceeding east, and then drown south down one of the smaller side streets.

"Never seen the Sheriff and deputy takes off like that before," Rooster said.

"What about the road north?" Nila asked.

"Ones with answers to that question just drove off."

Sheriff Knight approached the archery practice range on the Omega Ranch, where hunters came to practice during the prime hunting season. Visiting hunters considered the forest area east and south of Elysium as one of the best places in the western United States to hunt deer and wild boar. They weren't aware of the town's existence, bordering the natural and supernatural realms.

Surveying the landscape, two trees had a considerable number of arrowheads imbedded in the wide trunks. Impaled on the ground in two different locations were three more arrows. The Sheriff, holding his palm up, caused the projectiles to vibrate and release from the fertile earth, followed by their moving in reverse flight. Seconds later, they landed and rested in his hand; examined the wood-shaft darts. These were like the ones the store salesman had mentioned he sold to

Nila. *What would cause Nila, or whoever these belonged to, to leave these behind?*

"Hericulium, Archemedeium, Xanexerium, you three get up here now," Sheriff Knight commanded.

A breeze rustled the grass. Grayish dirt particles from between the blades rose from the ground, forming a mirage of shapes molded and remolded. Three distinct bodies of wolves manifested in front of the Sheriff.

Sheriff Knight's confident and determined stance caused the three creatures to whimper and drop prostrate, docile on all fours. The lead wolf inched up in front.

"Cammael, we know why you're here. You can't be here to dispatch us to the abyss; we're doing nothing more than our ascribed duties."

"For years you've been dormant, not having to execute your obligations. Now, suddenly you herd your prey through the main street of town. Who's behind causing those heirs of perdition to escape their destiny that you needed to shepherd them west?"

"The mayor decided to not let the spoiled packages acclimate at Barclay's and wait for the transport, but for them to proceed on west. Many rejected the walk and attempted to leave town, failing to admit their past lives had expired. They tried to go south and then east, out of the valley."

"Ok, the mayor shows he's an idiot. But there's no way he's the one behind the grand scheme of everything going on, like the high number of spoiled packages, and some residents acting strange."

"You should know a Destroyer is the designer and instigator of all you mention?" the wolf to the right noted.

"A Destroyer is behind all this? Which one? Is that why the Huntsman sent Chrishav and Nila?"

"We are not privy to such details," the wolf on the left commented, "but a Guardian and high servant of the Great Creator should know all."

"You know we're told what we need to be told." The sheriff didn't want to tell the beasts any more information than they needed to know.

"Is that all you have for us, or would you like to annoy us further? We must return to our sentry duties."

"Go."

The wolves turned and raced towards the forest before dissolving into gray dust particulates and dispersing into the earth that rippled where they had entered.

DEPARTURE

"Get outta here, Rory," Clarissa yelled out of her front door. Rory stood on the step to the porch landing; inside, a toddler was crying. "You already destroyed what little we had together by sleeping with that hussy girl. Don't destroy the relationship with your daughter by being an asshole."

"You're telling me I can't see my daughter? I should be able to see her anytime I want," Rory bellowed. "Listen to her; she wants her daddy."

"Why do you wanna break our arrangement? Now get out of here."

"I'm not trying to break anything. I want to see my daughter."

"I called the sheriff, so you better get outta here. And Dugan will be home anytime now from the lumberyard. I called him."

"Why would you do that? You know I don't want to cause you any trouble. I want to see Madison."

Clarissa stood in the doorway without saying a word. Her hardened stare and crossed arms showed her determination to remain unwavering in letting Rory in the house. She was worried that he seemed aggressive. Even during their earlier breakups before Madison was born, he would call to announce his arrival. Now he'd shown up unannounced, made belligerent remarks, and threatened to break the door down and barge into the house. Clarissa was concerned for her daughter's safety. Hearing that, she called for the sheriff and Dugan; he agreed. Rory went to his Mustang and drove off, not wanting to entangle with the local law enforcement.

A minute later, spotting Deputy Rutherford drive up, Clarissa stepped out onto the porch carrying a chubby, brunette, 30-month toddler girl straddled to her side. "I'm glad you're here. Rory stopped by and was scaring me."

Deputy Rutherford exited his patrol car. "Everyone okay?"

"We're fine."

"Did he threaten you or Madison in any way?"

"No, he didn't."

"What about Bailey and Henrietta?"

"No, they're still in school."

"Did he seem drunk to you?" Deputy Rutherford gingerly asked.

"No, I don't think so, just crazy."

Deputy Rutherford considered Clarissa's on again, off again relationship between Rory and Dugan to be unstable, if not irrational. Hearing Clarissa's panicked voice calling into the station about Rory being belligerent was not normal. Dugan was the one who tended to be explosive. Even though he was never abusive towards Clarissa or the girls, he was infamous for punching holes in drywall, kicking in the lower halves of doors, or slinging objects through windows.

"Did he say where he was headed?" Deputy Rutherford inquired.

"No, he drove away before you got here."

"I'll call the sheriff, and we'll keep an eye out for him when I head back to the other side of town. I bet he's at Lake Alice's or Carver's on the main strip."

"I'm so fed up with his crap. If he ended up at Barclay's, I wouldn't care."

"You know you don't mean that. He's still the father of your beautiful daughter there."

Clarissa paused before responding. "You're right. I'm upset right now," she said, with remorse in her voice.

"I understand. We'll sort this out."

"Thank you, Carlson."

"And take the rest of the day off. I don't think the Sheriff will mind."

Clarissa smiled and gave Deputy Rutherford a hug. "Thanks, I appreciate that."

Sitting in his hotel room contemplating the oddity with the tour bus, and Rooster mentioning seeing his sister, the severe emotional brunt of losing his sister again struck Randall. It was as if he were hearing it for the first time - magnified tenfold. Randall never took time to mourn and absorb the full psychological impact with the loss of Sherry. He had wanted to be strong for his mother, who herself was on the verge of breaking down before he left Chicago. Now, all he wanted to do was chase away the pain. He strolled over to Lake Alice's.

Strolling into the empty tavern, Randall took a seat at the bar and ordered a scotch and water. Ricardo placed the drink in front of him. Randall stared at the glass for several minutes before taking a sip. He couldn't get past the first couple of swallows despite the urge to get drunk. Randall pushed the glass to the side, placed his elbows on the bar top, and put his head in his hands, forcing himself not to display an embarrassing emotional outburst in public. Moments later, he grabbed the shot glass and gulped down the pale amber contents.

Two drinks later, Rory entered the near vacant tavern and pool hall and made a beeline to an open seat next to Randall.

"What do you have, Rory? Your normal""

"I'll take a dark stout, whatever is on tap."

"Dark stout? That's not like you."

"Just get me the beer."

Ricardo left and returned with a glass stein filled with a dark liquid.. Rory, noticing his barstool neighbor displaying a forlorn facial expression, now observed three empty shot glasses resting in front of him, with a fourth half-full.

"Everything alright, man?" Rory asked.

Randall kept quiet.

"That bad, huh?" Rory continued.

"Rather not talk about it," Randall responded standoffishly.

"Can't be that bad?"

Randall was a bit irritated. "Like I said, I'd rather not talk about it." He took another sip of his drink.

"Fine, don't talk about it. But maybe sometimes talking about something will help."

Finishing his drink and ordering another one, Randall continued to ignore Rory.

"Trying to help, that's all," Rory responded to Randall's silence.

Randall sat remaining quiet, contemplating Rory's remarks. Reluctantly, he elected to engage in the conversation because of Rory's persistence.

"I'm trying to come to grips with something that's happened."

"What happened?"

"My sister killed herself here in town. They think it was over some guy she met and had a fling with."

"Sorry to hear that, man."

"But I don't think that's what's got me upset. I never thought about how much I'm gonna miss her," Randall said, forcing himself to hold back tears.

"Man, my problems are nowhere near as bad as what you're going through," Rory said, attempting to sound sympathetic.

Randall downed another swallow of his drink. "What's up with you?" He asked, wanting to move away from the emotional distress regarding his sister.

"I blew it with my ex-wife again, and now she's moved back in with her ex."

"Ouch, your ex is with her ex. That's a bit messed up."

"Yeah, but sorry 'bout your sister," Rory said, taking a drink of his beer with a tattooed arm Randall hadn't noticed before. "That's gotta be a heck of a loss."

"I was so head-strung about trying to find out who it was my sister had the relationship with that I didn't let it sink in that she was gone. It's easier to be angry at whoever it was she was having the affair with than to be sad that she's gone. My dad died when I was young. My mom taught me to be strong, but I don't know if I can this time."

"Wish I could help you, man," Rory empathized.

"You can't. I don't think there's anything anyone could do?" Randall said, finishing the drink in his glass and ordering another round.

After a few minutes of uneasy quiet, Rory continued. "You know what, if you go north, you won't have to worry about anything else again."

"What are you talking about?" Randall asked.

"You need to get away from here, since this is where your sister died. North of here is a place where you can console all your worries."

Twenty minutes passed as Rory talked to Randall about the pros and cons of staying in town, heading back to Chicago, or going north. When they finished their discussion, Rory gave Randall such a deep and piercing stare it weakened him. Randall returned the stare with a gaze of complicity. "How far a drive north is it?"

"Not far at all. You can walk there."

"I'd rather drive."

"Didn't you arrive here in town with a couple of friends?"

"They're not friends of mine," Randall said sharply. "I met them on the way up here. They drove themselves into town."

"Didn't know. Meant nothing by it."

"Don't worry about it. You said north, huh?"

"Yeah."

Randall pulled his wallet from his rear pocket. "Think I'll go check it out."

"Don't worry, I got this," Rory offered.

"You sure? I can't let you do that." Randall hoped his new drinking acquaintance was persistent.

"Sounds like you're going through a lot. Ricardo put his drinks on my tab."

Ricardo nodded.

"I'm not gonna sit around here arguing with you about this. Much appreciated."

Randall shook Rory's hand and left, feeling relieved. As Rory watched Randall leave the bar, Deputy Rutherford walked in.

"Lovely," Rory said. He turned back around, facing towards the bar.

Rory expected Deputy Rutherford to come talk to him.

"You don't have to guess why I'm here, Rory, do you?" Deputy Rutherford asked, stepping up to the bar.

"What'd that skank tell you?"

"Whoa, that's not very nice now, is it?"

"I'm not worried about being nice, deputy."

Deputy Rutherford sat on the barstool vacated by Randall. He followed with taking off his hat and placing it on the bar top. "Just what are we gonna do? You never acted like this before."

"Don't know what you're talking about, deputy."

Ricardo interrupted the conversation between the two patrons. "Want anything to drink, deputy?"

"I'm good." Deputy Rutherford focused his attention back on Rory. "So, what about this situation with Clarissa?"

"What about it?" Rory quipped.

"We've never been down this road before. What the hell's gotten into you?"

"Is it against the law for a man to see his daughter?"

"If he's threatening or assaulting her mother, then I would say the answer is yes."

Rory faced Deputy Rutherford. "You gonna take me in?"

"Should I?"

"I'm gonna wanna see my daughter."

"I don't want to take you in. It's funny. I'd thought that I'd be having this conversation with Dugan. He's the belligerent one."

The two men stared at one another for a few moments.

"I'm gonna let you slide this one time. Work it out with Clarissa before going to see Madison," Deputy Rutherford said. He placed his wide brimmed deputy hat on his head.

Rory stared straight ahead. "Maybe I should head north like that visitor fella who left."

"Don't go talking like that. You know nothing good would come of that." Deputy Rutherford paused after the full effect of what Rory had mentioned hit him. "Whoa, whoa, whoa, whoa, what do you mean? That corn fed stranger isn't thinking of heading north, is he?"

"That's what he was mentioning. I don't know why he wanted to do that?"

"And you didn't stop him. You know, visitors to this town aren't supposed to head up there, just those destined to pass through."

"Not my job."

"Wait a minute, I know the sheriff was supposed to talk to you. He never mentioned to me the conversation; did you have an affair that man's sister?"

"You know a man doesn't talk about things like that. That's all I told the sheriff. Imply what you want."

Deputy Rutherford knew part of Clarissa being angry with Rory and wanting to keep him from seeing his daughter was because she believed Rory had an affair with Randall's sister.

"I need to get the sheriff so he can stop that man," Deputy Rutherford said. "Damn you, Rory."

The deputy jumped up from the barstool, bolted past the pool tables and out the door. He didn't hear Rory make the comment, "I already am, deputy. I already am."

Sheriff Knight's office was empty. Raising him on the radio was unsuccessful; there was no response. The Sheriff was good with answering if Deputy Rutherford called. Walking out of the station house, Deputy Rutherford debated on if to check over at Sammi's. Along the street, Rooster was in his normal spot, planted in his chair, leaning back on the rear two legs, against the wall.

"Rooster, have you seen the Sheriff?" Deputy Rutherford asked, walking up to the old man. "Did he get back yet?"

"Nope, I thought you know since you's both left together," Rooster answered.

"He went to go find out about that fog while I responded to a domestic call. What was all that about anyway? The sheriff told me to stay inside until whatever that was outside went by. In all the years I've been in this town, nothing like that has ever happened before."

"Don't think it's supposed to. That's why he went to goes talk to the sentries in the south. Then he had to go escort some young people back north."

"South sentries? I didn't know they existed."

"Son, you forgets, you're in Elysium. You never has to deals with them."

"Damn, I need the sheriff; it's important. One of those three visitors, I heard may decide to walk north."

For the first time, the deputy didn't expect Rooster's wide-eyed expression showing his genuine astonishment.

"That ain't good, especially if it ain't his time," Rooster said. "Which one?"

"The corn-fed white guy. I think his name is Randall."

"You should tells his two friends. They mights be in Sammi's."

Chrishav and Nila were in Sammi's as Rooster had guessed. Chrishav was drinking what appeared to be coffee. Nila's ivory-colored coffee cup had a string with a little square sheet of paper hanging on the side.

"Gentlemen, your friend may be in trouble."

"Our friend?" Chrishav asked, hearing the worry in the deputy's voice. "What are you talking about, deputy?"

"The friend you arrived with looks like he's determined to head north," Deputy Rutherford said.

Since their arrival in town, Chrishav and Nila learned to go north held some sort of finality.

"Why would he want to do that?" Nila queried.

"Don't know. I was told by one of our town troublemakers."

"Town troublemaker, and you believe him?" Chrishav asked.

"People around here don't joke about things like that."

Chrishav and Nila darted out of their seats, forgetting they hadn't paid for their meal. Deputy Rutherford told their waitress not to worry about the check. He'd make sure she was confident Chrishav and Nila would be back to pay.

After the three men entered the deputy's police car, Ricardo, the bartender from Lake Alice's, ran over to the vehicle.

"Ricardo, what's wrong?" Deputy Rutherford asked after rolling down his window.

"It's Rory. After you left, he had another drink, then went to find Dugan. He said he wants to settle the situation between him and Clarissa once and for all."

"Damn it, what's gotten into that man?" the deputy asked. He turned towards Nila sitting in the front seat, and Chrishav in the rear. "Gentlemen, you mind walking? All you need to do is head north from the roundabout and go as far as Barclay's."

"Which one is Barclay's?" Chrishav asked.

"It'll be the last house on the edge of town. Just don't go any further. Talk to Barclay. He'll let you know if your friend passed by."

"Will do," Chrishav responded.

Both got out and hurried towards the town circle and then north. Minutes later, they were at Barclay's. Knocking on the door, a dejected, sullen, and hostile Barclay answered.

"You know you don't have to knock. All the other packages don't, no matter the day, the week, or the time of day," Barclay said. "It's like being in a living hell here. I can't get any sleep."

"I'm sorry, but I think you have us confused with somebody else. We're wondering if someone we know passed through here."

"You're joking, right?"

"We're serious," Nila responded.

"What does he look like?"

After giving Barclay a description of Randall, Barclay grew sour. "Yeah, I know him, and thanks to the mayor's aide, he was prompted to play me in a few rounds of pool. Because of her possessed butt, I'm still stuck here in this town."

"Then we must hurry," Nila exclaimed.

"Nila, wait," Chrishav commanded of Nila. "What do you mean, possessed?" Chrishav asked of Barclay.

"I was told that something possessed her when she set up the pool game. She destroyed any chance for me to leave this god-forsaken place. All that's waiting for me now is my turn to head west."

Was Destiny possessed by a major daemon? Chrishav thought. *If so, was it the Destroyer? And is that why I couldn't sense it in the hotel?*

Where could it be now? We could be close. No immediate answer came to mind. *Was it skilled in blending and living within the victim's psyche while disarming his or her inhibitions?*

Nila watched his companion experience a moment of enlightenment. "Did you think of something?"

"I'm not sure," Chrishav responded, "but we can go now."

"Wait a minute. Which way did he go?" Nila asked.

"He tried driving north," Barclay replied, "but was turned around being he's a spoiled package. He went walking outta here a short while back to go west instead of waiting for the transport."

"He didn't drive," Chrishav asked.

"Cars don't do you any good where he's going. Along the way, they're nothing more than distant memories."

"Darn it, we didn't see him coming up here either. It may be too late to save him," Chrishav noted.

"Always do your best to help your friends and family, my father taught me," Nila said.

Nila took off jogging back towards town. Chrishav followed. Approaching the roundabout and heading west, they came up to the same brown brick, colonial revival style home that Chrishav had visited the day prior. The middle-aged Hispanic woman he had earlier met was wearing the same outfit. She was again working on all fours with a small hand spade in her rose bush garden in front of the raised porch. For Nila, this being his first time west, the neighborhood represented what he had already seen throughout the town.

"Oh, hello there young man, nice to see you again. I hope you're here to visit and not passing through this time?" The woman said, seeing Chrishav and Nila walk up from the sidewalk, focusing her attention on Nila.

"We're trying to find out if someone we knew came by this way."

"Dear lord, more and more poor souls seem to pass by this way lately. What did he or she look like?"

Chrishav described Randall to the woman. She appeared distressed.

"I saw him. He passed through here a short while back. I even tried to give him one of my flowers, but he seemed so depressed. No one ever takes any of my flowers."

"We need to hurry and try to catch up and stop him," Nila said.

"I don't know if you can do that, young man," the woman said.

"We must do something," Nila said.

"If it's his time, it's his time," the woman replied.

Deputy Rutherford drove up as the woman finished her comment.

"Nila, Chrishav, the Sheriff wants me to drive you near through the western forest to see if we can catch up to your friend. I can't take you any further."

"Are you sure that's a good idea, deputy?" the woman asked.

"It's what the Sheriff wants me to do."

"I guess he knows best," the woman said.

"What about your Rory situation?" Chrishav asked.

"Sheriff's gonna take care of that."

The three drove close to a mile and a half past the tree line after entering the forest as the road inclined upwards. Deputy Rutherford pulled the car over to the side of the Ponderosa pine and ironwood treelined road. "Gentlemen, this is as far as I can take you," he said with finality while getting out of the patrol car.

"What's up the road?" Chrishav asked, also exiting the patrol car. He was assaulted with a bout of queasiness, while an oppressive emotional weight bore down on him.

"Never been up there, don't plan to either," Deputy Rutherford responded.

Stepping away from the patrol car, Chrishav's nausea increased. Nila experienced mild apprehension if to go further. Chrishav's stomach further churned. He forced himself not to think about the sickness. Taking a couple more steps, he became distressed, unable to move any further.

"Are you alright?" Nila asked, seeing his friend's bronze complexion become insipid.

Chrishav ignored him, forcing himself to move forward. Taking another step, he dropped onto all fours. A torrent of vomit spewed from his mouth.

"Oh, that's not good. Looks like you had the special at Sammi's," Deputy Rutherford said, staying back as Nila pulled out an unused handkerchief from his pocket.

Chrishav accepted the contribution, wiping vomit from around his mouth and speckled remnants that sprayed onto his hands and arms.

"Are you alright?" Nila asked again.

"I don't know what it is, but I think I'm alright," Chrishav said, standing up with Nila's aid. "We need to get a move on."

Taking another step, Chrishav found himself on all fours again, this time dry heaving; his diaphragm and solar plexus region ached from the contractions.

"I don't understand," Chrishav said once he resumed breathing normally, and could talk without his abdomen muscles tightening. He returned to the deputy's patrol car. His discomfort passed. "Whatever is going on, it's keeping me from going up."

"Maybe I should do this alone," Nila said.

"Are you sure? You don't know what's up..."

Nila dashed off before Chrishav finished his comment, disappearing over the crest when the sheriff arrived. He got out of his vehicle and strolled over to Chrishav and Carlson.

"What's going on here?" The sheriff asked.

"That Randall character went west," Deputy Carlson replied, "and the African boy and his friend here were trying to stop him. Chrishav got sick, but Nila went on ahead a few minutes ago."

"Any passersby go up the road after Nila went up."

Chrishav recovered from his dry heaving and stood. "No, he's been the only one since we've been here."

"Good." The sheriff was relieved when the response was no. He stepped around to the driver's side of his patrol car. "Carlson, take Chrishav back to town. The lands here don't seem to agree with him. We'll be back soon. You're in charge."

WEST

N ila jogged for several minutes up the road to where it curved and protracted into the woods. Soon, the two-lane highway transitioned into a single lane compacted gravel and clay road that descended downward into a valley. His side of the valley, with plush, thick, and tall grass and scattered trees, carpeted the landscape. The road traversed down to where it met a bridge crossing a river flowing along the bottom. The landscape looked familiar. A man strolled on the bridge over the slow-moving, clear and pristine waters. It was Randall. Across the river, the valley wall appeared desolate, desert–dry, and rocky. No plant life sprouted from the barren earth. A pathway leading from the bridge was scarcely discernable from the surrounding terrain.

"Randall," Nila yelled. He hoped the valley would have provided an echo, but barely heard his own voice.

Randall crossed the river.

"Randall," Nila yelled again.

He was about to run down the road to the valley bottom when the girth of a large hand grasped his shoulder, pulling him back. Startled, Nila turned to see Sheriff Knight. For an instant, an immense shimmering aura had surrounded him.

"Don't go down Nila, let him go. He's already crossed over."

"We should be able to help him."

"There wasn't anything you could do. He was lost long ago before this day; to each man is his own destiny," Sheriff Knight said with compassion.

"Then why have Chrishav and myself come and try to stop him? Was it his destiny to cross over to the lost lands?"

"It was to help teach that you can't be responsible for someone else's decisions. Randall had decided this path before even coming up to Elysium."

"Why did he decide to do that?" Nila asked.

"When he walked the road north before spiritually preparing himself, he thought he was to take that path."

"What do you mean?" Nila questioned.

"He tried to go north, but never accepting the work of the great creator, was turned away."

"What's north? And why would he decide to go in that direction?" Nila asked.

The sheriff turned around, walking away, back towards the forest. "We need to get back before they miss you."

"We're not going to do anything?"

"Nothing can be done."

Nila stood fast, watching Randall walk up a compacted dirt path on the opposite side of the valley. About to turn away, Nila witnessed two shadow figures emerge over the crest ahead of Randall. Randall, seeing them, tried to run back down the hill towards the river. The two figures were so quick that they moved in a blur, leaving black streaks painted through the air in their wake. Each one seized Randall by his arms, dragging him from the hillside and carrying him over the crest. Randall's wails and moans echoed in the valley.

"Who or what were those two things that came and grabbed Randall?" Nila asked.

"Don't worry about them; you'll never have to encounter them," Sheriff Knight replied.

"But who?"

"We need to go." Sheriff Knight's voice was stern and forceful. It was with the same vibrato and intensity he heard from the Huntsman.

Nila obeyed and followed the sheriff. Walking down the hill, he found it hard to keep pace with Sheriff Knight's broad stride.

The sun seemed out of position for the little time Nila had spent during this undertaking. He got the impression from the sun rising and breaking through the trees that morning had settled upon the forest. It was the latter half of the day after leaving town to catch up with Randall. It should be dusk with a setting sun.

"What time is it?" Nila asked.

Sheriff Knight chose not to answer the question, but asked a question. "Nila, did that river look familiar?"

Nila tried to associate the question with his question; there wasn't any connection. "I don't understand what that has to do with the time?"

The sheriff's large six-foot three-inch frame stopped walking and turned towards Nila. "Nothing? I'll ask again, did that river look familiar?"

Nila recalled a similar landscape when the Huntsman who trained him in Africa escorted him to the valley, but he imagined there's no way it was the same river. After a moment of reflection, he realized it was the same.

"Are you telling me that's the river...," Nila paused, wanting the Sheriff to finish the answer.

"Yes, it's the river Purgo."

"How is it the same river is here, and in my native land? It's impossible."

"Because where we are is not in your native land, nor the land of America; where we exist is between the world where the ground you walk and the eternal lands exist. It is here in this realm where the sun and moon are silent in their duties to provide the semblance of day and night for those that pass."

"Is this where all men pass?"

"No, but we need to hurry and go before we waste too much time."

We waste too much time? Nila believed they had been in the region for only two or three hours. Yet, there wasn't enough time to save his lost companion. Nila was confused.

"Now look down that road," the Sheriff directed, pointing toward a path that forked to the left from where they stood.

Nila had missed seeing the trail, concentrating on his pursuit of Randall. Observing where the Sheriff directed, he distinguished the remnants of a campfire in the clearing of savanna grass, elephant ear plants, short palms, and other foliage. It wasn't simply the same river, but the same land where the Huntsman had brought him as part of his training.

The urge to walk down the alternative path swept through Nila. "Is that the way home?"

"It's not the true way, but it is to the land of your fathers."

Nila stood motionless, wanting to walk down the other path. He could see his mother again, Sogundu, and the townspeople.

Sheriff Knight placed his arm around Nila's shoulder. "We need to get going."

"But I get to go home, to see my mother, to see home," Nila replied as the Sheriff prompted they continue to walk down their original path. Nila craned his head around to look back as they moved further from the other path.

"As much of a temptation this may be, you must remain focused on what is ahead, not what is behind. The past should be a guidepost. Do not let it could become a hitching post that holds you back."

Sheriff Knight removed his arm from around Nila's shoulder and picked up his pace. Nila stopped for a moment and took a quick glance back. Returning his attention back to the road back to Elysium, he thought about how the Sheriff now reminded him of the Huntsman. They both exhibited a strong and confident demeanor, and a deep understanding of the realm of Himmon and the River Purgo. And both were frustrating with their cryptic comments, never fully explaining anything. The two could be brothers.

"Come, Nila, you know what needs to be done," the Sheriff said.

Nila reluctantly loitered behind the Sheriff, resisting the urge to turn around and trek down the path leading away from Elysium.

Sheriff Knight presented a question to Nila. "Did you come across three wolves on the south side of town?"

Nila stopped. The sheriff knew the answer from his reaction.

"How'd you know?" Nila asked.

"That's not important. What happened?"

Nila detailed the incident as they continued their hike through the woods on an impacted dirt path that later transitioned to an asphalt covered two lane road. When Nila finished, he bombarded Sheriff Knight with a volley of questions. The Sheriff's response was silence.

They arrived at the patrol car and drove back to town. The one question Nila kept circling around during their brief trip was why the discrepancy in time. Nila knew when he went out into the forest with Chrishav the day was fading away. The sheriff's patrol car dashboard clock displayed 08:33. With Nila knowing the sun was now climbing higher into the sky since leaving the valley, it meant it was morning. This begged the next question: how many mornings transpired? When he was with the Huntsman, a little less than two weeks elapsed. Real time for Nila during that period, three days passed. Nila wondered where to find Chrishav? And what had become of the destroyer?

"Sheriff, will you at least answer this one question? Why would I cross paths with Randall if there was nothing we could do for him? I feel like we should've done more."

A downcast frown flashed across the Sheriff's face. "Nila, people cross our paths every day. We learn each one makes their own decisions radiating outwards piercing thru the destiny of others; we are spectators. We can't change that. Many are mere ripples that don't affect us in the sea of our lives. Other times, the ripples disrupt our paths, altering our course. All we can do is live each day, and build upon our own decisions, and navigate our own paths."

The sheriff remained quiet for the remainder of the trip.

Nila reflected that if not for the sheriff showing up, he would've taken the trail back to his lands.

THREE DAYS

After Sheriff Knight followed Nila westward, the deputy returned Chrishav to the hotel and told him to be patient. A couple of hours passed, and Chrishav became worried not having heard from his companion. More hours passed, and now it was the middle of the night. Chrishav tossed and turned all evening when he didn't head to Nila's room to knock on the door, hoping he came in before his last attempt. The next morning, after getting only a couple of hours of sleep, he awoke and checked Nila's room one more time. There was still no response. After a shower and shave, he headed out to visit Rooster. Maybe he would know.

Rooster was unaware that Chrishav and Nila had traveled on the road west past the town in pursuit of Randall. He didn't think anyone who wasn't meant to go west would make it as far as they had.

When told the Sheriff followed Nila further west, Rooster smiled. "I wouldn'ts worries. Just go gets some breakfast. It'll be fine."

It was hard for Chrishav to shake the awkwardness of eating breakfast by himself. He smiled when Deputy Rutherford and his wife joined him, avoiding asking him questions concerning Sheriff Knight or Nila. They told him not to worry; it was common for the Sheriff to be gone for up to a week on his brief excursions. Chrishav worried anyway.

Chrishav asked himself, what was up the road, and where had Nila gone? And why wasn't he able to go any further without his stomach going into upheaval? When he tried to walk west the following two days achieved the same result, his throwing up onto the roadway. He returned to try the third day. The old woman working in her garden gazed at him with sad eyes.

"Dearie, if you don't need to go that way, don't go," she said. "Why do you keep trying?"

"I'm trying to find out what happened to a friend of mine."

"Son, if it's not time for you to walk north or west, you shouldn't walk. You need to stop trying."

Chrishav followed her advice. Here it was three mornings later, and still no Nila nor Sheriff. He debated if to pack and head back to the monastery in Mexico in defeat. There was no reason to stay here in town and remain bored. His task was to help find the Destroyer, and when a viable idea for tracking down the daemon manifested itself, Nila's disappearance derailed him from thinking about it. Accompanying a soul hunter on a spiritual mission now appears to have ended.

The previous two days were the most boring Chrishav ever recalled; he walked around the town several times before heading back to his hotel room with nothing to do. He wasn't interested in antique shopping, hiking, or hunting.

Finishing breakfast and paying his check the next morning, Chrishav walked onto the street thinking the town had become more tranquil. The level of activity down the main strip considerably reduced. Cars, pickup trucks, a periodic tractor-trailer, or perhaps a commercial or tour bus negotiated down the street. Many parked in front of Rooster's perch on the sidewalk, with everyone in the vehicle getting out to grab a newspaper. Most of the recipients smiled; they seemed relieved. The others became frightened, cynical, or disbelieving, quickly turning to anguish, suffering, and remorse.

Chrishav overheard one young woman saying, "I can't be going in that direction. I've done all kinds of good works during my life. There's something wrong with this." Rooster ignored her and continued his routine of dispersing papers. She drove west, angry and gnashing her teeth.

Catching up with the deputy in the bakery as he was buying a donut, Chrishav inquired as to if he'd heard anything concerning Nila or Sheriff Knight. Deputy Rutherford, still not worried that they were gone for a considerable amount of time, told Chrishav to be patient, and that he had other issues to take care of in town. The most important one was to let Rory out of the jail cell at the station house later. Chrishav learned Sheriff Knight had Rory locked up for a couple of days to cool off and detox. It was then Chrishav's earlier epiphany returned. He deemed an entity had possessed Destiny, and Rory, acting erratically, may be under a similar influence. Now with Rory locked up, and events in the town quieting down, he suspected the two events were related. The Destroyer possessed one of the two.

Chrishav surprised the deputy not focusing his next question on Nila. "Has Rory acted as strange before you locked him up?"

Deputy Rutherford raised an eyebrow. "What do you know about him being locked up and acting all strange?"

"Small town, people gossip," Chrishav responded. It was overhearing Destiny's gossip while she ate lunch with Chantrelle and a couple of coworkers while in Sammi's the day prior.

"So why are you int'rested in Rory? You've been bugging me about your friend Nila all this time."

"Nothing special; it just seems like he's the most interesting thing going on around here. People also seem to talk about special parties sometimes held at Barclay's."

"Yeah, those he hosts for the mayor. They can be quite eye opening when you have time to talk to the guests. It makes you thankful for the life that you have."

Chrishav attempted to sense anything unique regarding the deputy and his response, but all he could discern was that he seemed blasé about the parties. Deputy Rutherford attempted to excuse himself from the conversation. Instead, it presented itself as a discourteous exodus. Chrishav didn't mind; too many other concerns were on his mind.

While shopping at the bakery for a pastry, Chrishav asked the aged Slavic baker if it was normal for the Sheriff to be gone for this long. She told him there were times he would be gone for up to three weeks. When Chrishav mentioned Sheriff Knight going west, she was astonished and knew of his long trips north. She never recalled a time when he had traveled west. Chrishav then added that the Sheriff went to go after a friend of his. The baker told him to consider his friend passed on and not to expect him back.

Chrishav's frustration and boredom now turned to worry. He went to the hotel lobby to contemplate his next course of action.

Deputy Rutherford entered the cell block in the rear of the station house, where two jail cells were located. In the cell nearest the block entrance, Rory, who was shirtless, was performing pushups. Yelling cadence aloud, his count was at fifty-five and incrementing with each time he raised himself up. Deputy Rutherford didn't consider the possibility that Rory had inflated the count, knowing that he witnessed the completion of seventy-five pushups the morning prior. Rory had a slim figure; his tattoos highlighted his muscular physique. Clarissa considered him handsome, despite his having yellowed and crooked teeth. Mild acne spotted his face. Her major attraction to him was his being a grunge metal fan; many of his tattoos were symbols of his and her favorite bands.

"I guess I can let you out now, Rory. You've been in there a little longer than your normal stint to cool off. Are we good?"

Rory continued his pushups, finishing at seventy-five. He stood and put on his black t-shirt silkscreened with an image of a giant skull rendered with a white drop shadow adding depth, a candle for each eye, and the name Yo Yo Devils across the front. "Time's up already?" he responded, winded after putting on his shirt.

"So, are we good?" Deputy Rutherford asked again.

Rory grinned. "Yeah, we're good."

"Good. When you leave, head out the side. Clarissa's working up front, and I don't wanna have to bring you back in here."

Rory gathered his toiletry kit as the deputy unlocked and held open the cell door. The two stared at each other with mutual distrust as Rory exited the jail block. Deputy Rutherford realized that Rory, while jailed, didn't take advantage of the shower facilities. Glancing back in the cell, his breakfast delivered from Sammi's remained untouched.

The deputy escorted Rory from the detention area to a small hallway leading to an emergency exit. He watched him walk out the side door and into a narrow alleyway between the bakery. Deputy Rutherford locked the door and went back to the cells, where the stench of Rory's body odor still lingered in the air.

Damn, I'm gonna need some air freshener. Deputy Rutherford prepared to start his cell inspection before having Clarissa come back to clean. Getting her to clean would be laborious; she hated that portion of her job. Add having to come back to clean up after a stint by Rory or Dugan infuriated her, no matter whichever one she was with, to come to work and clean after the other. Over the last year, Clarissa's two suitors were frequent boarders in the cells, barring an occasional hunter or two who had gotten drunk over at Lake Alice's and caused a ruckus. Today, Deputy Rutherford believed she was fortunate. There weren't any signs of vomit.

Pulling up and parking in front of the small police station, Sheriff Knight had ignored Nila's barrage of questions. As Nila got out, his patience at not getting frustrated impressed Sheriff Knight. *Nila may need that level of patience later.*

"Nila, all I'll say is for you and Chrishav to be patient and stay true to your purpose," the Sheriff said.

Upon their return to the station, Nila assumed the Sheriff was going to send him on his way, saying nothing. "What is it we're to do?" he asked.

"I couldn't tell you, but with the way things are going on around here, I'm pretty sure you'll find out soon." With that comment, they both exited the car. The sheriff went inside, leaving Nila standing alone on the sidewalk.

Nila wasn't sure if to follow him inside, or head back to the hotel and maybe find Chrishav. He opted for the hotel.

The sheriff promenaded into the station house, not surprised to see Deputy Rutherford sitting at his desk reading a newspaper. If not here, he expected him at Sammi's eating. Clarissa's desk was empty.

"Where's Clarissa?" The sheriff asked.

"You're back," Deputy Rutherford said, smiling while putting the newspaper down on his desktop.

"Of course, I'm back. What's been going on?"

"Clarissa's in the back doing cleanup. Other than that, it's been pretty quiet around here. Been like that about the same time you locked up Rory to cool off again."

"He's still in the back?"

"Naw, I sent him home a short while ago this morning. Promised he wouldn't cause any trouble."

"Promised, did he?"

"Yeah."

"We'll see how long that lasts. He's been acting weird lately," the sheriff said.

"You know that Chrishav's character was asking a lot of questions about him? Why is he interested in him?"

"I have my ideas, but nothing firm," the sheriff said as he entered his office, greeted with an empty desktop. "There's no paperwork on my desk. No spoiled packages you were aware of?"

Deputy Carlson grinned. "You know what, Mayor Corbett hasn't been running in here the last two or three days, all irritated," he said gleefully.

"Sounds like that made you happy."

"Since the mayor hasn't been coming in all upset about any spoiled packages, it's been quiet around here. You'd may have to check with Rooster on the traffic report though, and how busy he's been to see if there's any type of coincidence."

The sheriff stuck his head out the door of his office. "You're saying there has been not one in the last couple of days?"

"None that I'm aware of; it seems everyone is headed in the right direction, no rejects from the north. There's nothing from the mayor's office saying otherwise."

Clarissa entered the office area foyer from the rear of the station house, not expecting to see the Sheriff, almost dropping the plastic food tray she carried. Atop the tray sat a plate of undisturbed scrambled eggs, sausage, biscuits and gravy, hash browns, and a glass of orange juice.

"Sheriff, you're back," Clarissa said.

"Yeah, what do you got there?" the Sheriff asked.

"Just cleaning up in the back. This was Rory's breakfast from Sammi's this morning. He hasn't touched it. I'm worried about him. Since being locked up, he hadn't eaten anything," Clarissa expressed with concern.

Deputy Rutherford extricated the worry from her voice. "You can't tell me you're feeling sorry for him?" he asked.

"He is the father of my youngest."

"And still a pain in the butt."

Clarissa glared at Deputy Rutherford and then stormed off out of the station house to take the tray of food back to Sammi's.

"Why would you want to upset her like that?" The Sheriff asked.

"Because she needs to grow up and stop dealing with those two miscreants. Besides, Dugan is doing better these days."

"You know she can't help herself."

"I suppose. Then again, sometimes I wonder if those two boys are whi..."

"Now that's enough, Carlson," the Sheriff said. "No need to be crude."

The sheriff withdrew back into his office, with Deputy Rutherford going back to reading the newspaper. A moment later, the Sheriff emerged and stood in front of the deputy's desk. Deputy Rutherford glanced up to see a rare quizzical look flash on the Sheriff's face.

"You say that Rory didn't eat anything the entire time we locked him up?" The Sheriff asked.

"Yeah. Why?"

"Anything else strange?"

"Just that he was doing a lot of pushups though out the day."

"Hmmm, he's done nothing like that before when we had him in here."

"Is that odd?" Deputy Rutherford asked. "I mean, he is strange anyway."

"It's not normal for him." The sheriff went back into his office.

Deputy Rutherford returned to reading the paper, finding the news trivial. A notion came to him concerning the Sheriff's trip. He placed the newspaper down again and stepped up to the sheriff's doorway to his office.

"My turn, I meant to ask. Don't know why I thought of it until now. You coming back from the west? Was that African boy with you?"

"Why do you ask?"

"I don't know. Curious, I guess."

The sheriff hesitated, trying to plan if there was a specific reason for Carlson to be asking the question. "Yeah, he was with me."

"Did he go to the west and back?"

The sheriff hesitated again. "As far west as allowed."

"I don't think anyone here's been able to do that before. Has anyone else ever returned from the west?" Deputy Rutherford was soft-spoken when he asked the question.

"Not west per se, but from the same place."

Deputy Rutherford didn't know how to receive the Sheriff's comment. "I don't get it."

"Not important. Anything else?" The sheriff didn't want to mention that Nila was a soul hunter. He could enter and out of the boundary between the realms.

Deputy Rutherford chose not to pursue anything further and left to make his morning rounds around town.

Nila made his way back to the hotel where Chrishav sat relaxing in one of the lobby lounge chairs, apparently daydreaming and unaware of his surroundings. Nila was almost upon him before he recognized his companion.

"Nila! You're back." Chrishav jumped out of his chair, rushed over and embraced Nila. "Where've you been?"

Nila wasn't sure why seeing him shocked Chrishav. He knew there was a time lapse while he had traveled near the river Purgo, but it seemed inconsequential. To Nila, only a few hours passed between going west after Randall, and then being retrieved by the Sheriff. Chrishav's reaction implied a considerable amount of time had passed.

"You've been gone for three going on four days now. What happened? And did you catch up with Randall?"

Nila pulled away from Chrishav.

Chrishav gauged by Nila's eyes, they were despondent, filled with sadness. He sensed a longing concerning Randall. "What's wrong?"

Nila gathered the mental fortitude before he could answer. "I've failed. Randall is lost."

"You didn't find him?"

"No, I found him, but he crossed over. The darkness took him to the darkness."

Chrishav's face scrunched with confusion.

Nila explained the circumstances regarding Randall to Chrishav, and that it seemed as if minutes passed. Nila didn't pick up that Chrishav pursed his lips and eyed him with skepticism. While chronicling the brief account of his excursion, Nila also remembered the comment Randall's sister made when he encountered her; *the water had been given, but she had refused to drink, and now was unable.*

Nila wondered if there was any way to tie in what had happened with their pursuit of the destroyer. "I must apologize to you, my friend."

"Why? What do you have to apologize for?"

"Because we haven't been able to do what we came here for."

"I wouldn't say that."

"Why is that?" Nila asked

"Here's the weird thing: I can soul read those who themselves are sensitive to the spiritual world. Here, it's as if I can somehow sense the emotions and feelings of most everyone. Yet, for the sheriff, mayor, and for a short while, Destiny, zilch. Wait, let me take that back. One evening with the Sheriff, I sensed something strong, but then it was as if he put up a brick wall. The same was with the mayor. Destiny was a different story. For a flash, there was an inky dark presence that I felt, but in Sammi's, it was her own self I encountered."

Chrishav forced himself to remember the preparation and training by his mentor, Orland. One lesson was that a soul hunter such as Nila could sense spiritual entities antagonistic towards men. This didn't appear to be the case. At no time did Nila mention he sensed any major incongruities between the persons they met and the spiritual impressions they emitted.

"Nila, since you've been here, has anything caught you as strange?"

"You mean like the wolves I ran into the other day, or my strange journey I just returned from? Then I would say yes," Nila responded with a twinge of mockery.

Chrishav had known Nila to be well-mannered, proper, and obedient, not expecting him to respond with sarcasm. "Wow; where did that come from?"

Nila took a couple of quick breaths. "I'm sorry, but I'm still getting over the fact that three days passed since I've been gone, when to me, two or three hours." Nila found the time variances disorientating, the same as when he was with the Huntsman.

"You're right, that is strange, and I can't get my head around that one either. But the last couple of days gave me a chance to think about a few things."

A major question came to Chrishav: why would the Destroyer be in Elysium? What was so unique about the town to draw himself, Nila and Randall, and their recent companion lost to the west? Another recurring thought was the recent dramatic change in Rory that he gleaned from overhearing several of the townspeople.

"You know what, let's see if anyone in town knows something about this Rory person."

Nila raised an eyebrow. "Rory?"

"I'm not sure, but it's instinct right now."

Heading out onto the main street, they came upon Rooster perched leaning back against the front wall of the bakery between the display window and front door, on the rear two legs of his chair. Chrishav considered maybe he would know something about Rory.

"Morning again, Rooster," Chrishav greeted.

"Mornin'," Rooster responded, setting his chair on all fours. Even though he appeared aged, Rooster still exhibited himself to be quite spry.

"Rooster, we're trying to find out more about our friend Randall, but also about a guy named Rory. What do you know about him?"

"I know that he ain't been himself lately. What you need to do is go up to Barclay's and talk to him."

"Barclay's? Isn't he the one on the north side of town in that lodge house?"

"Yep, he's the one hosting the get-togethers."

"We can't wait until this evening for the get-together."

Rooster smiled. "Who says about this evenin? These days, there always seems to be a get-together going on."

The two men took Rooster's advice and strolled up to Barclay's home. Once they arrived on the property, they passed through an array of vehicles-newer foreign sedans, a couple of domestic and foreign pickup trucks, an electric two-door coupe, and a large four-door Audi that sat on the rock and gravel imbedded driveway bordered by serpentine grass. As they walked up the home's front steps onto the small porch, a metallic blue Mercedes convertible with a young couple turned onto the lot after driving from the north. Both occupants, bickering profusely, berated one another as they slammed the car doors getting out of the vehicle. They then walked up to the house.

"I told you it was because of your driving we'd be here in this situation," the woman shouted.

"If you didn't keep distracting me with your damn nagging, I might've seen that damn truck," the male barked.

"Maybe I was nagging you because you were being an idiot."

"Calling me names isn't gonna help, and it's not gonna help us now, is it, since they rejected us. But why did we have to come back here?"

Chrishav and Nila didn't notice that the car had arrived from the forest in the north.

"You, I can understand, but I don't know why I wasn't able to go on," the woman said as she climbed the short set of steps up to the landing leading to the front door. "I've been a good person."

"Good at being a bi..."

"Don't you dare say it," the woman interrupted before he could finish.

The couple stormed into the house, unaware of Chrishav and Nila's presence, who watched the foray with interest. As the arguing couple passed by the two men, the male brushed against and bumped Chrishav without offering an apology. While the door was open, other houseguests stood around, most of them grumpy and miserable. Both heard the murmurings of the guests, but could not make out any of the conversations. Chrishav tried to follow the couple inside. The door slammed shut in his face.

"That was rude," Chrishav said as he knocked harder.

No reply. Waiting for what he considered a proper amount of time, he pounded on the door. Still no answer. The last time they visited, Barclay answered right away.

Several more people arrived at the house and entered. When Chrishav and Nila tried to follow again, the door slammed shut. Nila tried to turn the knob on the door. Locked. They went back to knocking on the door.

"What are you two redeemed meatbags doing here?" the mayor's voice croaked from behind the two. "And what are all these cars doing here?"

Turning around, Chrishav and Nila witnessed Mayor Corbett walking up, wielding a harsh and angry expression.

"We're here to see Barclay," Chrishav replied.

"Why do you wanna see him?" The mayor stopped; his expression changed from one of anger at seeing all the cars on the grass and driveway to one of astonishment. "Wait a minute; you aren't passing through to go west, are you? Because if you are, then things around here are messed up and me and the Sheriff would be in a crap load of trouble."

"No, we're here to ask Barclay a couple of questions. When go in, the door is locked. But we've seen other people go in with no problems."

"Whew, I was getting worried." The mayor said after exhaling a sigh of relief. "Of course, it's locked, you dummies; only townies and those destined west are allowed inside. What do you need with Barclay anyhow?"

"We want to see if he could clarify anything regarding our lost companion, Randall. We think it's odd that he'd end up doing what he did."

"Odd?" the mayor noted. "That's an interesting way of identifying what's going on around here. Eons of quiet, and this place is suddenly busy again. Hold on, I'll get him."

Mayor Corbett stepped inside with Barclay coming to the door a minute later.

"What do you two want?" Barclay snapped.

"I don't know if you remember us from earlier, but we were here about our friend," Chrishav said.

"Randall?" Barclay asked.

"Yes, did he mention anything about why he tried to go north?" Chrishav asked.

"He said that one of the town's residents, Rory, had talked him into it."

"Do you know where we could find Rory?" Chrishav continued with the questioning.

"Does your friend here talk?" Barclay asked.

"Yes, he does, but please, what about the question?"

"I'm not sure where he lives since most of my time here has been stuck in this house, except for a few conditional releases into town."

The mayor stepped up from behind Barclay. "Barclay, you need to get your butt back in there and work the crowd before the next transport and chaperone arrives."

Barclay dropped his head and turned, returning into the house. The mayor moved forward, standing proud and erect in the doorway.

"What is it you want to know?" the mayor inquired.

"We're trying to see if we can find out where Rory lives. We'd like to talk to him."

The mayor smiled. "Sure, I'll tell you. I bet it'll annoy the sheriff, but I don't care. If you can find out what's going on, you end up helping me as well. Rory lives on the south side of town on the Omega Ranch. It's located before you get to the practice archery range and the hunting grounds. He's the main handyman in charge and takes care of the cabin lodges."

As the mayor talked to Chrishav and Nila, a mini-van that drove from the north pulled up and parked with the other automobiles. A father, mother, and three adolescent children disembarked.

"No, no, no, no, no," the mayor shouted.

Chrishav and Nila turned around to see what had caught the mayor's attention.

"What are those kids doing here?" The mayor asked. "They're supposed to be let through."

"Someone in the forest stopped us and sent us all back, saying we weren't..." the father said before the mayor interrupted.

"That's a bunch of bull. Kids have an automatic pass since they haven't reached the age of accountability. You wait your butt over there until I can get the sheriff up here to clear this up. The Guardian of the Gate knows better." The mayor focused his attention back on Chrishav and Nila. "And you two, get over to Rory's and see if you can find out what's going on."

CONFRONTATION

C hrishav and Nila neared the archery practice range under half-a-mile south past the Omega Ranch and accompanying hunter's lodges. Nila was familiar with the area. This was nearby where he experienced the three mysterious gray wolves while practicing his archery skills. Chrishav had passed close north of the area during his walk-about, but never made it this far south past the outskirts of town.

Chrishav and Nila strode up to the ranch on a single lane road lined with Eastman oak trees, each one bursting with emerald and jade tinted foliage. Behind the trees, a white four-foot railing fence bordered well-manicured grass fields. Off in the distance to the right were several two-story log cabin style hunting lodges built in a semi-circle formation. Near the lodge on the furthest to the left was a massive double-door barn like structure with an adjacent waste disposal bin. Situated ahead, at the end of the road where it circled back upon itself, was a single story, amber-colored brick, ranch style home.

As the two men walked up to the front door, a brawny Hispanic male with an aged, creased face and day-old stubble greeted them. He rode a young, spotted, brown and white mare arriving from the direction of the lodge cabins.

"May I help you?" the rider asked with a slight accent.

"We're looking for Rory," Chrishav replied.

"Rory, huh? Well, so am I. He didn't show up for work again this morning, and we're still trying to get ready for the new season. What do you want him for?"

"We assumed this was where he lived. We didn't know this was where he worked."

"He lives on the backside of the ranch property."

"You mind if we go to see if he's in?"

"I already checked, but you can try. You see that dirt path over there?" the rider said, pointing to the right towards a small path leading in between the thick brush and trees. "That's a shortcut; take that for about a quarter of a mile, instead of following the dirt road all the way around. His place will be the tiny white house sitting next to a tiny creek." The rider galloped off over to the lodges to join a couple of ranch hands carrying lumber and tools from behind one of the guest structures.

Chrishav took the lead, walking over to the path leading through hedges and forest undergrowth.

"Watch out for poison oak," Chrishav warned.

"Poison oak? What does it look like?" Nila questioned. "I'm not sure if I know of such a thing."

What do you know? So far, this trip has been a bust? Chrishav couldn't explain why a surge of anger overcame him from Nila's comment. His remark didn't garner the unwelcoming emotional response. Yet, he became upset that he'd been the one putting in any serious effort to find the elusive daemon.

"Nila, are you sure you're who you say you are?"

"I don't understand," Nila replied, wondering if he detected a hinted of antagonism from Chrishav.

Chrishav had accepted Nila's subtle methods of trying to find the Destroyer. He imagined he himself had put more effort into their hunt, believing Nila contributed little, despite the missing days. Chrishav deliberated that maybe what happened down in Los Angeles with the dog might have been an anomaly.

"It just seems you haven't helped out much in tracking down the Destroyer," Chrishav said, turning around to face Nila.

Nila stopped in place and wasn't sure how to take the criticism. "I can't hunt that which I don't know I am looking for. We haven't come across anyone or anything to make me believe the Destroyer indwells him or her," Nila responded, defending himself, now feeling combative, but resisting the urge to strike Chrishav.

Chrishav didn't know why he had become so adversarial. It hadn't bothered him at all earlier concerning Nila and his limited input with trying to assist in their search for the covert yet powerful daemon. He knew Nila was inexperienced in their current endeavors. Chrishav knew he too was inexperienced as well; they were novices on this quest.

A small house came into view.

A fresh surge of uncomfortable emotions welled within Chrishav. The antagonism he was experiencing seemed nebulous. The emotions didn't emanate from Nila, nor did he know where they originated.

It reminded him of when he had been talking to Nila in the hotel room before the odd fog rolled in. The one potential source was the tiny abode ahead of them. A moment of clarity interlaced with déjà vu wrapped around Chrishav's thinking. Reflecting to being on the reservation, he sensed a similar radiated malevolence within the senior shaman on the council.

"Impossible," Chrishav said.

"What's impossible?" Nila was bitter when he responded, still upset over their previous quarrel.

"Why we're suddenly arguing, as if it's somehow coming from the house. Rory, or the Destroyer, may be in there."

Regaining his senses, Chrishav knew there was no reason to have reacted the way he did. "Nila, I'm sorry, but I think something else is causing us to feel this way."

At first, Nila wanted to reject everything that Chrishav had said, yet he had no reason to doubt him. They both internalized a short private prayer. Then, taking a couple of deep breaths, and pondering on the last several days, there wasn't an excuse to remain angry.

Arriving at the single-story dwelling, the house appeared unoccupied, yet secured. The two spent the next several minutes knocking on the door, walking around the perimeter, peeking through the windows where the blinds were open, and trying the front and back doors were unlocked. Nothing seemed out of the ordinary.

"We need to go," Nila cautioned. "I'm getting an uncomfortable feeling about all of this."

Chrishav agreed. He also maintained lingering thoughts as to the cause for both to become so antagonistic towards one another, since not finding anyone around.

Leaving the ranch structures and walking down the private drive back to the main road leading to town, Chrishav and Nila, thinking their trip was fruitless, both sensed a familiar portentous feeling accompanied by goose pimples and chills. Nila was the first to link the onslaught of uncomfortable feelings to his previous encounter on the archery practice range and during the fog covered street incident.

"Chrishav, do you sense that?" Nila warned.

"Then I'm not crazy, I do." Chrishav turned in whatever direction he perceived the smallest breeze or rustling tree leaves. He was wary, as if something would pounce on them from out of nowhere. "I swear something weird is going on," Chrishav said, with caution in his voice, the uneasiness building.

The two sped up their pace. Nila's instincts had him reaching over his back, wanting to pull an arrow from his quiver. He made the gesture and realized he was grabbing empty air. His stomach turned; he was unarmed.

"Whatever it is, we'll have no weapons to defend ourselves," Nila said.

"Defend ourselves from what?" Chrishav asked, a bit panicked.

"The wolves."

"Wolves, what wolves?" Chrishav snapped his head in all directions, freaked out and searching for any signs of creatures. Why had Nila mentioned wolves when the space around was open and spacious, barring the trees along the roadside?

Nila slowed down, his skin getting goosebumps. Chrishav emulated Nila's tempo and took measured and methodical strides down the lane. Nila witnessed a vaporous form emerge, rising from the compacted dirt of the private drive. A gray wolf with scruffy fur, sprinkled with black and brown strands and a white underside coating, and yellowish green eyes, stood growling, blocking the men's path. Nila stopped and put his hand on Chrishav's chest, who was continuing to walk forward towards the beast. Chrishav wondered why Nila had prevented him from continuing. "What's wrong?"

"Don't you see it?" Nila asked in response.

Chrishav scanned the surrounding landscape, seeing nothing but the treelined empty road and fence bordered fields. "I don't see anything, but something seems out of sorts, uneasy again."

Chrishav now recognized the full extent of the anger and ferociousness suspended in the air. It was the same as when the fog and moaning invaded the main street. In Nila's peripheral vision, two more wolves emerged and materialized in the fields, one on their left and one on their right, near doppelgangers of the fur covered apparition ahead of them.

"Chrishav, don't move. I don't think they'll attack. We're not their usual prey."

"We're not whose usual prey?" Chrishav quizzed with unease, seeing nothing around, but still apprehensive, sensing an unknown malevolence.

"The wolves."

Chrishav raised an eyebrow. "What wolves are you talking about?" Chrishav was worried about his companion. Maybe something more happened during his short disappearing stint.

The wolf on the road encroached up to the two men and sniffed.

"Just follow me," Nila said, nudging Chrishav to move forward. Nila took restrained side steps around the lead wolf, staring him in the eyes.

"Why are you back?" The wolf asked, continuing his sniffing.

Nila remained silent. The other two lurked on the sides, preparing their attack.

"The stink of Barclay's place is on your clothing," the wolf hissed. "Yet the odor of the natural world is on your flesh."

A snakelike tongue darted out of the wolf's mouth, taking a quick lick of Chrishav's left pants leg. Chrishav pulled his leg up and jumped back with quick reflexes when something brushed his left shin. "What was that?" He hollered, not seeing anything around him. "Something touched me."

"I taste the soul of one that is lost upon you," the wolf said, with Chrishav unable to hear the wolf's remark.

"Trust me when I say, prepare to run," Nila whispered to Chrishav.

"And upon you, dark one," the wolf said with a small snarl, its unnaturally long, serpent-like tongue again extending out from its mouth and licking Nila. "I smell the lands of Purgo, but taste not the forbidden side, yet you have journeyed there, where you should have stayed." The wolf's voice increased with intensity and fervor, letting Nila know it wasn't good to be standing around.

Nila did a quick scan to find a fallen branch, object, or anything he could use as a weapon. It would take too long to pull or kick a plank of wood from the fence lining the road. He ceded the faltering circumstances by mentally reciting a quick prayer for help.

The wolves tensed their muscles, low crouched on their front paws, and raised the hairs on their backs and necks. Each one snarled, brandishing their front canines. An attack was imminent.

"Chrishav," Nila said in a warning voice. "Run!"

Chrishav agreed it was a wise idea; both sprinted down the private lane to the main road. The wolves gave chase. Chrishav sensed something ominous approaching from their rear, reminiscent of the fog that rolled through the town. The two wolves on the side angled in for their attack. The wolf on the road lunged and clamped Chrishav's left leg, forcing him down to the ground. The wolf maneuvered its snouted mouth to tighten its grip on his ankle, pulling him in the field's direction. It found it difficult to drag its catch with Chrishav's weight increasing with each tug.

Nila stopped, knowing he had to help his friend. How would he handle the other two approaching wolves? Turning around to aid Chrishav, Nila thought he saw out of the corner of his eye the Sheriff's police car speeding onto the private drive entering from the main road. Racing back to Chrishav, he spotted the wolves attacking from the side, pouncing, lunging high in the air. Nila ducked. The two beasts collided head-on in mid-air, yelping and rolling on the ground. Nila knew he wouldn't be that lucky again. He continued to figure out how to defend himself and Chrishav.

The wolf attempting to pull Chrishav away was still having difficulty doing so. The other two wolves recovered and maneuvered to pounce again, this time angling for a better attack. Nila knew they wouldn't make the same mistake.

The arriving car and the opening of its door yards away caught Nila's attention. A quick glance revealed the sheriff exiting his vehicle while wielding his baton. He took one step and leaped a distance of what appeared to be twenty yards. At the highest point of his arc, the baton transformed into a large and eloquent Flamberge styled sword with a hilt wrapped in the finest leather and three etched characters of an unknown script. The polished yard long blade glistened in the sun. The Sheriff landed in front of the wolf on the right as it tried to re-attack. He stepped to position himself and swung; his blow found its mark, striking the wolf's midsection. The creature dissipated, this time not into a cloud of gray dust, but as if in a minute explosion of sparks and fiery streaks. The Sheriff pivoted to the wolf on the left, which now cowered back towards the field. The beast that had latched onto Chrishav's leg released its grip.

"Cammael, why banish one doing his duty?" The wolf next to Chrishav said.

"These two are not lost, nor yours for shepherding west," the Sheriff answered.

"We were dispatched and stalked these two from when they were milling about the house by the creek."

"Dispatched by who?"

"The house's owner. He said two would come from Barclay's and..." The wolf stopped speaking and sniffed the air, no longer interested in his immediate surroundings. "Xanexerium, the true spoiled packages are coming."

Releasing a quick howl, both gray wolves dashed towards the main road. The two animals became visible to Chrishav as they sprinted down the lane. Through the haze of coming to grips with the preceding incident, he knew they were the origin of malevolent emotions that surged earlier through his soul. They somehow caused him to lash out at Nila. Chrishav now realized his being in the mind's eye of the wolves; the image of the young couple they encountered arguing at Barclay's was approaching in a vehicle. An outright hatred of the wolves towards the driver and passenger washed over Chrishav, as if the couple were attempting to cheat their destiny.

Once the wolves entered onto the two-lane road, they stood in the center facing north. The shifting gears of a speeding vehicle echoed in the distance. The Sheriff, Nila, and Chrishav watched a metallic blue Mercedes convertible hurtling down the road. The two wolves readied themselves, lowering their heads and raising their rear quarters. The sensation of defiance by the driver flooded Chrishav's emotions. The convertible shifted gears and increased its speed. The car impacted into the two wolves, who hammered forward with their heads, forcing the front of the vehicle to crumple and pummel down into the asphalt. The rear of the vehicle flipped upwards, catapulting the two occupants forward. The wolves leaped upwards, one snatching the driver, the other the passenger, while still midair. They landed and dragged the two west into the outlying forest, with their prey shrieking and wailing. The convertible faded.

"What the heck was that?" Chrishav asked, his emotions and mind's eye perspective exiting the wolves.

"They must've been the ones the sentinels were waiting for. You two came along and ended up as a distraction, almost allowing the two in the car to go by undetected," the Sheriff answered. "I don't know if I believe it was all a coincidence, though."

"How come Chrishav wasn't able to see the wolves at first?" Nila inquired.

"He hasn't walked the lands you've walked, nor has he experienced the realms whence they exist."

"But I could see them just now," Chrishav said.

"Because you've been bitten by one," the Sheriff said, amazed. He glanced at Chrishav's ankle. "Oh man, didn't expect it to be that bad."

Chrishav and Nila observed the jeans fabric torn around the injury site on Chrishav's lower left leg with puncture wounds on his ankle, accompanied by torn flesh. One of the entry points exposed bone.

"You gotta be kidding me," Chrishav shouted, noticing the severe wound. Pain radiated throughout his leg. "Damn, this hurts."

Nila bent down to help render first aid.

"Hold on, Nila, I can take care of that," the Sheriff comforted.

"How? By cutting my leg off?" Chrishav questioned with angry skepticism. His leg throbbed as if someone were inserting thousands of needles at the wound site.

The sheriff glanced into the distance. "Look, there's another wolf."

Startled, Chrishav and Nila turned in the direction of the Sheriff's stare. Nothing resembled a wolf.

"All done," the Sheriff said, brandishing a smile exposing perfect, straight, and brilliant white teeth.

Chrishav pulled back the shredded jeans on his injured leg to expose healed and smooth skin. The pain in his leg subsided.

"How did you do that?" Chrishav asked, helped up by Nila.

"Don't be worried about how. It was by the same means and power the sentinel wasn't able to pull you away."

"And how was that?" Nila asked, recalling the wolves pulled the couple in the car away with ease.

"The two in the car were destined west; you aren't," the Sheriff replied. "Being believers and having faith in the Great Creator, it's impossible for you to end up there."

"How'd you know where to find us?" Nila asked.

"I went to Barclay's to catch up with the mayor on an intuition. I came out right away after taking care of the issue with the children and sending them on their way."

"On their way where?" Chrishav continued with the questioning.

"North. Children who pass through and are not here to visit or hunt with their family go north. Except someone is trying to disrupt things around here."

"And if he's successful?" Chrishav wondered.

"That would be bad."

"How bad?" Nila asked.

"Very bad," the Sheriff noted with a foreboding tone.

"That doesn't sound good," Chrishav said. "Are we talking about end of the world type bad?"

"What we're talking about is you need to focus on what's ahead of you," the Sheriff said, wanting to change the subject. The two men caught the Sheriff's hint.

Chrishav took a 360-degree survey of their current situation—himself, Nila, and the Sheriff standing in the middle of a private road surrounded by trees and grass fields, and the sheriff's police car, still running yards away.

"Now what?" Nila asked.

"What brought you both out here, anyway? I think once you answer that question, that'll give you all the answers that you'll need."

"We came out here to talk to Rory," Chrishav chimed in.

"I don't think he's out here. I'll give you two a ride back into town. Did you walk out here?"

"We're used to it," Nila answered.

"Never-the-less, get in the car. It may not be too safe out here."

Chrishav got into the front passenger seat; Nila hopped into the rear.

"I'm concerned with what Hericulium said about their being dispatched by the owner of the house on the backside of the ranch. That means Rory is involved," the Sheriff said as they drove away from the ranch property.

"Sheriff," Nila interjected, "the first time I encountered the wolves, they mentioned the Destroyer being behind a lot of what's going on?"

"You didn't mention that before?"

"I didn't know you'd be as involved as you are, but seeing that baton trick of yours changed my mind."

"What baton trick?" Chrishav wondered. *It's of no concern,* entered his mind, followed by the forming of a mental wall. He knew it was the Sheriff's interloping.

"Nila, we need to get you to your hotel room so you can grab your hunting gear. It's time, soul hunter," the Sheriff said.

"Sheriff, who or what is the Destroyer?"

"You don't know?" Sheriff Knight replied, surprised at Nila and Chrishav's unfamiliarity with the class of daemons. Maybe there was a reason their dispatchers didn't inform them.

"No," Chrishav and Nila said in near unison.

"Foremost, Destroyer daemons focus on those who don't believe in the Great Creator, destroying men's hope and souls. They influence the unsuspecting to condemnation with no possibility of eternal light, the souls to live forever in eternal darkness. This destroyer is of a class that exudes a sense of hopelessness, the recipient believing all is lost. He blinds men from ever seeing the deliverance that rests in the divine good of the Great Creator. The sad part, men allow themselves to be deceived because they shut out and don't want to hear the truth."

"You mean as with Randall and his sister?"

"Yes, but that's not all. If, like the preceding Destroyers, like the one that possessed your friend Sogundu, they revel in the carnage they create for the short time they deprecate on this world. There are some-they wait patiently, days, weeks, months, sometimes for years, and instigate minute changes rippling to major life altering events."

"Why are they dangerous for us, like with what happened with my father?" Nila asked.

"They attempt to dispatch those who are servants of the Great Creator. They tend to react openly against those who may try to stop them, because you're gifted with the ability to send them back. With a destroyer in town, he must be trying to disrupt those who pass through on the road north or west, and undermine the power of myself and the mayor."

"And if that happens?"

"For the town, cataclysmic. For the throne of heaven, I don't even want to imagine. The enemy never gives up, even though the greater war is won. You two need to find him and stop him."

"Sheriff, how come I couldn't sense the Destroyer when I read the Destiny's soul the night we met on the road? I knew there was something dark and empty, but nothing that had led me at the time to think the Destroyer possessed her. Wouldn't the same be true for Rory?"

The question also made Chrishav wonder once again why it was so easy to sense the souls of most of the town's people, yet the mayor, the sheriff, and even Rooster were enigmatic personality domains, revealing nothing but impenetrable barriers.

"That's why they're great deceivers," the sheriff answered. "Those possessed, their body and soul more times than naught, is a willing vessel. Because of that, the destroyer can hide deep within the soul of his quarry, making it even more elusive."

The three remained quiet for the rest of the trip to the main drag of town. As the sheriff executed a U-turn to pull in front of the Hotel Metropolis, Chrishav broke the silence. "What do we do now?" he asked.

"Nila, you need to prepare your weapon," the Sheriff directed. "Soul reader, you'll need to be ready to back him up."

BANISHMENT

Mayor Corbett paced back and forth behind his office desk. Administrative functions within the town weren't his major concern. It was the large number of spoiled packages passing through the town. There should be zero. They were supposed to be non-events. Now, passersby proceeded west after being turned around from somehow believing they were to go north. Then there were the sentinels who found themselves busy from those trying to escape their dismal immortal destiny. The sentinels had manifested themselves as wolves. Many years had passed; the mayor had forgotten their last manifestation. Bears? Mountain lions? He didn't remember.

The mayor hated his residency in Elysium, metamorphosed into a human body. Many of his body's frailties squelched his true essence, limiting what he could display or control in relation to his power over the physical world. He wasn't happy the sheriff had restricted him from talking with the sentinels over the years, for reasons he didn't understand.

Mayor Corbett elected not to worry about the number of spoiled packages anymore, wasting an hour pacing back and forth. He'd leave it up to the sheriff to figure out what's going on. Now would be a good time to check on the staff in the building to see how things were operating, and an excellent opportunity to check up on Destiny to see if whatever entity had re-infected her had returned. If so, maybe it was possible to quell its influence and prevent the flow of spoiled packages.

At her desk, Destiny, wearing no makeup, wore a wrinkled, flower-patterned blouse, her hair haphazardly combed and frizzled, sat staring out the window dazed. The mayor stepped over, grabbed her thin neck with his massive hand, and pulled her up and out of her chair—her face was in front of his.

"What is your problem!?"

The mayor didn't answer. He stared into her incensed green eyes, convinced no entity possessed her.

The mayor's actions confirmed to Destiny he was a pain in the rear. She pushed back away from him and mentioned she needed to head home, not feeling well.

"Fine," he said.

Destiny grabbed her purse and scampered out of the office. The mayor finished his rounds visiting the other offices, then left the building to stroll over to Sammi's.

Sheriff Knight's patrol car drove past as he was about to turn the corner onto Main Street. Two other people accompanied him in the vehicle. The mayor knew them to be the recent visitors to town who had a companion unexpectedly head west. They were also the same two who, at Barclay's trying to discover where Rory lived. The timing for the mayor was perfect.

The patrol car pulled up in front of the hotel, flipped a U-turn after letting passing traffic clear, dropped off its two passengers, and then parked in front of the sheriff's station.

"I know why you're here, Hannibal," Sheriff Knight said while getting out of his vehicle, seeing the mayor standing on the sidewalk.

"Alright, then tell me, what's going on?"

"You know what, Hannibal, you tell me. What is going on around here? Why does there seem to be a destroyer roaming around?"

The mayor's small eyes widened in astonishment. "What do you mean, a destroyer? My hierarchy didn't tell me anything about a destroyer. Do you know how disruptive a destroyer is?"

Sheriff Knight returned a piercing stare of disbelief that the mayor had asked such a question. The Sheriff knew. The dominion where the mayor and destroyer lived was a house divided. From his previous assignments, transition liaisons, such as the mayor or his peers, had to contend with self-serving daemons departing from their pre-destined realm and going rogue. As a result, it caused the Sheriff or his counterparts to coordinate its expulsion and force the errant entity's deportation to a temporary internment before their final conscription to the abyss.

"I'm not surprised you didn't know. It seems like you and your friends can never stay harmonized on anything anyhow. By the way, I've dispatched a sentinel to the valley of darkness."

"What the heck, Sheriff? Was that necessary?"

"Your cohorts took to go after our two special visitors in town. One even tried to attack me directly."

"Why would they do that?" the mayor asked, bypassing the remark the Sheriff made about the attacking sentinel. Many times, he himself wanted to become aggressive with the Sheriff. Mayor Corbett knew the consequences—permanent retirement beyond the valley.

Sheriff Knight headed towards the station house front door. "They mistook our two visitors for spoiled packages trying to make a run for it. That's not a minor mistake."

"What are you going to do about all this?" The mayor asked.

"We're already working on it."

The Sheriff wanted to seek the solace of his office, once again finding his time with the mayor irritating. For decades, maybe they would see each other on the street, but wouldn't acknowledge their association. Now, with reluctance due to all the recent incidents, they had to spend more time collaborating with one another.

The mayor followed the sheriff up to the doorway. "Doesn't look like you're working it to me," Mayor Corbett said.

The sheriff stopped and turned around. His neck veins throbbed as his eyes narrowed. He stepped up to the mayor and stared him down face to face. "You, better than most, know that your cousin of perdition isn't going to come here and say, 'Here I am, take me. I'm turning myself in.' He's able to possess most anyone or any creature; you know that only certain talent can track and banish a destroyer."

"And why can't you? You had no problem with the sentinel?" The mayor asked.

"Because they're in the realm of my jurisdiction, just like you imps, a destroyer isn't."

The mayor backed away. "Damn, maybe that's who possessed Destiny."

"What do you mean may have possessed Destiny? Why didn't you mention anything? We could've dealt with this much earlier."

"Because I deemed it had been a minor daemon trying to cause a little mischief."

"A minor daemon? You misjudged that one."

A voice hollered from down the sidewalk several yards away. "Sheriff, I heard you were looking for me? Here I am, take me."

Sheriff Knight and Mayor Corbett turned to see Rory standing several yards away, holding his arms extended to the side and hands up.

"What the...the timing would've been ironic," the mayor quipped.

The sheriff raised his right arm towards Rory and gestured in a swiping motion with his hand. Rory flung to his right, slamming into the building with his backside, immobilized against the brick wall.

The sheriff and mayor rushed over to Rory. The mayor stared into Rory's bloodshot eyes with enlarged pupils.

"That was too easy," the Sheriff said. "What do you see in there, Hannibal?"

The mayor stared into Rory's glazed eyes. Within the irises, pupils with vertical slit irises stared back. "Oh yeah, something fierce is in there, very fierce. I think it's him, but I'm not sure."

The mayor smiled.

Sheriff Knight slowly stroked his chin. "If he's turning himself in, this destroyer is up to something, or already started some mischief. I don't trust him. Hannibal, go get Carlson. He may be at Sammi's. Have him get our two friends from out of town and bring them to the station. They're staying at the hotel."

"Why do you want to do that? How are those two meat sacks able to help?"

"Just do it. I'm going to put Rory behind bars for now."

"Do you think a jail cell will hold him?"

"It won't hold the Destroyer, but it'll hold the man. That's all I'm worried about right now."

Deputy Rutherford walked into the hotel lobby, relieved to find Chrishav and Nila. Both were tired and downcast, sitting on a couple of plush early century lounge chairs. He wouldn't have to track down their rooms. Chrishav sat back deep in one chair with his lower left pants leg bottom shredded. He was nursing a small Styrofoam cup of coffee. Nila sat in a similar chair opposite Chrishav, leaning forward, his fingers interlaced as if he were praying.

The cavalcade of events at the ranch had exhausted the two. They were stuck in their progress with tracking down the Destroyer. The sheriff told them to prepare to move forward in their search. Up to this point, they considered themselves inept. Chrishav had conveyed to Nila he suspected the Destroyer had possessed Rory; their search for him was fruitless.

"Gentlemen, let's go," Deputy Rutherford ordered, startling both men. Deep in thought, they were unaware of his arrival in the hotel lobby.

"Why? What's going on?" Chrishav responded.

"I don't know, but it's got to be pretty important if he sent the mayor to find me to track you two down."

Chrishav and Nila followed the deputy out of the hotel and down the street past Rooster, who didn't wish them to have a good day or anything similar, but said, "Good luck. You're gonna need it." They pondered the context of his comment. Why would they need good luck if going to see the Sheriff?

Walking into the station house, Sheriff Knight sat on Clarissa's desk with his legs dangling from the front., leaning back, supporting his upper body with his arms extended to the rear, calm and relaxed. The mayor, who was pacing back and forth in the room agitated. He pondered if it was the destroyer possessing Rory, and why was he in Elysium?

"Here they are, sheriff," Deputy Rutherford announced as they entered the room.

"Good, I need you two to do me a quick favor."

"What's that?" Chrishav asked.

"Follow me. I need you to look at someone."

Both returned puzzled looks, but followed the sheriff. The door to the station house swung open with Clarissa, panicked, rushing in. "I heard Rory was brought in again. Where is he? What did he do this time?"

"Why're you so concerned about him? I thought you were back with Dugan?" Deputy Rutherford asked.

"Things aren't working out between me and Dugan. We're thinking of breaking up again."

"You got to be kidding me," Deputy Rutherford replied, sounding off angrily. "Rory was bothering you and the girls."

"Carlson, calm down," the Sheriff directed to his deputy.

"Sorry, Sheriff, but I was a bit surprised by Clarissa's man situation. Girl, you need to leave those two men alone."

Clarissa's squinting eyes, crinkled nose and flushed face established she didn't care for Deputy Rutherford's remark. "Go to hell, Carlson."

"We need to get back on track, folks," the Sheriff interjected. "Clarissa, the best thing you can do right now is to head home. We got this all under control."

"So why is Rory here? Why do you have the father of my baby locked up again?"

"Carlson, take her home."

"Sheriff, I'm not going home until you tell me why you got Rory locked up again," Clarissa petitioned again.

"Clarissa!" the sheriff bellowed, jumping off the desk and planting his feet on the floor. The room vibrated with the resonance of his deep baritone voice. Everyone silenced.

Never had the sheriff raised his voice to Clarissa. It brought tears to her eyes. Deputy Rutherford and the mayor were speechless to hear the sheriff respond with intensity.

"Go home and we'll discuss this later," Sheriff Knight said, now in a softened, but tempered voice. "Carlson, take her home," the sheriff commanded.

Deputy Rutherford guided Clarissa by her shoulders, leading her out the front door. Once they had exited the building, the sheriff continued. "Chrishav, Nila, I need you two to talk to Rory."

The mayor was curious about the sheriff's request but remained quiet.

"But, sheriff, that's what we've been trying to do: track him down so that we can talk to him. The problem is that we don't know where to find him," Chrishav said.

"Don't worry about that; he's locked up in back. Follow me."

"Rory's here? The one we think to be indwelled by the destroyer?" Chrishav asked, revealing a small grin.

"That's what we're about to find out."

The mayor jumped in. "I told you, Sheriff; I sensed something in there. Who else could it be?"

"Let's make sure," the Sheriff replied. He never trusted the mayor. He was a specialist in deceiving others, especially when it was for his or his mentor's advantage. Then there was also the possibility that the mayor himself might not be aware of whom, or what, he sensed indwelling Rory.

In the jail cell, Rory sat on the floor, meditating in a lotus position with his eyes closed. The four men walked up to the bars, trying to gauge Rory's actions of sitting and acting as if they weren't in the room. Several minutes elapsed. Chrishav discerned an empty void while attempting to determine if there was a presence within the incarcerated man.

"This is what it's like to see through these miserable mortal eyes?" Rory said as he opened his eyes, the whites now tinted and had turned black within black. The tinted eyes returned to white and the irises to their natural amber brown, remaining in the shape of vertical slits.

Chrishav trembled; a surge of rage originated from Rory. Nila didn't know why, but there was a sense of familiarity with Rory. It was as if they had crossed paths before.

"It's good to see all of you again," Rory professed. "I didn't think all four of you would show up."

"What do you mean, see all of us again? When have we met?" the mayor asked, not of Rory, but of whomever possessed him.

Rory replied with an impish smile.

"Let's get straight to the point, why don't we?" the Sheriff said. He pulled out his baton, knelt on one knee, and used his long truncheon as if it were a staff to support himself. Nila witnessed it appeared as if it were the beautiful sword he observed earlier on the roadway, then back to a baton. He wasn't sure if the mayor or Chrishav perceived the same since the transformation occurred in the twinkling of an eye.

"In the name of the Great Creator, I bind thee," the Sheriff commanded, staring at Rory.

Nila witnessed golden threadlike filaments radiate from the Sheriff's baton. They wrapped around Rory's torso, and then faded. Once again, Nila wondered if anyone else observed the manifestation.

Rory stiffened; his eyes narrowed. "How dare you," he said, his facial expression flashed disgust towards the sheriff.

The intensity of Rory's eyes broadcasted to Nila's whom they reminded him of; the sharpness of the stare was distinct. A wave of anger and repulsion flooded Chrishav's emotions. He had experienced the malevolent feelings before and recalled their source.

"The wolves," Chrishav and Nila blurted out in near synchronicity.

A name flashed into Chrishav's mind. "Hericulium. Sheriff, I sense the name is Hericulium."

Rory glanced up at Chrishav, displaying an angry scowl.

"Wait a minute; you're saying Rory is possessed by one of the Sentinels?" The mayor asked.

"Something told me this wasn't right," the Sheriff responded.

"You knew it would be one of the Sentinels?" the mayor continued.

"I wasn't sure," the Sheriff said. "But I had a feeling, considering Nila here mentioned the wolf talked to him about the destroyer. They've had to have been working together," the Sheriff said.

"So, is Hericulium the Destroyer?" Nila questioned.

The Sheriff stood worried. "This is not good. I bet all of this was a distraction. If Hericulium and the destroyer swapped, the destroyer is out there in the semi-temporal body of a Sentinel wolf."

"Can he do that, Sheriff?" Nila asked.

"You bet he can. Didn't quite expect it, though."

"You gotta do something, Sheriff," the mayor demanded.

"I don't see you going to talk to your supervision," Sheriff Knight countered.

"Just like you, you know I can't get involved. My job is to prime the way west for my packages," the mayor said.

"Exactly, so worry about your job, and I'll worry about mine. Now let me take care of this," the Sheriff said.

"You don't need to be so flippant. I think that..."

The sheriff cut the mayor off. "Shouldn't you be concerned that there are more spoiled packages as we speak?"

"Yeah, but if they're spoiled, that means they tried to go north, but were sent back," Mayor Corbett responded.

"Meaning they're not my problem anymore; they're yours. And it seems the Destroyer is causing your side more problems than mine," Sheriff Knight said.

The mayor knew the sheriff was correct in his estimation.

"What about Rory here?" Mayor Corbett asked.

"I have to banish the Sentinel Hericulium within Rory."

The mayor fidgeted, becoming anxious. "Wait a minute, that'll mean there's just one Sentinel guarding the south when there should be three, at a minimum, two. With one, there's a real possibility that someone who has the gumption and tries to head south could make it out of town."

"I know what that means if someone escapes their trip west?" the sheriff said. "It could open the floodgates for others to escape, and their tormentors along with them, causing all types of hellacious havoc."

The mayor feigned concerned. "We need to do something." He hoped the circumstances could lead to the sheriff losing his influence over Elysium.

"I think we have nothing but one option for the mayor's friend indwelling Rory."

"You need to return him to his duties as a Sentinel," the mayor demanded.

Sheriff Knight glanced over at the mayor. "You know what happens when one of your brethren goes outside of their ascribed domain. Geesh, how many times do we have to go over this, and how many of your ancient brethren are locked up in Tartarus for that reason?"

The mayor knew the protocols for daemons to remain within their sanctioned boundary. Sheriff Knight quickly expelled him. The destroyer class was one class of daemons allowed reign to roam across the various realms. No one knew why the Great Creator allowed the malevolent entities to do so. Also, the previous potentate, the mayor's predecessor, had attempted to overthrow the sheriff.

"You can't leave the way south unprotected," the mayor said.

"You more than most know better, Hannibal, I'm not worried about that. First things first though, I need to drive Rory west."

Chrishav sensed a surge of despondency and hopelessness flow through Rory, masked behind a wall of anger and fury. The saddened emotions originated deep within the captive, in the soul of the one held in the jail cell.

"Sheriff, about Rory, are you saying…" Nila asked, troubled by Sheriff's implication.

"What I'm saying is that there's no way of separating the two safely, at least not out here. I must do that on the bridge. I'll leave a message with Carlson when he returns to give Clarissa the bad news. There's nothing we can do."

Chrishav felt as if he was going to have a panic attack, but knew it wasn't from his own emotions. It originated in Rory's psyche. "Sheriff, I think Rory senses you're about to do something he's not happy about."

Sheriff Knight looked over at Nila, who grasped what was in store for Rory, and then turned towards Chrishav. "I'm sorry, Chrishav, but Rory is lost."

"What do you mean, lost?" Chrishav questioned. Then he realized. "Ohhh."

"Chrishav, Nila, you must search out the wolf," the Sheriff responded, not answering the question. "Do you understand the ramifications of your going out to find it? It's important that you're successful to prevent more from befalling the same fate as Rory. Don't worry, I know you have a lot of apprehension, but you must be strong. The destroyer isn't out to destroy the world or anything like that. He's focused on destroying individual lives. But it also looks like he may have a second goal to crash the gates of Heaven. However, his primary focus is to disrupt the lives of those who may have a greater destiny before them. The ripple effects, the smallest winds of his disruption can become mighty storms throughout human history."

"What do we need to do?" Chrishav asked.

"Nila, grab your gear. I fear you'll need it. You'll need to search him out."

"Where?" *Maybe I can do this*, Nila thought.

"Just go get your gear and get back here as soon as you can. I'm going to take our friend here on a little trip west."

Nila and Chrishav left and returned to find the mayor alone at the station house, the sheriff already having left to usher Rory west.

"About time you two got back. Sheriff Knight wanted me to tell you to wait here for him."

"He left already?" Chrishav questioned.

"It seems so; I gotta get out of here. With all these troublemakers running around, I have a feeling I'll have to deal with some packages up at Barclay's." With that, the mayor stormed out, slamming the door.

"So, do we wait?" Nila asked, jittery and pacing back and force, wanting to do more.

"We wait," Chrishav answered, searching for a chair to sit down on. Finding one next to Clarissa's desk, he sat.

A few minutes later, Chrishav became overwhelmed with an overpowering sense of loathing, revulsion, and hatred. Nila's skin crawled as if pricked by thousands of needles, a sensation he hadn't experienced before. Both men stared at each other.

"I sense something's wrong," Nila said.

"Me too," Chrishav followed.

UNEXPECTED VISITOR TO TOWN

A massive, husky gray wolf, its fur mixed with brown and white on the underside, sauntered down the middle of Main Street in town. Several vehicles followed at a distance, two and a half car lengths behind. Every so often, one honked. When it did, the wolf turned its massive head and snarled. Spectators gawked from the storefront windows, with no one staying outside brave enough to witness the encroaching animal, except for Rooster. As the feral canine sauntered past and glanced over, its eyes narrowed and then widened in surprise, as if a wolf could display a look of surprise. Rooster stood alone on the sidewalk, glaring at the creature.

The wolf snarled.

Deputy Rutherford frantically rushed into the police station. "Good, you two are here," he said in an excited voice.

"What's wrong?" Chrishav asked.

Instead of answering Chrishav's question, Deputy Rutherford noticed Nila's bow and quiver of arrows laying across Clarissa's desk. "African boy, we need you outside, and bring your gear. There's a wolf running around on the street, it's disrupting traffic. I talked to the sheriff on the radio; he said you need to take care of it."

"What's going on?" Chrishav asked.

"Just get out there," he snapped, and then hurried back outside.

Chrishav helped Nila put on his quiver; they then rushed out the door, following Deputy Carlson.

"You're not dead?" The wolf asked as it growled. Without wasting another second, it pounced, and in a single leap, landed on top of Rooster, who lay on the ground with the beast's full weight on his body. Sharp, unnatural, long talons extruded, curving downward out from the wolf's forepaws; they pierced Rooster's shoulder muscles. Blood oozed from the puncture wounds.

"How is it you're still alive, and I didn't recognize you before?" The wolf said.

With one quick snapping action, it attempted to strike down on the neck of its victim. As it lunged, two bullets penetrated its torso midsection, forcing the beast to roll to the side onto the sidewalk. Rooster maneuvered himself away, back up against the bakery wall.

The wolf recovered and stood on all fours to see Deputy Rutherford down the street with his weapon drawn and pointed towards him, with two men standing next to him. Nila, having finished inserting an arrow and drawing back on his bowstring, took aim. Just as he was about to release, a couple of patrons rushed out of the bakery, helping Rooster by pulling him into the shop.

"Deputy, I was going to shoot him," Nila said, irritated he no longer had a clear shot.

"We didn't have time, did we?" Deputy Rutherford responded.

Chrishav moved behind his two companions, gazing at the wolf. He sensed a distinct set of emotions than what he encountered at the ranch. These were more malevolent, serpent-like evil with no soul to hide behind.

"Guys, I think this is the destroyer," Chrishav whispered.

The wolf snarled. "You think a couple of bullets are going to harm me, dark one?"

The two patrons attempting to assist Rooster froze with fear at hearing the wolf speak.

"However, you hunter..." the wolf continued.

"Nila, shoot the damn thing," Deputy Rutherford commanded, getting over the momentary shock of the wolf not going down despite taking two rounds.

Nila hesitated. *I barely have a clean shot.* Although not in his direct line of sight, he deemed Rooster and his two rescuers to be too close in the flight path compared to moments ago. The steadiness of his hands faded; his aim relaxed; this situation wasn't the same as when at the archery range, or with the Huntsman. On the range, his view of the attacking wolves was unencumbered.

The wolf took advantage of Nila's timidity. It leaped onto the street and ran across the roadway in front of a car driving down the road. Nila overcame his hesitation. He pulled back on the bowstring to give it more tension. The wolf darted down the opposite sidewalk, traveling westward. Nila attempted to keep his arrow targeted towards the creature. Obscured by parked cars, a trashcan, a light post, and a bench mounted to the sidewalk, he found it hard to aim. Nila kept the arrow tip sighted on the running beast, waiting to seize the perfect time to release. The Huntsman had trained him on following a target as it moved through the density of his native lands' vegetation; the foreign townscape with man-made obstacles disoriented him, but he refocused.

As the wolf passed across the street from their location near the front of the station house, Nila released his fingers. The arrow flew and grazed the wolf's hind quarter, impaling the wood door of an antique shop. The beast stopped, glared back at Nila, and growled. Witnessing Nila reaching back into his quiver and pulling out and nocking another arrow, it sped off again, continuing west towards the traffic circle. Nila reacquired his aim and released. The wolf broke to the north just as the arrow in flight would have struck.

Darn, Nila thought. He would have to go after it, not having an opportunity like this again.

"Chrishav, go make sure Rooster is okay. Deputy, can you drive me to follow the wolf?"

"You bet. Get in the car."

Nila pulled the quiver from his back and followed the deputy over to his patrol car. Nila placed his gear in the rear seat and jumped in. Deputy Rutherford rushed getting into the vehicle, starting it up; the screech of tires breaking contact with the road surface filled the air.

Chrishav hurried over to Rooster to help. While on the reservation, his short time in the good graces with the Shamans guided him on how to administer first aid. He was thankful for that part of his training—their willingness to aid wounded creatures, more so fellow man.

The bakery shop owner came out with a first-aid kit. Chrishav dressed Rooster's injuries once he finished cleaning out the puncture wounds. While placing the last dressing and bandage, he couldn't help but wonder about the comments the wolf made before it attacked.

"Rooster, what was all that about?" Chrishav asked.

"You's got to explain yourself, young man. What's all whats about?" Rooster replied.

"What was all that the wolf spouted off to you before he tried to kill you?"

"Oh, that ain't nuthin. He's tried to kills me before in a previous town."

Chrishav halted applying the final bandage, gauze, and adhesive tape, confounded by Rooster's remark. "You've met the wolf before?"

"Nots the wolf, but the Destroyer. Thank you all with helpings me."

A young, skinny man of Asian descent, who was in one car while the wolf walked down the street, drove up and parked in front of the newspaper stand. He stepped out of his vehicle and meandered onto the sidewalk, overcoming his mild disorientation.

"Where am I? What am I doing here?" he asked in Mandarin, his eyes glazed over.

"You're in Elysium, my friend," Rooster responded in perfect Mandarin. He picked himself up, went to the wireframe newspaper stand next to his sitting chair, pulled a newspaper, and handed it to the young man. Chrishav glanced at the front page and saw what he assumed to be a Chinese typescript. The man's eyes watered as he read the headline and the accompanying article.

"Sorry, young fella, but you know the direction you need to go from here," Rooster said, again in Mandarin.

Chrishav didn't understand the conversation, except that he sensed deep remorse had overcome the man.

The young man returned to his vehicle and drove off, downcast. A newer model black Ford Taurus drove up and parked next to the sidewalk.

"Why don't you handle this one, young man?" Rooster encouraged Chrishav.

"What do you want me to do?"

"Justs give him the paper."

"How do you know they want a newspaper?"

"Trust me," Rooster gloated.

The Ford Taurus driver, leaving the car running, got out and walked up to the two men. "Excuse me, but where am I, and how did I get here?"

Chrishav, feeling inadequate, glanced over to Rooster, who pointed to the newspaper stand. Chrishav then knew to pick up a newspaper and pass it to the Taurus driver. He expected to see Chinese lettering again, but this time, the newsprint was in English. Scanning the headlines, it read, "Black Ford Taurus Rear Ends Semi-Trailer." Chrishav read the article's first two sentences. It described the car and driver standing in front of him.

"Uhh, is that for me?" the Taurus driver asked.

Chrishav handed off the newspaper. "Sorry."

"Damn, I knew I shouldn't have tried returning that text," the driver said after reading the article on the front page. He followed the same routine as with the previous car, getting back in and driving off towards the town circle.

"Rooster, what is it you do here?"

"I help guide those who may not be sure of where they are, how they got here, or where to go..."

"How long have you been doing this?" Chrishav asked, unaware of Rooster's improved diction.

"Sheriff's here," Rooster said, seeing the sheriff's patrol car driving up next to the station house down the street. "Better go talk to him and tell him what happened. I has a feeling your friend might need some help."

PURSUIT

"Do you see him?" Deputy Rutherford shouted to Nila, focusing on trying to find the wolf, losing sight of him while attempting to drive at the same time.

"He took off into the trees...wait, there he is, back near the side of the road," Nila said.

"I see him."

The wolf continued his hectic run, weaving in and out of the tree-lined road north past Barclay's. A mile later, the wolf shifted directions, turning up a compacted dirt road. The patrol car turned and followed, navigating with surety through each turn and dip. Suddenly, the road ended. "Looks like this is as far as we can go. We need to get back to the station."

Nila hurried out of the stopped car.

"What are you doing?" Deputy Rutherford asked, not expecting Nila to exit the car.

"I'm going to track him down. I have to stop this wolf."

"You know the Sheriff warned no one from town is ever supposed to go further north than this?" Deputy Rutherford said. "Ever."

Nila pulled his equipment from the patrol car's rear seat. "Do what you must and get the Sheriff, but I'm going after him." He slung his arrow quiver over his shoulder, put on his archer's glove, and then strapped a large Bowie hunting knife in its carrier around his upper leg.

"Do you think it's smart going in there by yourself?" the deputy asked.

Nila didn't answer. He sprinted into the forest to where he had observed the wolf enter. Breaking his way through brush, ferns, wild berry plants, and other low growing shrubbery forced him to slow down to make sure he reconnoitered for signs of his quarry ahead of him.

The forest, old and majestic, provided a canopy of shade from the indiscriminate sun. Pine, honeysuckle, and the earthy aroma of mulch invaded Nila's nostrils, wanting to embrace and explore the surroundings. He followed the trail of displaced leaves, crushed grass, pieces of snagged fur and branches broken by someone or something passing by. Every so often, imprinted in the soft soil, were the impressions of a wolf's paw prints.

It struck Nila this was his first major hunt by himself. His father or the Huntsman weren't here to help guide him. It would be up to him to find the wolf. One problem, the wolf was faster. Would it slow down now that it was under the cover of the woods and use its concealment to its advantage?

Nila wanted to make sure he didn't lose the trail of his quarry. He slowed his progress and listened for any sounds of rustling or activity masking his own movements. He imagined something moved every time he advanced. Now, stopping to gather his bearings gave him a chance to scan the area, and also to determine if the wolf was stalking him. The wolf, not feeling threatened, could have caught his scent, then turn around and attack.

It was best to stay out in the open of the scattered trees, reducing the chance of an ambush. Since his bow and arrow were weapons of distance, Nila was at a full disadvantage if attacked at close range, possibly not having time to load an arrow. He would need to resort to using his knife.

To follow the correct tracks required intense concentration so as not to end up pursuing the wrong animal, as he did once during his training when he was younger. His father let him follow them until he realized his blunder. Nila suppressed his feelings of insecurity, reminiscing of what he had experienced then to not make the same mistake.

The forest here differed from the tropical forest and dense vegetation of his native land. It didn't change the fact that the animal life seemed almost non-existent. What came to mind was the silence. The birds chose not to reveal themselves when Nila expected to hear the melodic chirping of the feathered creatures seducing one another, the ingratiating cawing of scavenging ravens, or the other trills and tweets from creatures of flight speaking their secret language. Maybe because of their nature, they sensed danger in the vicinity, and the air was silent of birdsong. And where were the woodland creatures living in the forests that should be scavenging or mulling about? There should be their scurrying away upon hearing or smelling an oncoming human? Yet not all creatures are afraid of humans.

Nila's training told him he'd at least come across the remnants of other creatures; it may be their scat, distinct paw prints imprinted upon the soil, or the devoured or decaying remains showing the life and death cycle of nature. He came across none of that; the visible signs of snapped branches with fresh breaks on shrubs, a tuft of gray and brown hair snagged by a thorny bush, or the recent impressions of large paw prints in the dirt showed he was on the track of the wolf.

The further Nila traveled, the dense forest changed to scattered pine trees with their cast-off needles blanketing the ground. Underlying bush and native saplings diminished. It was now easier to view greater distances, giving Nila some comfort. The breeze of mild, humid air carried the scent of pine and evergreens. Relaxed being out in the open with distance between him and his quarry, would give him time to use his bow and arrow. He considered rearming.

The sole hindrance now was a slight mist in the air confounded with the hazy sky, unable to tell if it was morning or night. This affected his ability to orient his direction of travel. Without a watch or other means of telling time, he knew a considerable amount had already passed.

Nila was confident he was on the destroyer-infused wolf's trail, believing the paw prints he tracked were fresh with the lack of other animal prints. When he came upon a road he did not expect, Nila panicked. *What if the wolf ran onto the* road, *leaving no trail?*

Regathering his focus, Nila surveyed the roadside. The same size tracks of the animal he'd been pursuing ran parallel to the asphalt. Following the canine prints stamped in the dirt, they veered onto the roadway. To Nila's surprise, they were like fluorescent paw shapes painted on the blacktop surface. *How could that be?* The ones immediately in front of him faded as he followed. Further up the road, they beamed brighter. Nila picked up his pace to make sure he didn't lose the trail.

Behind him, the sound of an automobile engine from a vehicle speeding up the roadway echoed in the light mist. Nila stepped onto the roadside. A burgundy red Toyota Forerunner pickup truck with a silver stripe containing two occupants drove by. The driver was a young redhead, his face dotted with freckles and cheeks pockmarked from acne. The passenger was a young, ebony skinned man, somewhat overweight with a short afro and wearing a shirt silk-screened with skull and crossbones. The vehicle continued up the road and disappeared into the fog.

Nila resumed his pursuit, noticing the glowing prints continuing to fade. If he were to lose the trail, he needed to follow the road back to town. It would be difficult to backtrack on his original route from his current location with little to no tracking markers.

He heard a vehicle approaching from ahead of him. Breaking through the mist, the same Toyota pickup truck from what he estimated five to ten minutes earlier had returned. The truck rolled to a stop next to Nila; the passenger rolled down his window. "Are you the one we're supposed to meet?" he asked in a mournful voice, ready to crack as if he were about to cry.

"I don't think so." Nila was curious why they had turned around. "What happened behind you?"

"We were told we couldn't go any further," the black man noted, his words laced with sorrow.

"Did you see a wolf back there?" Nila quizzed.

Both stared at Nila with incredulity. "No. Someone so different...so...I can't explain it," the passenger replied.

"We asked him where were we?" The redhead continued, noticing his companion didn't finish his last statement. "He told us we're not allowed to go further on this road. We're supposed to head back to meet someone to show us where we're supposed to go."

Nila wondered about the destroyer's ability to send lost packages if it were here in the forest. "How did you end up coming up here instead of the other direction?"

The two young men remained quiet, not having a response. The passenger rolled up his window. They drove off. Nila returned his attention back to the road. The prints faded and grew darker. He risked sprinting to meet up where the tracks luminesced with intensity, letting him know he was getting close once again. The blanket of light fog hugging the ground and haze obscuring the vista through the scarcity of trees still limited overall visibility.

Nila heard a commotion echo in the air ahead: snarling, a swatting noise, and the movement of two distinct creatures, sounding as if they were engaged in a scuffle. Nila drew an arrow, primed his bow, and advanced with caution towards the noise. There was a horrific growl, followed by a low, breathy woofing sound. More scuffling sounds followed, ending with a loud swooshing noise in the air, trailed by a thud and a yelp as if a creature was in great pain. Amid all the activity, a commanding voice bellowed, "Be gone."

Although Nila didn't know why, the air smelled sweet with new aromas of fragrant flowers, sweet spices, and myrrh that overtook the forest scents of pine and moss. They evoked a memory of training with the Huntsman.

Approaching close to where he believed he heard the commotion, scattered fluorescing paw prints littered the roadway. For a quick instant, before they all disappeared; they intermingled with several human shape footprints of someone wearing sandals. Because many of the residents in his town wore simple sandals whereas they couldn't afford shoes, he recalled similar footprint patterns on the dusty roads.

Dark spots of a viscous liquid that lay splattered on the ground and upon the road top caught Nila's attention. He squatted and dipped his finger into the mysterious substance. He then rubbed it between his index finger and thumb. Its consistency resembled blood. Was it blood? If so, was it the wolf's blood? The droplets left a trail leading off the road and back into the forest. Nila stood and resumed his tracking. He found fresh impressions of paw prints formed on the soft earth. They were similar in size to the same one's he'd been tracking, accompanied with droplets of blood.

If the wolf is injured, how? Nila prepared himself not to be surprised at how different the beast you're hunting can become. It'll try to run and evade if it feels there is a chance to escape. If cornered, you'd almost think you were facing a different creature altogether, one with increasing aggressiveness. Considering one wounded with any strength remaining, and feeling threatened, it becomes more vicious. From this point on, he needed to exhibit greater caution. It was important to remember not to focus too much on the wolf attacking and miss key markers on the trail.

The droplets of blood spattered on the ground were spaced closer together. This could be a good sign. The wolf, if wounded, must be slowing down. Nila did the same to make sure he didn't come upon the beast unexpectedly and cause it to attack.

Visibility improved throughout the sparse forest. This helped to quell the likelihood of a surprise attack. But where was the wolf? Roaming for several more yards, no new blood droplets or recently formed paw pad impressions were visible in the semi-hardened soil. The trail stopped. Only a light dusting of pine needles covered the forest floor.

It couldn't have disappeared. Nila's heartbeat thumped aggressively in his chest.

He glanced up and then remembered that wolves don't climb trees. So, if the wolf didn't go up, where was it? Nila recalled the first time he encountered the pack of sentinels while practicing at the archery range. They appeared to have emerged from the ground. Was the wolf toying with him? During the pursuit, did it dissolve into the ground, ready to manifest nearby to gain an advantage? If it did, why didn't it already attack?

Nila prepared himself by repositioning the arrow nock on the bowstring, raising his weapon to the firing position, and drawing with enough force so as not to tire his grip. He moved forward with caution, turning if he imagined seeing something move out of the corner of his eye, or heard an unexpected rustling sound. Pressing forward, a foul, musty odor let him know he was close. Off to his right, out of his peripheral vision, was an unnatural disturbance at ground level several yards away. Nila aimed, pulled back on the bowstring, and released his arrow. The projectile impaled into the semi-hardened soil. Nothing happened. He loaded a fresh arrow into the bow and continued forward. There were still no visible signs of the wolf.

Nila returned to where the tracks stopped. It was now that he became confident the wolf was turning from evader to pursuer, setting up for an ambush attack. He walked several steps, followed by his turning in a 360-degree pattern with his arrow aimed forward to make sure nothing snuck up on him. Doing this several times, he doubted if the wolf was still around. Or was it being patient? Nila was determined to be patient.

Nila wasn't sure how much time had passed when, from below where he stood on the ground, belched a putrid and musky odor that assailed his nose. The moist earthen soil rippled as the form of a canine's head materialized while trying to maul at his leg. The wolf's snout grazed Nila's calf as he shifted his bodyweight to the left, pivoting while releasing his grip on the bow, bowstring, and tail of the arrow. As his bow fell to the ground, the barbed-headed shaft launched, sailing through the air in a haphazard flight path. Nila reached, grabbing the hilt of his hunting knife, and snatched it out of its carrier while dropping to his knees. He plunged the blade into the semi-formed wolf's back of the neck.

Nila scooted back from the creature. Its head and upper neck section up to the shoulder had solidified as if sprouting from the earth. After a couple of labored breaths, the wolf's eyes closed shut with its final exhale. Nila waited for the remains to form into gray dust as in times prior when he had defended himself. The other expectation was for a mist or other ethereal form to evacuate from the creature.

Nothing happened.

A few minutes passed, Nila retrieved his bow and combed the area for his wayward arrow. While searching, he checked to make sure the earthen-submerged wolf remained expired. Finding his errant projectile, he checked its integrity; the shaft was undamaged. He placed the arrow back into his quiver.

Nila returned to the semi-formed wolf, verified its death, withdrew his knife from the canine's neck, and wiped the blade clean. He was prepared to backtrack so that he could find his way to the road when a brilliant light illuminated the forest. The unexpected, intensified sweet smell of flowers and spice filled the air. Nila was about to turn around to determine the source of the radiant light when an authoritative bass-like voice said, "Do not move. Stand where you are."

The command's forcefulness squelched Nila's desire to look.

"Who are you?" Nila asked, since the mysterious arrival didn't prohibit him from talking.

"That is not your concern. But you must deliver a message to Sheriff Knight," the voice said.

The unknown visitor sounded familiar. Nila wanted to place it as the Huntsman, yet this iteration was more majestic, its tone more musical.

"What message is that?"

"The wolf that you slayed is not the vessel brandishing the Destroyer. When Sheriff Knight displaced the one called Archimedium, who attacked you and Chrishav at the ranch, it materialized at the River Purgo in the Valley of Himmon. Archimedium, with not his time to cross over, then worked his way over to where we are and met with the destroyer as soon as it came upon the roadway in these forests to lead you away. The destroyer then doubled back."

Nila's ego had soared, thinking he had accomplished a magnificent feat and ended the destroyer daemon's vessel. Now, to find out that the destroyer had tricked him by swapping with a sentinel, allowing the more dangerous daemon to escape, he became emotionally deflated.

Nila's emotional high deflated. "I failed."

"Do not think that you failed. Not all of that occurred until after the Guardian of the Gates wounded it when he attempted to crash the hallowed entrance. The current wounded vessel of the wolf containing the Destroyer is now more dangerous than a legion of daemons; it departed from this realm, returning to Elysium. This wolf's intention was to lead you astray, to kill you."

"Why didn't the Destroyer attempt to kill me here in the forest himself?"

"It changed its focus, occupied with someone in town—as for this evil incarnation before you..."

Violet and gray flames erupted and engulfed the half-buried, half-exposed wolf. They licked and danced in the air seven feet high.

Nila thought his eyes were playing a trick on him; within the fire was a broad, muscular, naked male human form with wings, writhing in agony and pain. The winged male and wolf's body disappeared.

"Who are you?" Nila asked of the unknown entity.

"Worry not about who I am. Know that you've done well since the time in Africa."

Nila was positive–the voice resembled Huntsman. "Huntsman, is that you?"

The aura of light disappeared.

Nila wasn't sure of his next actions. His stomach was queasy, and for an instant, his eyes flooded with tears before he suppressed them with the help of taking a couple of quick, deep breaths. *I need to do better next* time; he thought.

He spent several more minutes meditating. He then secured his gear, traced his tracks back to the road, and headed off towards Elysium.

New Revelations

Chrishav finished dressing Rooster's wounds. He was comfortable leaving the old man to tend to his undertaking of delivering his personalized newspapers. Now, instead of going down to see the Sheriff next as intended, the Sheriff was walking towards them.

"What's going on here?" the Sheriff asked

"One of the gray wolves came through here and attacked Rooster. Deputy Rutherford tried to shoot it, but nothing happened. It ran away with the deputy and Nila going after it," Chrishav explained.

Chrishav expected more of a surprise reaction from the Sheriff. His response was a simple raised eyebrow. "Which way did they go?"

"I thinks they chased the wolf north," Rooster replied.

"Really," the Sheriff responded, turning around and staring at the traffic circle. "Think I might have to go take a trip."

"Can I join you?" Chrishav entreated.

"Nope, I bet going north on the road will cause the same problem as when you went west. I don't think it'll be a good idea."

"Right now I feel kinda useless," Chrishav said.

"Don't worry, right now you are."

Rooster chuckled.

Chrishav didn't find humor in the remark. "Sheriff, I want to help somehow."

"There's nothing you can do right now but pray. But don't worry, you'll be needed sooner than you realize. Trust me, we have to work out some sort of game plan to resolve all of this when I return."

"Sheriff…"

The sheriff flashed a stern stare at Chrishav, who accepted the conversation was over. He was trying to avoid sitting around doing nothing while Nila went off on a new pursuit. The last jaunt when the Sheriff and Nila departed was three long boring days of waiting.

During that time, events around the town stagnated. Even the number of passersby seemed to have diminished to where Rooster had sat around during long bouts of doing nothing but watching visitors in the town antique shop. Chrishav wasn't sure how long Nila would be gone this time.

"What's this I hear about a wolf attacking the old coot?" the mayor asked, approaching the mini crowd hanging around Rooster's chair in front of the bakery. Sheriff Knight flashed an expression of repulsion at the mayor's arrival.

"Everything's under control, Hannibal," the Sheriff said.

"You may think so, but it seems like everything here is messed up from what I heard."

"And what did you hear?"

"A wolf ran through town, scaring all these poor residents. Then it attacked Rooster. Deputy Rutherford tried shooting it, but it up and ran away."

"It may seem like that, but depending on what happens to our friend from Africa, this wolf situation could soon be resolved. I'll have to head on another trip west."

"Whatever, sheriff, can we get things back to normal around here?"

"Don't be so dramatic, Hannibal. Everything is normal around here."

The mayor observed Clarissa walking up from behind the Sheriff, but didn't warn him. "You say that? How are you gonna explain Rory to Clarissa, for example?"

"I'll have to break it to her easily, that's all."

"Break what to me, Sheriff?" Clarissa asked, nervousness apparent in her voice.

The Sheriff pirouetted around to find Clarissa's petite face staring at him. "Clarissa, you should be at home. How long have you been standing there?"

"Sheriff, what do you have to explain about Rory?"

Sheriff Knight hesitated before replying. His lack of a response added to Clarissa's anxiety.

"I'll tell her," the mayor said, jumping in. "Rory's been taken to the west. He won't be coming back," the mayor divulged in a gruff and harsh tone.

"Hannibal, I have a good mind to send you back. I was going to tell her when all of this is situated."

Clarissa's eyes saturated with tears, she attempted to hold back.

"Oh, don't tell me you're gonna miss him?" the mayor said.

"How dare you say something like that? He's not gone," Clarissa said, hollering at the mayor. "You're a heartless son of a b." She held back the urge to go over and slap the mayor.

"Hannibal, stop," the sheriff said.

"I'm only stating the truth," the mayor said.

Clarissa ran out of the station house crying.

"You and I aren't done, but right now I gotta go follow up with Nila," Sheriff Knight said.

He dashed to his patrol car and drove towards the traffic circle, and proceeded north. Driving up past Barclay's, Deputy Rutherford was driving back down from the forest. They pulled up aside one another and lowered their driver's side window.

"What's going on, Carlson? I heard about the incident with the wolf." Sheriff Knight asked. "Where's Nila?"

"We chased that thing after it was walking down the main drag and then attacked Rooster."

"So, I heard."

"Nila and I chased after it. It ran down Simpson's Road, up to where it ended. Nila jumped out and charged into the forest after it."

"Was he armed?"

"Yeah, he took his bow and arrows and knife."

"Good." The Sheriff sounded relieved.

"Sheriff, what's going on around here?" Deputy Rutherford questioned. "I know Elysium is a strange town, and I expect strange stuff, but I popped that wolf with two rounds, and it got back up and then ran out of here like a banshee. Oh yeah, did I mention that the damn thing talked?"

"What do you mean, it talked? You heard it speak?" The sheriff questioned.

"Yeah, I heard it speak. I know you don't like cursing, sheriff, but that was some strange stuff."

"Don't worry, Carlson; I know you don't have any malice behind it."

"Now what?"

"I'm gonna go up and see if I can find Nila and help with that wolf."

"Shooting it won't help, so I'm not sure that bow and arrow of his is going to do any good," Deputy Rutherford noted.

The sheriff didn't want to tell Deputy Rutherford that it wasn't the weapon making the difference in terminating the wolf; it was the person accomplishing the kill. Nila, because of his background, and having traveled to the Valley of Himmon and the outer reaches of the realm, he would be capable of killing the wolf.

The sheriff was curious about the wolf's visit. "By chance, did the wolf do anything else?"

Deputy Rutherford recalled the wolf walking down the street, attacking Rooster, himself shooting the wolf, and then the creature darting off across the street and towards the roundabout.

"I'll be," the Sheriff said, observing the road leading to the forest. Deputy Rutherford tried turning around in his seat, but could not get a good view. He adjusted his rear mirror to center its focus behind him. Nila was walking down the thoroughfare, carrying his bow down at his side and his quiver of arrows slung across his back.

"He's back already? I dropped him off a few minutes ago." Deputy Rutherford said. "He must've lost the wolf."

The sheriff and deputy stepped out of their vehicles, engines still running.

"At least you're alive. What happened back there in the woods?" Deputy Rutherford asked.

"I killed the wolf sheriff, but I didn't get rid of the destroyer," Nila replied, staring into the sheriff's beaming eyes.

"What do you mean you killed the wolf? Already? You were gone for five, maybe ten minutes. What does he mean by that, sheriff?" Deputy Rutherford asked.

"It means something strange is going on," Sheriff Knight said.

A rhythmic chiming sound originated from Deputy Rutherford's pocket, disrupting the conversation. He pulled out his cellphone. The caller ID displayed it was the mayor. Deputy Rutherford knew the Sheriff ignored the mayor's phone calls, so he didn't think it strange for him to be calling his phone.

"I better get this. It's the mayor, boss." Deputy Rutherford stepped away from the background noise of the running cars and the other two men talking to focus on the call.

The sheriff re-engaged in his conversation with Nila. "How's that possible? If Hericulium jumped to Rory, allowing the destroyer to possess that wolf and the one you chased down, you should have encountered a distinct manifestation of our adversary."

"Because it wasn't the same wolf sheriff; it was the one you sent away when Chrishav and I were attacked at the ranch," Nila said. "It didn't return to regular patrol."

"Then the Destroyer-possessed wolf could still be anywhere. How did you find out about the swap?" The Sheriff asked.

"Someone came up to me in the forest. He wouldn't let me see his face," Nila said.

"You don't know who it was?"

"No, he was the one who warned me about the Destroyer-possessed wolf."

"Hmmm, I might know who that was. I think you do too," the Sheriff said.

"How could it have been him?" Nila asked.

"Sheriff, we got a problem," Deputy Rutherford said, returning to the two men and rejoining the conversation. "You wouldn't believe it, but according to the mayor, they spotted another enormous wolf in one neighborhood near the school. He says the residents are going ape sh..."

The Sheriff's expression displayed to Deputy Rutherford he didn't appreciate hearing the intended vulgarity. "Sorry, sheriff, but that's about as best as I can explain it."

"Where was it last seen?"

"In the neighborhoods on the south side of town," Deputy Rutherford passed on.

Sheriff Knight speculated the destroyer may try to indwell the final wolf of the three sentinels, but that would cause the immediate banishment for both. So, what was the destroyer's intention?

"Carlson, I need you to go back to town and pick up Chrishav, and then meet up with us at Juniper Elementary. We'll start our search there."

"Why do we need him?"

"Just do it. I don't have time to explain. Nila, you're with me," Sheriff Knight commanded with force.

Nila jumped into the sheriff's patrol car. Deputy Rutherford hesitated for a few seconds before getting into his vehicle, attempting to absorb the Sheriff being exacting and demanding. He'd been accustomed to how his boss had acted when responding to previous issues in town. Even when several hunters were involved in a major fracas at Lake Alice's, the Sheriff remained subdued throughout the incident and follow-on arrests.

Sheriff Knight and Nila drove up and down a couple of blocks attempting to find their quarry, but encountered streets devoid of human activity. Periodically, while glancing at the houses as they passed by, panic or fear-stricken faces stared out of the front living room windows. Nila surmised word had gotten around about a strange creature walking along the streets. Everyone hiding inside must be waiting for the all clear, signaling the wolf's capture or killing. The residents knew wolves lived out in the surrounding forests, but never known of any this massive encroaching into town before.

Before heading over to meet up with Deputy Rutherford and Chrishav, the Sheriff did a quick drive by the Omega Ranch. He wanted to make sure the remaining sentinel was where it was supposed to be. Staying off in the distance, and watching from inside the car, the wolf was accomplishing its patrol on the main road leading out of town. Corporeal cars passing through town were unaware of its presence, unable to see the sentry pacing back and forth.

Speeding down the road, Nila recognized a burgundy red Toyota Forerunner pickup with a silver stripe. Seeing the red-headed driver, it was the same vehicle from earlier in the woods.

"I know that truck," Nila said.

"You do," the Sheriff replied.

"Yeah, it was in the forest. They were turned around sent back to town."

"Probably Barclay's. Looks like those two didn't want to wait for their transportation west."

The wolf moved to the roadside, and as the truck passed, it leaped into the driver's side window, snatching both the driver and passenger, and then exited through the passenger window. With its prey, it pranced into the woods, heading westward, leaving the wailing and moaning of the two men in the wake. The truck drifted forward, fading into non-existence. Moments later, the wolf materialized, walking patrol along the road.

The sheriff, confident the Destroyer did not influence the third sentinel, drove off. It took a couple of minutes to reach the elementary schoolyard. This area of town was foreign to Nila; it was several blocks from the main road heading out to the Omega Ranch. As before, the Sheriff remained quiet for the entire duration of their drive. His one conversation was with a corner store owner along the way to see if he had witnessed the wolf. Two customers claimed to have seen the gray creature, but steered clear, making sure it was heading away before they continued on.

The Sheriff and Nila exited the patrol car to scan the area to find any signs of the creature, or of Deputy Rutherford and Chrishav. The parking lot and schoolyard were desolate. An expression displaying worry painted itself on the Sheriff's strong-featured face-Deputy Rutherford hadn't arrived.

Nila didn't recall seeing the sheriff show apprehension before. "Shouldn't they be here by now?"

"Yes, they should."

The sheriff reached into his patrol car to grab the handheld microphone for the dispatch radio when an inbound radio announcement blared from the speaker. "Sheriff, this is Carlson, come in."

"Go ahead, what's your location?" the Sheriff responded.

"We're over here at 7th and Butler. You may want to get over here."

"What's going on? We have a wolf to track down."

"That's just it, sheriff, we found it."

"Keep an eye on it and don't try anything crazy. It can be dangerous."

"That's not going to be a problem."

"What do you mean?"

"Just get over here, sheriff. Carlson out."

Sheriff Knight and Nila jumped into the patrol car and drove over to the intersection identified by Deputy Rutherford. A small crowd had formed around something of interest; they were all gawking at the ground. The sheriff and Nila made out a gray, furry mass on the front lawn of a corner Victorian-style house. Getting out of the car and strolling up to the spectators, the carcass of a lifeless gray wolf laid on the grass.

"Everyone head home," the Sheriff ordered.

The onlookers scattered. Their compliance impressed Nila. It reminded him of his hometown's complicity when Sogundu barked out similar requests during town gatherings or meetings. Here, the local townspeople trusted the Sheriff and followed his instructions, leaving the four of them standing around the lifeless, hulking, and furry carcass. The body brandished two fresh slashing wounds deemed to be non-fatal. There was no blood on the remains, nor anywhere near where they stood.

"Sheriff, is this the same wolf that attacked Rooster earlier?" Deputy Rutherford queried.

Sheriff Knight glanced at Deputy Rutherford for a quick second, then bent down and flipped the expired creature over. Two gunshot wounds were visible.

"What's going on, Sheriff?" Deputy Rutherford asked. "Did I kill it? And why did it take a while to die after I shot it? And how did it get those cutting injuries?"

"No, the gunshots or whatever cut him had nothing to do with this. Something else is going on." Even though the wolf manifested into the physical, corporeal realm where men could see him, the Sheriff knew natural weapons weren't involved with its demise.

"Is it pretending to be dead?" Nila asked.

"Nope, this puppy is dead," Chrishav said. He sensed nothing but a cold, empty husk.

"You're sure you don't sense anything, Chrishav?" The sheriff asked.

"Nobody's home."

The Sheriff grabbed the wolf by its scruff and, lifting with ease, raised it to view the lifeless hulk face to face. "This is strange. Any other time when a daemon infused vessel expires, the daemon returns to its own realm. This isn't the case this time."

"Are you sure, sheriff?" Chrishav said. "Maybe we got lucky, and it died from its injuries."

"I don't think so." The sheriff carried the wolf over to his patrol car. "Just as important, the dead carcass should have dematerialized."

It amazed Nila at the strength the Sheriff showed not appearing to strain. With a single hand, he lifted what appeared to be a creature he estimated weighed 150–170 pounds. He knew that a typical wild, large gray wolf weighed up to 100 pounds.

The sheriff opened the car trunk and tossed in the canine remains.

"Hmmm, why here?" the sheriff said, just above a whisper, while closing the trunk. He turned almost in a full circle when something caught his attention. His three companions focused in the same direction he'd been staring. They gazed upon a Victorian style home on a corner lot. The front door was ajar; the screen door's bottom half ripped open.

"Carlson, you know whose home this is, don't you?" By the sheriff's tone, he was being rhetorical when he asked the question.

"No, I don...," Carlson paused for a few seconds. "Wait a minute, do you think she's inside?" Deputy Rutherford unholstered his .45 and rushed towards the front door. Chrishav was going to follow, but was told to stand fast by the Sheriff, who then pulled out his cell phone and hit a speed-dial number icon.

"Hannibal, do you know where your assistant is right now?"

Chrishav and Nila heard the mayor's voice blaring, laced with expletives, through the Sheriff's cell phone speaker.

The sheriff broke in on the mayor's ranting. "You could have said no, Hannibal, instead of going off on a tirade like that. If you see her, try to bind her. She's not herself again." The sheriff didn't wait for a response–he disconnected the phone call. "Call was getting boring anyway," the Sheriff continued.

"Whoever possessed the wolf left of their own accord. Nila, we need to find your girlfriend," the Sheriff directed with determination. Nila wasn't sure how to receive the comment, but suspected sarcasm. Chrishav was flabbergasted.

Deputy Rutherford came rushing out of the house and rejoined the three men, noticing Nila and Chrishav were viewing the Sheriff with displeasure. "Destiny's not inside? What do we got here?"

"Nila, concentrate," the Sheriff directed to the youngest of the three men, placing his hands on each side of Nila's face. "Now is the time to be the hunter that you are. See!"

Nila's mind jolted. The sheriff released his grip on the side of Nila's face. Everything blurred, then doubled, almost as if one set of everything he was witnessing was hyper-realistic, and then phased back into single objects. The anxiety of seeing a dreamlike perspective to the world around him confused Nila. The sheriff radiated an aura like that of the unknown entity he encountered in the forest while pursuing the wolf. Glancing down at the holstered baton on the Sheriff's utility belt was the beautiful sword, glistening in the sun, almost appearing as if flaming. Chrishav appeared normal. The impression of the deputy troubled him. It was as if he possessed an aura, yet ebbed or subdued, almost as if the flickering light of a candle was about to expire.

"This is weird," Nila said.

"Focus," Sheriff Knight said.

Nila took a couple of quick steps back from everyone; it was unsettling to view everything in a surreal manner. Withdrawing from the three men, something stood out-slowly fading luminescing paw prints on the ground trekked towards the front of the house. Coming back out to where the wolf's body had rested were female footprints, he suspected to be Destiny's. From there, the footprints proceeded up the street.

"I'm not in the forest." Nila asked. "How's that possible?"

"What's possible?" Chrishav asked, sensing Nila's unease.

Nila stayed focused on the footprints; he deduced from what he was witnessing. "She went this way." Nila took off running, tracing the footsteps.

"We need to follow him," the Sheriff said.

Chrishav jumped into the sheriff's patrol car. Deputy Rutherford took up the rear of his vehicle. They restricted their speed to lag Nila.

"Sheriff, what was that between you and Nila back there?" Chrishav asked, the Sheriff keeping his focus both on Nila and the road as they were heading towards the main street of town.

The sheriff didn't answer. Chrishav returned his attention back to Nila, who was jogging along the sidewalk while looking down.

"I think I know where Destiny's going." The sheriff sped up to the side of Nila while opening the window on the passenger side. "Nila, get in. I think I know where the trail you're following is going."

AFFRONT ON THE GATES

With the earlier attack on Rooster, many residents were hesitant to walk outdoors. Word later spread that the sheriff had found the wolf roaming on the streets, now dead on the south side of town. With this recent news, the residents returned to their outdoor activities. For the unknowing passerby or unsuspecting visitors doing antique hunting, sightseeing, or driving through on a simple outing, everything seemed normal.

Rooster observed Mayor Corbett stroll along the sidewalk across the street, with his shoulders squared and chest puffed out; he knew the mayor wanted to give the impression he was the one responsible for eliminating the earlier threat roaming through town. Rooster then watched the mayor walk up to a disheveled Destiny. With her out of the office, the mayor recalled she had taken off early. The Sheriff had also instructed him to restrain his assistant, but opted not to bother her. He had become more of an annoyance over the last couple of days. The mayor didn't want to make a direct assault against him, yet the current circumstances provided an opportune way to annoy his nemesis.

Rooster grabbed the next newspaper atop the stack for the driver of a Cadillac that had pulled up. With a quick sideways glance, Destiny crossed the street down the block.

She's not herself, Rooster thought.

Destiny approached with haste, distracting Rooster before he could pass off a personalized newspaper to the recent arrival, a portly older man with two days of bearded stubble, and a bald top head with dark brown hair streaked and silver strands. The vacant stare in Destiny's eyes confirmed Rooster's suspicions: she was not in control of herself. The same entity that had possessed the wolf and tried to kill him earlier was revisiting him.

"You're back?" Rooster said. "Have you come to finish what you started last time?" he continued, not speaking in his rustic slang.

"You had died," Destiny said.

"You forget, for many here in Elysium, we are between life and death. I have not crossed over to the afterlife, an afterlife governed by our Great Creator, one where you and your brethren attempt to make an affront. I have a purpose now — to ensure those destined north make the journey. In the grand scheme governed by the Great Creator, there is no way you will win."

"I disagree," Destiny said in a husky voice. "I've been successful in causing mayhem in the man-infested world and for those coming up through here and other locales."

"It's clear you've been trying to have those who should go west attempt to escape their lot in the afterlife, yet none could. I wouldn't call that successful," Rooster countered.

Several spectators watched the old man and young woman engage in their verbal sparring that now sounded as if they were talking in a Middle Eastern language. One observer, a sightseer in town and a seminary student on vacation during a break in school, knew their dialogue resembled ancient Hebrew. He understood portions of the conversation.

The spectators, except for the balding man, couldn't notice that after Destiny's remark, a green gaseous fog extruded from her nose and flowed as if a river of mist. Nor did they see the misty discharge flow into the semblance of a human form, the arms reaching forward and wrapping around Rooster's body. The slow constriction of force caused Rooster to stiffen. The balding man waiting for the newspaper backed away, fearful of what he was witnessing. Disoriented from being in a town he had no recollection of traveling to, he believed this was all a dream. Yet, his surroundings and everyone around appeared lucid and vivid. To the other three spectators in the area watching, they only saw Destiny smile and flash a roguish grin while standing in front of a paralyzed Rooster, bones sounding as if they were making a cracking sound. The gentle, fresh, and vibrant mountain breeze changed; the acrid odor of decay and sulfur laced the air.

"Hey man, are you alright?" a witness standing nearby asked of a distressed Rooster. Rooster couldn't move or make a sound. The man sensed an indescribable fear and stepped back.

Destiny's upper left torso radiated severe pain of something piercing through skin, sinew, and bone. An arrow had impaled her through the shoulder blade. The misty constrainer released its grip and then retreated into its host; while doing so, she released a shrieking yelp. She turned to determine the projectile's origin. The sheriff's patrol car sat in the middle of the road by the traffic circle with the front driver's side and passenger side doors swung open. The sheriff stood behind the driver's side door; Nila stood behind the passenger side door with his bow out, readying another arrow.

"You see, Nila, I told you that you wouldn't hit anyone else," the Sheriff said, gloating.

I need to make sure I focus, Nila thought. He finished setting the arrow nock onto the bowstring and took aim downrange towards Destiny. "Wounding her again, I could kill her," he said. It was more so to reinforce to himself the finality of his actions.

"Nila, she's already lost."

Destiny, with an arrow protruding from her shoulder from the rear to the front, horrified the spectators. Adding to their disbelief was that up the street, following the path to the arrow's origin. It was back to Nila, who had armed another arrow in his bow. The sheriff stood next to him, appearing complicit in what had happened.

Destiny took her hand opposite the pierced shoulder blade, grabbed the arrow's shaft behind the minutely barbed head, and forced downward, snapping the metal shaft in two. With ample dexterity, she reached around to the tail, extracting the arrow fragment from her body. She then flung both pieces onto the ground and held her hand above them, palm down, from where she stood. The two arrow pieces glowed red; they disintegrated into dust.

"I was afraid of that," the Sheriff said.

"You were afraid of what?" Nila asked with concern. The arrow had no observable effect on Destiny. Where the arrow penetrated her clothing and skin, only a small semblance of blood oozed from the wound, like a slow-drying creek.

"Don't worry, just shoot. And don't aim to wound this time; you need to shoot to kill."

Nila was hesitant. Chrishav, walking up with Deputy Rutherford, sensed Nila's reluctance to release his grip on the bow.

"I never killed anyone before." Nila stated.

"You must do it, Nila," the sheriff said in response to Nila's comment.

Chrishav glanced downrange to see Rooster backing away from Destiny, who herself focused on the four men with intensity and took a stance as if ready to charge.

A name surrounded by vile anger, deceit, and malevolence, swirled in Chrishav's mind. It originated from within Destiny. The name was Midiochonion. He assumed the arrow must have disoriented the destroyer-daemon spirit to drop its guard.

With the full capacity of his lungs, Chrishav yelled out the name. Destiny's muscles stiffened – she froze.

"Nila, now!" both the Sheriff and Chrishav shouted.

Nila never imagined he would have to take a human life. The first shot he released because of straight adrenaline, and he didn't consider his actions. He had aimed to wound. When hunting, he believed he would have to contend only with possessed animals, such as the wolf in the forest. Even though a daemon had possessed Destiny, her humanity blinded him; he only saw a beautiful, slender woman, one he almost became intimate with. Yet Nila knew the Destroyer, or at the least a major daemon, must have possessed her. Chrishav's commanding of its name and the follow-up rigid response of Destiny, its host, and the same as with the dog in the airport back in Los Angeles, swayed Nila.

"Nila, do it now, for the sake of all," the Sheriff petitioned, in an urgent and boisterous manner.

Forgive me. Nila's belief and purpose in removing the evil overrode his reluctance. He released the arrow. With laser-like precision, it flew true. Destiny, with lightning reflexes, snatched the arrow from the air before it struck and flung it to the ground.

"You waited too late, boy," she said, her normally mild, squeaky voice sounding octaves lower.

Nila looked over to the sheriff. "I messed up."

Sheriff Knight kept his attention on Destiny. "This is turning out a lot different from what I had expected."

"How was it supposed to turn out?" Chrishav asked.

"Not like this," Sheriff Knight said. He pulled out his baton, striking the ground.

Nila witnessed the baton once again transform, appearing as a well-crafted, Flamberge type sword. Golden filaments emanated from where the tip struck the ground. Radiant threads flowed along the asphalt toward Rooster and Destiny. Destiny raised her right foot and stomped on the ground. A green aura wave of energy expanded from where her foot landed. The golden threads dissipated. Both Deputy Rutherford and Chrishav witnessed the Sheriff striking the ground with his baton, thinking it was a strange maneuver.

"You fool, I am a Dominion of the second sphere; you mere archangel wannabes cannot bind me."

Destiny walked up to the balding man who had stepped back to his car. She grabbed his collar, hauling him to the passenger side of his vehicle and forcing him in. Still disoriented, he didn't resist. Destiny ran back around and jumped in on the driver's side. The Cadillac reversed back into the street and then sped towards the sheriff's car parked blocking the entrance into the traffic circle. Sheriff Knight hurried to get into his patrol car to head off the approaching automobile. The Cadillac lurched to the right, up onto the adjacent sidewalk, navigated around the patrol vehicle and then back onto the road, speeding north.

Sheriff Knight jumped out of his patrol car before giving chase. "Rooster, where was that man Destiny commandeered destined? North or west?" He hollered, Deputy Rutherford, Chrishav, and Nila all thinking his voice resembled a booming trumpet.

Rooster read the newspaper, scanning the article to find the answer. The article read *Retired, beloved and faithful pastor and father has a heart attack while driving back from store...* A little further, *his congregation noted he had a genuine love for...* That was enough for Rooster to speculate. "North," he replied.

"Thanks."

The powerful projection of the sheriff's voice astonished Nila and Chrishav.

"Nila, you're with me," the sheriff commanded. He jumped into the car, Nila following along on the passenger side.

Chrishav was curious about his role in everything that was transpiring. "What did you want me to do, Sheriff?"

"Not sure there's anything else you can do at this point. Wait until I return."

Chrishav contemplated what the Sheriff had said about he would return. He speculated he was to return by himself, with Nila to follow several days later, as they had done when they traveled west. Chrishav didn't think about the fact that when Nila pursued the wolf into the woods north, and he returned to meeting the Sheriff and deputy while walking back, ten minutes passed. For Nila during that time, two and a half hours transpired.

Trees blurred by as the patrol sped down the narrow roadway. The Sheriff focused on his driving, slowing down where the road became winding. This didn't deter Nila from wanting to question the sheriff about the current situation. "I know you probably won't answer me again, but why is it I have to be the one to dispatch the daemon?"

"It's because of your bloodline, Nila."

"My bloodline? I don't understand."

"Millennia ago, there were those daemons, the fallen ones, and watchers that transgressed their realm, all in rebellion against the Great Creator. They came down, seduced, and procreated with women found them fair and desirable, many having unholy offspring. For those who didn't have direct involvement with the daemons, they succumbed to the unholy revelry and evil they sponsored, their hearts corrupted, barring the faithful few."

"I remember Parsons teaching this during one of my Sunday school lessons. A massive flood wiped away the evil offspring of those unions along with all those in rebellion of the Great Creator from among the world, except for the ark builder, his wife, their three sons and their wives. But aren't all men descendants of the ark builder and his sons?"

"A while before the flood, one of the ark builder son's wife had a sister who wanted nothing to do with the seduction; a fallen one raped her. The sister, violated and learning she was pregnant, was repulsed and affronted by what happened. She self-aborted, not wanting to bring the abomination into the world. Though she self-inflicted so much damage to herself, and the love between her and her sister, who was to marry one of the three sons, the Great Creator delivered mercy for her faith before she died."

"What do you mean, delivered mercy? if she died?"

"I'm sure Parson's mentioned through one son and his wife, our redeemer would be born? Through the sister of the one who died, the promise that the line of her offspring could contend with the brethren of certain daemons equivalent to the one that violated her sister."

"Those daemons? Destroyers?"

"Yes, not all daemons rebelled in the same way and are in Tartarus, only those for their severe transgressions."

"Did Sogundu and Parsons know all of this?"

"No, they were faithful in doing their duties, never knowing the full backs..."

The patrol car jolted to the side. Glass fragments sprayed inside the vehicle. Nila, disoriented with shock, didn't understand that one instant he was listening to the Sheriff, the next he's watching the outside rotating before his eyes, his body feeling as if tossed like a die in a backgammon cup. As abruptly as the commotion started, they stopped rolling. The patrol car rested on its roof.

The sheriff recovered his senses, then looked over at Nila. "Are you ok?"

"I don't think so. Feels like my shoulder is broken, and I can't feel my legs." As Nila made the remarks regarding his injuries, the Sheriff placed his hand on the top of his head; a warm sensation bathed legs. The pain subsided. Nila felt. "What did you do?"

"That's not important. Hurry and get your gear. We need to get a move on."

Peering through the front windshield, the Sheriff watched Destiny scurry away down the road, manhandling the balding man she had accosted back in town.

The Sheriff and Nila witnessed the full scope of the collision after crawling out of the overturned cruiser. They had plunged down an embankment at the edge of the denser portion of the forest. Several yards back, a Cadillac Seville sat in the middle of the road with its front end crumpled; antifreeze fluid was leaking onto the ground, and the driver's side front tire was at an angle, indicating a broken axle.

The Sheriff suspected Destiny had waited off in the distance along Simpson Trail, a dirt road that ran perpendicular to the road from Elysium, then raced out and rammed the sheriff's vehicle as it passed. She timed the collision perfectly.

"Why do all of that instead of trying to make a run for it?" Nila asked.

"Any chance to cause trouble, destroy, or impair, sometimes for no reason, they will. More so now that we're following it."

Nila finished collecting his equipment that had ejected from the patrol car, surprised to find his bow was undamaged. However, the quiver of eleven arrows was short three. Sheriff Knight stood on the roadway, clean-dressed and presentable. His combed hair remained impeccable. His uniform shirt and pants, and high gloss black shoes experienced no sign that he was involved in an accident.

Nila climbed up the short embankment, joining the Sheriff. "Why did she take that man with her?"

Sheriff Knight stared at Nila, who was dusting himself off. "She's going to try to crash the gates protected by a guardian to the way of the Great Creator. We need to hurry and get a move on. I know a shortcut through the woods so that we can try to cut her off. When we catch up to them, are you ready to do what needs to be done?"

Nila grew emboldened, armed with the new information regarding the history of his bloodline. "Yeah, I think so."

"Are you sure? You can't hesitate like you did in town. Too much is at stake."

The forcefulness of Sheriff Knight's voice caused Nila to reevaluate his earlier answer. He had assumed he could fire the arrow at Destiny, but now he wasn't sure. "I don't know."

"Good, that's the answer I wanted to hear. You're being honest with yourself. Let's go." The sheriff launched into a fast walk along the road, taking long, confident strides. Several yards later, he peeled off into the woods. Sheriff Knight slowed down when the vegetation in the forest thickened, hindering their progress. His aggressive strides through the underbrush showed he wasn't interested in stealth. His concentration going forward was determined and focused. Yet, although the Sheriff was tall and muscular, his movements were smooth and graceful. He scarcely broke any twigs, crumpled any leaves, or stepped on any dried natural remnants that revealed their location. Nila tried his best to mimic his actions, but found each step landed hard, making noise much louder than expected. The sheriff didn't seem to mind.

To Nila, the landscape looked familiar. Sheriff Knight was confident of every step and the direction they were heading. They soon arrived in an area where the trees thinned out and the undergrowth was almost non-existent. Trudging along, they came upon a road; it looked as if it were a river of blacktop asphalt streaming through the forest. Stepping onto the single lane roadway, to the right it flowed into a veil of the all too familiar low-lying fog and mist. To the left, it curved and emerged from amidst a multitude of trees.

"Which way do we go?" Nila asked.

"Shhh. Listen."

Nila concentrated on trying to hear anything audible. Their surroundings were silent, the air stagnate; all was still. Nila recalled his earlier excursion into the forest, where no wildlife stirred.

"I can hear them. They're coming." The sheriff was undeterred in not removing his attention from focusing on the empty roadway.

Nila listened. "I don't hear anything."

"Give it time," the Sheriff responded.

Waiting for a few minutes, off in the distance, a female voice scolded or berated someone responding in a compassionate tone. The voices got louder the closer they approached the turn in the road.

A large cavity of clear air distended within the fog and mist that had encompassed the two men. The area now reminded him of his earlier encounter with the wolf.

"Now what?" Nila questioned.

"Do what you were trained to do," the Sheriff said. He placed his hands on Nila's shoulders from behind, turning him to face down the road toward the oncoming individuals. "It's up to you now. You must stop the Destroyer. Now prepare an arrow, and remember, what happens here in this forest is not the same as in Elysium." He paused and presented Nila with a reaffirming smile. "You can do this."

Nila pulled out and inspected the integrity of an arrow, making sure there was no damage to the shaft because of the earlier car accident. He armed his bow and took aim. "Must I kill her?"

There was no response. Nila turned around to find no one was there. The sense of calm the Sheriff provided by his presence fled. Nila dropped the aim of his arrow, rubbernecking, searching for his enigmatic guide. He was at a loss at what to do next, but then recomposed his thoughts; the training of his father and the Huntsman flooded his memories.

Nila heard Destiny and her hostage coming up through the murkiness of the mist into the corral of clear air. She was forcing the balding man to walk in the lead, grabbing him by the nape of his neck. Her long fingernails bit into the man's skin. Nila deployed his bow and arrow into the ready-fire position, pulling on the bowstring and aiming at his target.

Destiny flashed Nila a large malicious grin as she hid herself behind the man, peeking over his shoulder. "Well, look at what we have here. What do you think you're gonna do with that arrow, boy? You couldn't finish shooting me back in town, what makes you think you're gonna do it now?"

Nila remained quiet.

Destiny continued. "You think you can finish the job like a real man? A real man would have slept with me instead of listening to some pathetic spirit reader."

"Son, don't worry 'bout me," the man said. "Through all of this, I figured it out. On the way over here, she talked so much, and after hearing her story, I feel sorry for her. In the end, to each man is their own destiny, and my journey is complete. I am safe and confident I will be in my Redeemer's care hereafter. There's nothing she or anyone can do to hurt me anymore."

"You're right, I can't hurt you, old man, but I can use you to crash through the gates protected by the guardian. He dare not attack to drive me away with you in tow. He must allow us through."

Nila wondered what Destiny and her hostage were referring to regarding the idea that no one could hurt the man. Yet, did they reveal how to wound or inflict damage to herself? Nila remembered what the Sheriff had said: don't expect the same things to happen here in the forest as in town. When he last struck Destiny with an arrow, she seemed unaffected by the projectile. Maybe now would be different. They were north of Elysium, where most men couldn't walk.

The older man shielded her body, and Nila again considered what he had said about his not being able to be injured. If he couldn't since he was destined north, could the destroyer possessed within Destiny have transgressed its boundaries and it was possible to injure her?

Destiny tried navigating around Nila, taking miniature side steps while keeping the man in front of her as a human shield. She was effective in hiding most of her petite body behind the man's stocky girth. Nila was confident she was afraid, because of her fearful actions. He focused on the man's center mass and pulled the bowstring until it was taut. Destiny's eyes widened, witnessing the confidence in Nila's eyes.

Nila released his fingers. The bowstring's tension released, launching the arrow. The full force of his pull allowed the metal-shafted projectile to sail the short distance through the air and pass through the man as if he weren't there. Instead of skewering him, tearing through the man's clothing and flesh, the arrow impaled Destiny. She looked down to see the metal-shafted dart protruding from her center torso. Her eyes bulged with surprise, mouth agape, confirming his arrow found its target.

The man blocked Nila's view of being able to see if the strike was successful. Destiny reached down with her free hand and grabbed the shaft to remove the projectile; it wouldn't budge. Instead of blood flowing out of her wound, a green mist ebbed from her pierced skin.

Destiny's eyes again widened. She panicked and released an ear-splitting shriek, grabbing harder onto the back of the man's neck and scurrying down the road clutching his arm. Nila pulled out another arrow from his quiver, charged his bow, exerting extra force, aimed, and released. Once again, his accuracy was on the mark; the arrow struck Destiny in her right shoulder blade, with its momentum sling Destiny to the ground with her captive. He tried to break free, but remained restrained by Destiny's abnormal strength. She continued holding onto his arm, almost losing her grip. More green vaporous secretions oozed from the fresh wound.

Destiny launched back up to her feet and attempted to continue her run down the road. Through the fog and mist, the manifestation of a tunnel made of pure white light appeared. Nila had enough time to load another arrow and aim. Destiny made a dash towards the tunnel entrance with the old man in tow. Pulling back on the bowstring and zeroing in center mass once again, Nila released the arrow. Destiny bellowed in agony as it struck her lower back. She released the grasp on her captive. He strolled down the road, entering the light, smiling.

Green ethereal vapors poured from Destiny's wounds and formed into the shape of a serpent, then transfigured into an obscure naked figure with a male physique and four expansive wings extending from its back, immobilized, and surrounded by a milky haze. Destiny's body collapsed onto the roadway; the arrows in her body disintegrated.

Her wounds faded, replaced with smooth skin. The tunnel of light dissipated.

"Well done." A tenor voice said, surprising Nila from behind. "I can take it from here."

It was Sheriff Knight walking up the road. He proceeded over to the waiflike figure and then stared into its face. "It's time for you to go, Midiochoneum. Tartarus awaits."

The figure stared back with repulsion and disgust. "You betrayer of the cause, men should worship us. We were the first of his creation, being born of light, greater in stature. They were born of mud. Here you are defiling yourself by serving them. We will prevail."

"You defiled yourself when you rebelled against our creator; and here at the gates, I have dominion over you."

Sheriff Knight pointed with his index finger to a small pond resting yards from the roadside that Nila hadn't noticed. A massive globe of water emerged and ascended, disrupting the mirrorlike surface. Sheriff Knight motioned with his hand, control of the sphere. He glided it over onto the road where it enveloped the detained personage. The liquid orb shrunk smaller and smaller until it was a baseball-sized globule. The sheriff clenched his hand into a fist; the globule atomized.

The Sheriff and Nila helped Destiny, who was waking up, stand to her feet.

"Sheriff, what are you doing here? Wait, where are we?" she asked, disoriented and unfamiliar with the forest surroundings. "I don't recognize any of this. Are we lost somewhere?"

"Not we, you. You'll need to head back to town to Barclay's."

Destiny's watery eyes and long, pouty face revealed her sorrow. "I thought I'd have more time?"

"Most everyone believes they have more time before they realize the end of the journey is upon them." Sheriff Knight said. "Your days of reflection are over. Your life story is written and archived in the Book of Works. Your newspaper is waiting." The Sheriff extended his arm, palm up, gesturing for Destiny to begin her walk on the road leading back to Elysium.

Destiny glanced north and wept, grinding her teeth in despair. "But I...giving in like I did...I didn't..." she said. "Must I?"

"Your path is west across the river Purgo."

Unable to find any other words to say, she strolled down the road and disappeared into the mist.

"I guess we need to be heading back to town ourselves," Nila said.

Sheriff Knight closed his eyes and cast his head downward–his expression became mournful. He reached over and gently grabbed Nila's shoulder. The bow and quiver of arrows disappeared. Nila didn't understand why.

"I'm sorry, Nila," the Sheriff said. "You've done well, the same as your father, but you've also seen much more than he ever had."

"What are you saying?" Nila's voice was shaky.

"Back down the road when we got sideswiped, since it occurred on the boundary where we entered the forest, you experienced the finality of the accident."

"I don't understand. What do you me..." Nila understood the Sheriff's comment. "Am I not to see my mother again, Sogundu, Parsons, or even the town of my fathers?"

"My friend, you are heading to a greater city where the streets have no name."

The tunnel of light re-manifested itself.

DIMINISHED RESOLUTION

C hrishav and Deputy Rutherford followed the Sheriff and Nila by several minutes to see if they needed help. The two men did not know how their companions were faring on the road north, nor did they expect to see Destiny walk up to Barclay's. More so, she yielded no discernable answers after interrogating her. The lone remnant of information she recalled was last seeing their companions a way up the road. She remembered walking away from the two men, and the next instant, she was at the outskirts of town.

"How do you feel?" Deputy Rutherford asked Chrishav as they entered the deputy's patrol vehicle at Barclays.

"Fine, why?"

"I remember when we were heading west, you got sick. You're not gonna throw up in my cruiser, are you?"

"It's not my intention to."

"If you need to get out, let me know," Deputy Rutherford said as they departed the driveway.

Chrishav noticed Deputy Rutherford sneaking long glances in his direction the further they traveled up the road. "I'm fine," Chrishav announced, not waiting for the deputy to ask the question.

This didn't deter the deputy from his continued scrutiny of Chrishav. He wished they were traveling faster than the posted 35 miles per hour on the treelined winding road. Entering the turn prior to Simpson's Road, the deputy glanced over to see Chrishav's eyes widen and jaw drop. "You're not about to throw up, are you?" Deputy Rutherford barked.

"Stop!" Chrishav screamed while pointing straight ahead.

Deputy Rutherford snapped his attention forward, seeing the road blocked by a Cadillac Seville. He slammed his foot on the brakes, causing the tires to lock as they screeched to a stop. The pungent smell of burning rubber wafted into the passenger compartment of the patrol car. Ahead of them sat the Cadillac with its front end crumpled in, the driver's side tilted down, almost resting on the ground; radiator fluid dripped onto the road. Glass fragments, along with the shrapnel of red and yellow plastic, lay scattered along the asphalt and roadside sod. Getting out of the vehicle, Deputy Rutherford and Chrishav noticed the sheriff's vehicle overturned down the embankment on the right side of the road.

"What happened here?" Deputy Rutherford said as the two men surveyed the crash scene. The deputy started a closer inspection of the Cadillac to search for injuries. Chrishav sprinted down to the overturned patrol car, seeing a dark-complexioned arm sticking out of the passenger window. Dropping to his knees and checking inside the vehicle, he confirmed it was Nila. Was he unconscious, or worse?

Chrishav grabbed Nila's wrist and searched for a pulse. "Nila!" The temperature of Nila's arm worried Chrishav–cooler than he expected. There was no throbbing reaction to a heartbeat. It was now that Chrishav noticed Nila's eyes were motionless, unblinking, and lacking any sparkle; his head twisted around, faced towards the back.

Deputy Rutherford joined Chrishav, kneeling next to the vehicle. "Is he alright?"

Chrishav remained quiet, almost unable to answer. "No," he responded with despondence.

"Then we need to get him out."

Chrishav backed away from the car, tears watering his eyes. "It's too late."

"What do you mean, it's too late?"

Deputy Rutherford surveyed Nila's body and understood Chrishav's comment. "Damn. What happened here?"

Chrishav didn't want to think about the answer. He sat in the grass off the roadside, moving away from the wreckage, still trying to comprehend Nila's death. He prayed.

Deputy Rutherford stood on the road, his hands on his hips, slowly turned a full three hundred and sixty degrees surveying the area, still trying to fathom what had happened. There were no signs of anyone ejected from the car–no blood, nor any other signs of anyone sustaining injuries.

Where's the sheriff? *Where's Destiny? And what about the man she shanghaied? Did the remaining three continue to head north?* Deputy

Rutherford then comprehended he was at the point where the sheriff told him never to travel. He complied with this one of the many rules the Sheriff had established.

Deputy Rutherford saw a downcast Chrishav sitting in the grass, his head bowed down and eyes closed, not having moved since discovering Nila's remains.

Chrishav was still experiencing the gut-wrenching impact of finding his friend passed away. He never had to face the death of anyone he knew personally. Even the passing of one of his sages when he first arrived at the monastery down in Mexico seemed impersonal compared to his current situation. Chrishav had considered Nila a friend, not a mere companion during their undertaking in Elysium.

"I'll be damned," Deputy Rutherford said, staring along the road towards the forest. "You gotta be kidding me."

Chrishav turned to see the same thing the deputy witnessed, Sheriff Knight walking towards them. With the amount of damage to the sheriff's patrol car, they knew he should have displayed an injury or damage to his uniform. There was none. The creases of his clean shirt were sharp and crisp; his pants spotless and unsoiled.

"Sheriff, what's going on? Where'd you go?" Deputy Rutherford asked.

"We had to take care of that nuisance polluting Destiny."

Chrishav wanted to know more about what happened to Nila and joined the two men on the road. "We? You don't mean Nila, do you?"

The sheriff caught the derision in Chrishav's voice, but refrained from reacting.

"How can you say that sheriff when he's still in your police car? You left him there," Chrishav said.

"Trust me, I didn't leave him."

Chrishav attempted to suppress the volcano of an emotional outburst from erupting, followed by his trying to hold back an onslaught of tears. He failed. "He's dead, sheriff."

"Listen to me when I tell you I didn't leave Nila in the car. He traveled with me and continued his journey north."

Chrishav was too distraught to grasp and comprehend the Sheriff's comment. Deputy Rutherford knew what the Sheriff inferred. Sheriff Knight placed his hands on Chrishav's shoulders and forced him to stare into his eyes.

For the first time since arriving in Elysium, and attempting to scan the Sheriff, Chrishav found he wasn't met with resistance. Echoing in his mind, Chrishav heard, *"He's crossed through the glorious gates and was greeted for a job well done."*

"He'd been dutiful in his work against the destroyer," the Sheriff said aloud.

A shuddering wave of calm engulfed Chrishav. Yet, it didn't relieve the sense of loss. "Sheriff, it doesn't help that Nila is gone."

"Carlson, take Chrishav back to town. I'll oversee the cleanup of this scene."

Arriving back in Elysium, Chrishav witnessed Rooster folding up the empty wireframe newspaper stand and resting it against the building. He didn't believe how spry the old man seemed moving about, and swore he appeared younger.

"What are you doing?" Chrishav asked.

Rooster smiled. "There won't be any need to pass out papers anymore. The passersby will know which direction they need to go without my help when they pass through. Traffic is going in the right direction now. Visitors are visitors, hunters are hunters. I can head on up the road. My destiny to help dispatch the Destroyer is complete."

Rooster walked away.

Chrishav didn't know why, but he sensed a close familial familiarity with that of Nila, followed by inexpressible joy. *It can't be.*

"Rooster," Chrishav called out. "Tell Nila goodbye for me and that I'll miss him."

Rooster smiled and continued his walk towards the roundabout.

Chrishav decided not to watch the old man's departure, but to head back to the hotel and pack. There was no reason to stay in Elysium.

Mayor Corbett walked into the police station to find Clarissa's desk was vacant. He went to the sheriff's office and walked in without knocking. Sheriff Knight sat reclining in his office chair, reading paperwork removed from several file folders laying atop his desk. The mayor considered it insolent that Sheriff Knight didn't get up to receive him, or at least acknowledge his arrival. During most of his visits, the Sheriff continued whatever he was doing and acted as if the mayor wasn't there.

"Do you know why I called you here, Hannibal?" the Sheriff asked, still reading the papers in his hand.

"I don't know. Maybe to waste my time."

Sheriff Knight didn't appreciate the retort. Directing his attention away from the paperwork he'd been perusing, he gave the mayor an accusatory stare. "Is there any reason I shouldn't exile you right here and now from Elysium?"

"What are you talking about?"

Sheriff Knight laid the papers down on the desktop. "I'm talking about how I directed you to restrain Destiny before she went and kidnapped that passerby going north."

"How do you know that?"

"Rooster told me you let her walk right by you and did nothing to stop her."

The mayor raised an eyebrow. "Did he?"

"He did. Lucky for you, Rooster is no longer here for me to use as a witness to bring up a censure against you. Are you and your brethren planning something larger?"

"What do you mean?"

"You know what I mean; to have a destroyer here in town being subversive; the sentinels were working in league with the super daemon, and you acting as if you're not involved. Yet, knowing the potential of your prominence being undercut, you let the offender of your undermining go unimpeded. What's a guardian to think?"

"I think you've been around your goody- goody two shoe friends too long, thinking we're interested in continual connivances, or up to some sort of mischief."

Sheriff Knight raised an eyebrow in disbelief. "Aren't you? It's in your nature. Look how many poor souls you sent west."

"They all go west of their own volition." The mayor displayed an impish smile. "I help facilitate."

"Yeah, and most times, prodding their downfall. The day you and your brethren are all expelled beyond the great chasm will be a great day of rejoicing."

"Keep wishing; you know things can go differently."

Sheriff Knight chuckled. "Your arrogance never fails to surprise me. Do you think your side will succeed?"

The mayor presented Sheriff Knight with a smirk. "I know we will."

Sheriff Knight stood, placed his hands palm side down on the top of his desk, and leaned forward towards the mayor. "You can keep dreaming that, but like today, you and your brethren will fail. Your schemes will come to naught. Now get out of here."

The mayor left the sheriff's office annoyed, but not at the accusations brought forth against him concerning the alleged conspiracy. If there were larger machinations at work, his colleagues hadn't advised or consulted him. Maybe all the recent chain of events was fortuitous, yet the destroyer's overall impact in Elysium was minimal compared to other incidents occurring outside of town the mayor had heard about through other colleagues from their realm. Could the sheriff be right?

In the yard by the side of a large two-room mud house, Nila's mother squeezed a young goat's teat, filling a dented and banged up bucket with milk. She looked up to see the Huntsman walking down the road in her direction. He was alone.

Glancing away, she thought to herself, "*He's not coming here. He's not coming here. He's not coming here.*"

The Huntsman was getting closer. It convinced her she was his intended destination, but hoped he would pass by. She had dreamed the night prior of visiting the home of someone familiar, but could not reconcile whom it belonged to. A neighbor saw her knocking on the door and walked over to mention that the owner had moved to a beautiful new estate. Nila's mother was sad she didn't have time to say goodbye. She then awoke crying, but didn't understand why.

Seeing the Huntsman, she was afraid of what the dream had foreshadowed. Each squeeze of the goat's teat was firmer than the previous one. The goat bleated in distress and attempted to pull back.

"Keep walking, just keep walking," she whispered to herself. "Don't stop."

The Huntsman entered the yard through the recently repaired gate; the wood appeared less aged than the fence constructed with random planks made from local species.

"Where's your son?" the Huntsman asked.

"Since you oversaw Nila, I imagine you mean Milali? He's inside taking a nap."

Nila's mother stopped working on filling up the bucket. "Why are you here?" She asked.

"I'm sorry, he has pas..."

Nila's mother interrupted the Huntsman. "Leave." She went back to milking the goat.

"You must know he was successful in his duties for the Great Crea..."

Nila's mother interrupted again. "Do you not understand? Leave."

"You would've been proud of Nila," the Huntsman said, as he was about to exit through the gate.

That night, she cried herself to sleep.

The next morning, sitting outside her house weeping while milling corn in a rough, hand hewn bowl and pestle, was Nila's mother with her year and a half old son, who was sitting in her lap. Sogundu approached, wondering if she had already heard the news.

"You don't have to tell me, Sogundu," Nila's mother said, while catching her breath through the persistence of her tears.

Sogundu didn't want to present his news in case her comment was about something else. "I mustn't tell you what?"

"Don't play silly. It is unbecoming. I know Nila has passed on," Nila's mother replied.

"How'd you find out?"

Nila's mother lifted her head upward to face Sogundu, the sunlight glistening in her tear-filled eyes. "The Huntsman told me."

Sogundu trembled. He hadn't expected to hear about the Huntsman. It was out of the ordinary for him to journey to the town unsolicited. He didn't know the Huntsman had stopped by occasionally to see how Nila's mother was faring.

"What did he tell you?" Sogundu asked.

"He told me Nila has gone to be greeted by the Great Creator. I imagine he has gone and joined up with his father." Nila's mother sniffed from the runny nose before continuing. "I am not sacrificing another son."

Sogundu sat feeling light-headed. "I don't want to lie to you; I don't know what providence the Great Creator has in store for your son. I pray he doesn't call for him. For the Huntsman to come means he is preparing his way to come back."

Nila's mother's searing stare through her water-filled eyes unnerved Sogundu. "Leave," she demanded. "I gave up my husband and allowed my son to follow what was to be his father's path. No more."

"But..."

Nila's mother did not want Sogundu to continue. "I said leave." She adjusted the weight of her son on her lap, moving him to the opposite side, and went back to grinding dried corn into meal.

Sogundu accepted the finality of her statement, stood, and walked away.

ΩΩΩΩ

ACKNOWLEDGEMENTS

I first want to thank Joe H. and Monika R., so much for their input and feedback.

Just as important, I really have to thank Bethany Amber for her sprinkling of observations and contemplations that yielded wonderful insight.

Of course, I want to thank the readers who continue to provide feedback during the progress of each work, and hope they receive enjoyment from the stories.

OTHER WORKS BY JERRY J. K. ROGERS

Novella and Novels
Legend of the Salad Traveler
The Fallen and the Elect–Book I: The Eulogy of Angels
The Fallen and the Elect–Book II: The Aurora Strain
The Fallen and the Elect–Book III: Aurora's Child

Under Pen-Name Ray Jorge Ryes Jr.
House Xrion
Arising: Deviant Beings Series (Early 2026)

ABOUT THE AUTHOR

Jerry Rogers retired as career airman and civilian technician working both in the United States Air Force and in the California Air National Guard, with over 31 years' experience working in technology supporting legacy and state-of-the-art telecommunication and data-communication systems. He also worked for nearly seven years at two post-production film companies working in Information Technology. One of Jerry's greatest joys is being able to teach at a small church in Orange County. He's also traveled across the vast country to each of the contiguous 48 states and across the world to both Asia and Europe.

Ever since he was a teenager, Jerry's always had a fascination with religion and Science Fiction and has enjoyed writing, starting with writing short stories over the years. He took the next step and wrote a humorous novella called "The Legend of the Salad Traveler." He later began working on his first novel, the Fallen and the Elect, in 2011 developing the concept after months of research, building notes, and jotting down ideas. The story has now blossomed into a full supernatural mystery and religious surrealism story blending both religion and a sprinkling of Science Fiction.

See what else is brewing at his website at http://www.jjkr-writings.info.

www.ingramcontent.com/pod-product-compliance
Lightning Source LLC
Chambersburg PA
CBHW051436170626
46809CB00006B/2492